Praise for *The Chain*

The First Book in The Kinship Series

FOREWORD REVIEWS 2013

BOOK OF THE YEAR AWARD FINALIST

"A great read for lovers of mystery novels—with the added bonus of being an eye opener about life in a slaughterhouse town."

- **NORM PHELPS**, author of *The Longest Struggle*

"From the first page I was caught in the grip of this fast-moving tale. Robin Lamont is a smooth operator who cleverly navigates a subject too often swept under the rug."

- **JONATHAN BALCOMBE**, author of *Second Nature: The Inner Lives of Animals*

"Robin Lamont is a master of suspense, and her latest novel is no exception."

- **PAUL SHAPIRO**, Vice President of Farm Animal Protection, The Humane Society of the United States

"The Chain is a page turner ... Just go buy it and read it, because it's really, really good."

- **MARIANN SULLIVAN**, Our Hen House

"A gripping suspense novel which will hold readers rapt from page one, *The Chain* is a must read for both animal activists and the public at large."

- **GAIL EISNITZ**, author of *Slaughterhouse*

"Do yourself and the animals a favor. Read this book."

- **BRYAN MONELL**, Farm Animal Rights Movement (FARM)

Also by Robin Lamont

The Chain

Wright for America

If Thy Right Hand
(Named Suspense Magazine's Best of 2011)

THE KINSHIP SERIES

THE TRAP

ROBIN LAMONT

Award winning author of *The Chain*

The Trap

Disclaimer: This is a work of fiction. Names, characters, places and incidents either are products of the author's imagination or are used fictitiously. Any resemblance to actual events or locales or persons, living or dead, is entirely coincidental.

Cover and Interior Design: AuthorSupport.com
Cover Imagery: Shutterstock/Helen E. Grose

Grayling Press

ISBN #978-0-9858485-6-9 (print version)

LCCN #2015902805

Printed in the United States of America

Acknowledgements

The Trap was set in motion by a personal story told to me by Anja Heister about freeing a marten from a brutal neck snare only to be later threatened with prosecution for trap interference. And thanks go to Tom Knudson for his bold expose in the *Sacramento Bee* which served as inspiration for incidents and characters in this book. For patiently answering all my questions, I am indebted to Brooks Fahy and his organization *Predator Defense,* which has taken on the mammoth task of shining a light on Wildlife Services. Much gratitude to Maggie Howell and the *Wolf Conservation Center* for her insights about wolves and the challenges of wolf conservation. Good luck to Brooks, Maggie, Camilla Fox, and all the other good people of the Northeast Wolf Coalition in their efforts to ensure that wolves will have a place in our country's vast landscape. Thanks to Stephanie Boyles-Griffin at *HSUS*, to Suzanne Asha Stone at *Defenders of Wildlife,* and to the *Natural Resources Defense Council* for the advance screening of *Wild Things.* And to Martin Rowe, I appreciate his ongoing support and advice. Finally, thank you, Peter Young. This book took some twists and turns from where it started. But isn't that the way with all journeys?

The Trap is dedicated to Ken.
Without you, none of this is possible.

Chapter 1

Charlie Ferrow whistled for his dogs. They should have been back by now. It was getting cold – the kind of cold you might not see coming until its knife edge was at your throat.

The late evening sky had gone from charcoal to black and seemed impossibly clear, stars shimmered brighter, sounds carried farther. The other hunters had gone home and it was just him and his "boys" huntin' raccoons. Pelt prices were on the rise, nearly thirty dollars for a good size skin, and the meat brined and barbequed, wasn't half bad. Best though was times like this, listening for the excited squall-bawl of his hounds catching the scent, then trailing and treeing a coon – the sweetest music he'd ever known. But now the tips of his ears were starting to burn. Time to pack it up.

Ferrow called again, and the veteran coonhound Grit bounded in from the trees. "Atta boy," crooned the veteran hunter, reaching down to scratch Grit under the chin. "Where's Jocko, eh? Where's your brother?" Expecting the young 'un to appear any moment, Ferrow leaned his .22 against the back of his greasy, mud-splattered truck. The bumper sticker glowed pale green in the dark: *I Got a New Coon Dog for My Wife–Best Trade I Ever Made.* He tied off the garbage bag that held two dead raccoons and swung it onto the truck bed.

Just then, he heard Jocko, still deep in the woods. His urgent yelps cut through the crystal chill. Something wasn't right, and Ferrow felt the hairs rise up on his neck. Grit heard it too and bolted off to investigate. Ferrow grabbed his rifle and went after him.

The headlamp fitted over his cap paved the way across the snow-crusted ground. As he got closer, he could hear the two of them. Winding his way through the trees and pushing aside low branches, Ferrow gripped his rifle tight, hoping Jocko hadn't stumbled on a predator in a trap. The young coonhound wouldn't have the sense to stay well clear of the slashing jaws of a cornered coyote or worse, a wolf.

About fifty yards in, the headlamp caught the darting figures of his dogs in a small hollow between two big lodgepole pines. They were anxiously circling a mound of snow at the base of one of the trees, their tails held high and stiff with warning.

"Com' here," snarled Ferrow. "Git back."

Only Grit obeyed.

What the hey? No coyote. Had to be a coon. Ferrow shined his light up into the tree where it would reflect the gleaming eyes of the cornered animal. He raised up the .22, ready to fire. But the sparse branches over his head revealed nothing. As he moved in to get a better look, his foot kicked something. He looked down and saw raw, bloated fingers reaching out of the snow.

Ferrow dropped to his knees and hurriedly uncovered the hand, then an arm clothed in stiff flannel. He brushed the snow from a face he recognized. The man's eyes were open, ice crusted on his lashes and mustache, his skin waxy, the color of chalk, his mouth half open as if trying to scream. Very, very dead.

Heart pounding, Ferrow began to sweep the rest of the snow from the man's body. What the fuck happened here? Suddenly, he cut his hand against something hard and sharp – the rusted tip of a wire spring. With the body now partially exposed, the glare of his lamp revealed a gruesome sight. Soaked in blood, the man's lower leg was caught in the locked jaws of a coil spring trap. A big one, ten, twelve-inch jaws – a device that could have taken a bear or a hundred-twenty-pound wolf.

Holy Christ. Craig Eberhardt had stepped in his own trap.

Chapter 2

A young woman stood on a ridge overlooking the canyon floor peppered with rabbit brush and dried grass, tips poking through the snow cover. In the dawn that coated the landscape with a dreamy, blue-gray film, Jude Brannock peered intently through her binoculars, oblivious to the wind that painted bright pink patches on her cheeks. She wasn't pretty by conventional standards, her high cheekbones too angular, her chin too strong. But there was a spirit in her dark hazel eyes that captivated anyone who cared to look beyond the tabloid definition of beauty.

Next to her, Lisbet trained her spotting scope in the same direction. "Keep focused on that knot of elk by the curve in the creek," she told Jude. "See how they're all bunched together? Could mean they're uneasy ... they sense something. Be patient."

No problem there. Patient was what Jude did for a living. You couldn't conduct investigations into animal cruelty and not have a high tolerance for watching and waiting. Watching for the right moment to snap the photo. Waiting for the right time to approach a reluctant witness. She worked for The Kinship, a small group of animal rights investigators based in Washington, D.C. This week, however, Jude was taking a much-needed vacation and had decided to visit Yellowstone National Park for a chance to see wolves in the wild, a lifetime dream for her. The Kinship's founder Gordon Silverman had steered her to his old friend Lisbet Hammond, one of the park's wolf biologists.

Today, Lisbet had taken Jude to the Lamar Valley where a pack had been sighted mid-week. As they studied the elk, the biologist quietly relayed the history of the Yellowstone wolves. Throughout North America, the gray wolf had been hunted to near extinction before being given federal protection. Then in 1995, wolves were re-introduced to the vast landscape of the national park where they began to thrive. In that time, Lisbet saw the ecosystem in the park rebound as well. The wolves kept the herds of elk, moose, and deer from overgrazing near rivers and streams; in the newly flourishing undergrowth, bird species and beaver colonies returned, the rivers filled with fish. The *Canis lupus* kept the coyote population in check, they left food for scavengers, and the park saw a resurgence of eagles, lynx, cougars, grizzly bears, wolverines, and great gray owls. Such a landscape rich with wildlife needed the wolf. But two years earlier, pressured by the ranching and hunting lobbies, the federal government had removed wolves in the Northern Rockies from the endangered list and their numbers were plummeting again.

The two women shifted their feet to keep themselves warm as they continued to watch and wait. After a few more minutes, Lisbet pulled the scope away from her eyes, "It may not be our day," she said. "We can try again tomorrow."

The disappointment hit Jude like a punch. She'd planned this visit even before her last investigation. Wolves had fascinated her since she was a child, but she'd never seen one in real life, not even in a sanctuary. Her wolves always galloped across a TV screen on Animal Planet or National Geographic. Just once in her life she wanted with her own ears to hear the sound of a wolf howl, she wanted to breathe the same air, perhaps look into a wolf's eyes.

She became aware of Lisbet packing her scope away, but couldn't seem to move. A ball of sun emerged between two peaks twenty miles to the east, casting a pink glow on the mountains. And as if summoned by the light, they emerged from a stand of pine trees on the far side of the creek. Jude caught her breath. The wolves had come.

The leader had a thick pearl gray coat and a white muzzle that accentuated his almond-shaped eyes. Cautiously, he stepped out into the open, and one by one the others followed.

"Hello there," whispered Lisbet, back at Jude's side. "Meet the Stone Mountain Pack."

Close behind the leader trotted another wolf, lighter in color, her tail capped with a distinct black tip. Her head was thrust forward and low to the ground. Two more came into view, one with a reddish coat, the other nearly all black. They were followed by a pair of identically patterned, charcoal gray wolves, smaller than the others. All were fixated on the elk who huddled close together and sent bursts of foggy, anxious breath into the chilled air. The energy between elk herd and wolf pack hummed.

"Are they going to try to take down an elk?" asked Jude.

"I think they're just window shopping for now," said Lisbet, moving closer to tell Jude their story. "The big guy in front is 945M. He's the alpha male. We're pretty sure he originally made the trek from Montana."

Through her binoculars, Jude could see his rippling shoulder muscles, bits of snow on his whiskers, and his intense gold eyes ... inquisitive, watchful. So close, she could imagine reaching out and stroking his fur. The light colored wolf came up to sidle against the alpha male, and Jude asked, "Is that the alpha female?"

"Yes, at least we hope so, which is why we call her Eetsa, which means 'mother' in the Nez Perce dialect. She replaced a beautiful female 944F that we collared the same time as this alpha male. But we lost her last spring. She was shot by a hunter."

"I thought there was no hunting in Yellowstone," said Jude, never taking her eyes off the pack.

"There isn't. But the wolves don't know boundary lines. Yellowstone extends into Montana in the north and Idaho to the west. If the elk or deer wander outside the park, the wolves follow. We know that hunters set up just outside the park's borders and as soon as they spot a wolf on their side..."

The alpha male turned to make sure he had his pack together, his dominance displayed in his tail held high, his ears erect. Eetsa touched noses with him and then lay down. The two smaller wolves seemed to lose interest in the elk and began to play. One would nip at the other's thick ruff, then sprint away, looking back to see that his brother was following. Then they'd reverse roles. They ran to the edge of the river and tumbled in a mock fight, sending up sprays of water. Whenever they separated, their tails wagged furiously.

"Those two are the juveniles," Lisbet pointed out. "They're part of 944F's litter from last year."

The rust-hued member of the pack bounded up to the pups, then lowered his head and gave them each a quick, subservient lick to the muzzle. One of the young ones snapped at him for interrupting their fun and he quickly retreated off to himself.

"Poor Mika," said Lisbet tenderly. "They're always picking on him."

"Why?" asked Jude.

"He's the omega of the pack, the lowest ranking member. Always the last to eat, and always at the bottom."

"That's sort of sad."

"Sometimes I feel bad for him, but Mika is actually quite important to the family. He diffuses the tension when a fight is brewing and he's the absolute best babysitter. The pups are from a bigger litter. Maggie – that's the alpha female I was talking about – had five pups. But when she was killed, the pack kind of fell apart. No one was in charge of getting the babies food and three of them died. Then Mika, who's Maggie's brother, stepped up and helped feed them even though he was pretty distraught himself. He carried one of the dead babies around in his mouth, showing the others before he buried it. Wolves adore their pups and they were all heartbroken. We could hear them howling for days."

Almost on command, the alpha male threw back his head and let loose a mournful howl. His feral cry swept through an octave of notes and echoed on all sides of the valley, coursing through Jude's body like an electric charge. The others took up the chorus, sounding like an army of twenty or thirty wolves, not just the Stone Mountain six. An unearthly music, so wild and primitive, so utterly beautiful, it made Jude gasp.

Just as suddenly, they stopped. The pups went back to wrestling and jawing at one another, and the herd of elk began to move away, still in a tight group. A wisp of Jude's long auburn hair blew in front of the binocular lenses, obscuring her vision, and she brushed it back impatiently. For someone who cared so deeply about animals and had waited so long, nothing could intrude on this moment, not even a single strand of hair. Every cell of her being was concentrated on the wolf family circling, playing, nuzzling. She pushed Lisbet's sad tale of Maggie and her dead pups to the back of her mind. Jude wanted to revel in the wolves so full of life, right here, right now.

"Looks like they're on the move," noted Lisbet.

She was right. This time it was Eetsa who led the way back into the protective shadows of the pine trees. The juveniles, with Mika in tow, trotted obediently behind at a respectful distance. Finally, the alpha male – the *Canis lupus* who had no name, just a number, the majestic creature who carried the burden of keeping his family safe, fed, alive – took one last look at the valley and disappeared.

"So what do you think?" Lisbet asked.

Jude finally lowered her binoculars, her eyes brimming with tears. She didn't respond, afraid her voice would crack with emotion. Lisbet smiled in understanding and they stood silent on the ridge, watching the sun continue its climb, the light shimmering through the frost that coated the sagebrush and cottonwoods.

A rattle of stones beneath the tires of a Land Rover drew their attention away from the valley. The jeep came bouncing up the dirt road and pulled over behind Lisbet's vehicle. A young man bundled in a green bomber jacket and a National Park Service cap got out. "Sorry to interrupt" he said, heading over to the two women. "But we've got a situation you should know about."

"What's up?" asked Lisbet with a frown.

"Just outside the park, over the Idaho border in Stanton," he said. "Some hunter found a Wildlife Services agent dead."

"Who?"

"Craig Eberhardt."

"Oh, God," said Lisbet. "That's terrible."

"It's worse than that," said the young ranger. "He was killed."

"What?"

"He was shot and then stuck in a leg hold trap."

Lisbet exchanged worried glances with Jude before asking, "Do the police know anything?"

"I don't have any details," said the young man. "Only we heard that a couple of FBI agents from Boise are on their way."

"That's odd. Why wouldn't the cops handle it?"

"There's a rumor that Eberhardt was killed by animal activists," he said, sneaking an apologetic glance at Jude. "Your office also called, ma'am. Someone named CJ? He says you're to sit tight. Your boss is on his way."

Chapter 3

Jude buried her cold fingers into the warm fur of Finn's neck while the ninety pound dog sat contentedly at her feet, happy to be of service. They were usually inseparable, but Jude had left him at the park station so his mere scent wouldn't scare away the wildlife.

It was nearly midnight. Gordon had gotten a flight into Jackson Hole, and Lisbet had put together some food in case he hadn't eaten. But he brushed his plate aside and retreated to the corner of Lisbet's office with his computer. He hadn't yet said why the rush out here, but his long, narrow face, lit by the computer screen, looked serious.

Jude was trying to pry more information from Lisbet. "Tell me about the victim," she prompted.

Lisbet brought a cup of tea over to Gordon, who took it without raising his head, then she put another on the table in front of Jude and perched on the edge of her desk. "I knew Craig Eberhardt," she said. "Not well, but we'd crossed paths. He worked for Wildlife Services.

"I've heard of them, but what exactly do they do?"

"We've been asking ourselves that for years," was the caustic reply. "Wildlife Services is a federal agency that used to be called Animal Damage Control. Their stated vision," Lisbet said, accenting the word with finger quotation marks, "is to 'improve the coexistence of people and wildlife.' But as you probably know, conservation in this country is not about helping wildlife flourish, but about managing it in a way that doesn't interfere with human endeavors." She took a sip of her own tea. "Sorry if I sound bitter, but we put our hearts into bringing the wolves back from extinction, and now we're at risk of losing them again."

Jude looked over at Gordon talking on the phone while tapping out a message on his computer keyboard. Despite being fifteen years her senior, Gordon was as tech-fluent as a teenager and was armed with an arsenal of digital devices that connected him to a constant flow of information.

"Gordon helped with the reintroduction of wolves to Yellowstone, right?" asked Jude.

"He did, and probably saved our skins as well."

"How so?"

"A lot of folks around here were very upset about wolves coming back. And when we finally got the authorization to release six Canadian wolves into Yellowstone, the opposition was in a frenzy. More than once we were confronted by wolf hunters in camo gear, shotguns, the whole works. They even wore KKK hoods like they were some self-appointed militia. We actually had to keep the location of the penned wolves secret, so we set up camp for ourselves a good distance away. The night before we released the wolves, a group of armed men surrounded our camper. They thought we had the wolves and they wanted to kill them right there. When we wouldn't tell them where the wolves were, they were so enraged I thought they were going to shoot us. Thankfully, Gordon was able to turn them around. But it was pretty tense."

Across the room, Gordon closed his computer, deposited his lanky frame onto a chair next to Jude's and gratefully reached for a tomato and avocado sandwich. Finn sidled over to him to see if his hands needed warming. Apparently they did because Gordon began to absently stroke Finn's big black and brown head while he ate. After a few mouthfuls, he tore off a piece of crust for Finn, who thanked him by taking it gently from Gordon's fingers.

"CJ was able to ferret out some information from a law enforcement source in Salt Lake City," said Gordon soberly. Everyone at The Kinship relied heavily on CJ Malone, their resident tech nerd, intelligence officer, logistics man ... lifeline. "Eberhardt is definitely being treated as a homicide. I'm sure the cops are handling it, but there are rumors that animal activists are interfering with traps in the area, so the FBI is inserting themselves into the mix."

"That should go over well with the local police force," Lisbet commented dryly.

Gordon turned to her. "Give us a little background on Stanton."

She pulled out a map from her desk drawer and opened it. "Here's Yellowstone," said Lisbet, pointing to the northwest corner of Wyoming. Stanton is about twenty-five miles from our border a little south of here. The town itself is small, about three thousand residents. But it's a hub for hunters because of a big elk ranch, and for trappers who come in to the fur auctions in Saint Claire. Hunting season for big game is just about over, but not for wolves and coyote. In fact, a local sportsman's association is gearing up for a wolf and coyote shooting derby, and I hear it's not sitting well with a few of the residents. Because of the relative proximity to us and the other state parks, Stanton also draws tourists and wildlife watchers, so there's always conflict between them and the hunting community."

Gordon's face darkened in a frown. "Maybe this derby is drawing a few hardcore activists. I wouldn't be surprised since Idaho is ground zero right now, especially after they passed an ag-gag law. I'm guessing the FBI is interested because they believe that the ALF is working in the area."

There was a moment of silence as Jude and Lisbet took in this information. Finally, Lisbet said softly, "Animal Liberation Front? I heard about a couple of fur farms that were raided in Wisconsin, and there was some trap interference in Wyoming. It's a pretty radical group."

Jude's naturally translucent complexion had paled a shade. "Well, it's not really a group, it's more of an ideology. But why would anyone think the ALF had something to do with this guy's death? I mean, come on," she spluttered. "The ALF is opposed to violence. They … they don't do that."

"They did firebomb that place in California a while back," Lisbet said. "And they were linked to an arson attack in Colorado."

"That was ages ago. And no one has ever been killed in any of their actions," insisted Jude.

"Murder is not their style, I agree," said Gordon, the muscles in his jaw working. "But systematic trap interference is. It's direct action – it's what they believe in." He began to pace the office. "I hope to God they don't have anything to do with the Wildlife Services killing." He looked directly at Jude. "And I don't have to tell you why."

Lisbet looked back and forth at the two of them. "You have to tell *me* why."

After taking a huge breath, Jude said, "In a couple of weeks, Gordon's going to testify at a Homeland Security hearing on terrorism. They're looking to put more teeth in the Animal Enterprise Terrorism Act."

Gordon picked up the thread. "Bush signed the AETA into law in 2006 as a gift to the meat and pharmaceutical lobbies, both of which would like to get animal activists off their backs."

"They're afraid the public will learn too much about what's happening to animals in factory farms and testing labs," threw in Jude. "Because when people start to learn, they stop buying."

"As of now, the AETA is designed to punish anyone who 'damages or interferes with' an animal enterprise," said Gordon. "The language of the statute is so broad that the term 'interfere' could cover almost any activity, as could 'animal enterprise.' And they went so far as to title the statute in a way that labels animal advocacy as 'terrorism.' Under an earlier version of the act, six people were thrown in federal prison for running a website that reported on some questionable actions by animal activists. The government alleged they were encouraging the activists. Quite honestly, you'd be hard pressed to find any state court that would call that criminal conspiracy, but there it is on the federal law books. And it's making everyone in the animal protection movement worry about getting similarly arrested just for speaking out." He blew out his cheeks in frustration. "It gets worse. There's a Republican named Olander on the Homeland Security subcommittee panel who's pushing this new AETA amendment hard. He's been trying to shut down the animal protection movement for a long time and he's got some real corporate power behind him. They're determined to criminalize undercover investigations on a federal level. I'm the only voice at this hearing trying to convince the committee that it's unconstitutional – and nothing more than corporate repression..."

Lisbet finished his thought. "And if an animal activist is arrested for a murder, not to mention the murder of a federal agent, it damages your case before the subcommittee."

"It does more than that," Gordon threw back. "Just the perception that the ALF is escalating their violence makes it difficult for all animal protection groups."

Jude felt compelled to throw in, "Well, we don't know anything for sure yet. It may turn out to be an accident–"

"They put Eberhardt in a leg hold trap!" exclaimed Lisbet somewhat shrilly. "If that isn't making a statement, what is? For all the animals he's killed in traps?"

"If CJ's sources are correct and someone is sabotaging traps in Stanton, I want to know who's behind it," Gordon said. "I want to know what ties they may have to the ALF and if they had anything to do with this Wildlife Services agent. I hope it's not true, but if it is, we need to be the first to know."

His tone left no room for negotiation and Jude sensed trouble heading her way even before she looked up and met his eyes.

"That's why you flew out here?" she asked softly.

"You could do it," said Gordon.

Jude's heart sunk. "Oh, Gordon, I waited a long time for this week off. I really need it."

"Jude, this is important."

"I know, but what am I supposed to do? Just waltz into Stanton and start asking around?"

"Go in under a pretext."

Jude's stomach tightened. "I ... I couldn't put a cover story together in time."

"CJ will help you with that."

Lisbet broke in. "What are you two talking about?"

"We send Jude to Stanton undercover," Gordon explained. "If anybody can unearth ALF connections, she can."

"I can't leave Finn," Jude protested.

"CJ will put something together that will include him."

"Gordon, please. I don't feel comfortable with this. It's too quick."

He stepped over and crouched by her chair, so that their faces were level. "What's up, Jude? This is not a big deal, you're not using a cover to get hired. You're just going to see where things are at. This murder has to be a huge event in Stanton, and like Lisbet said, it's a small town, people talk. If the ALF is around, you'll find them before the feds do."

She shook her head. "I just don't think it's ... a good idea."

If Gordon saw her blush, he didn't see anything behind it. He knew Jude well, but he didn't know everything. "Listen, we need someone there, ears and eyes on the ground, and we need to do it soon. Hey, you usually jump at these things." He looked at her keenly.

Lisbet broke in apprehensively, "Gordon, I have to agree with Jude. She'd have to have an airtight story. Yes, it's a tourist town, but mainly in the summer. Not now. Now it's gone over to hunters and trappers. They do not like animal activists."

But he had already made up his mind. He stood and pulled an iPhone out of his pocket. "Nobody does," he replied.

Chapter 4

Jude glanced at the speedometer and was surprised to see she was bulleting along ten miles over the speed limit. She'd left Yellowstone midday and driven west, crossing the southern tip of Montana before turning south into Idaho. She eased up on the gas pedal, keeping an ear tuned to the soft, persistent whine of her old Subaru engine. The mechanic back home in D.C. told her not to worry too much about it, any vehicle with a hundred-and-thirty-thousand miles was bound to be a little cranky. But she couldn't afford to break down. The road ahead, coated white from road salt, was just one long, straight line that disappeared into the base of a mountain range that never seemed to get any closer and wisps of cirrus clouds feathered an empty pale sky – all reminding her that she was on her own now.

She'd been here before. Finn in the back, the two of them driving down a lonely highway to another investigation.

Her last assignment had taken her to North Carolina, where a worker at a Marshfield Industries hog slaughterhouse had promised to give her a video he'd made with a concealed camera, footage clearly documenting the terrible treatment of the animals and the miserable conditions for the workers. The meeting never happened and events turned ugly – she became the target of a whole town's animosity towards animal activists. This time she was going in undercover. But it didn't make it any safer. Trying to get the information she needed while maintaining a pretext would be like trying to dance in a straightjacket, and as she cruised closer, she could feel the straps tightening around her chest. She took a deep breath and went over her cover story again.

A few miles outside of Stanton, Jude drove into the parking lot of the motel where CJ had booked her a room. It looked nearly abandoned and was so dismal, she circled the lot and got back on the highway.

"Give me some other options, CJ," she said, putting the phone on speaker.

"How about the Ritz-Carlton?" he grumbled.

"They take dogs now?"

"Why are you doing this to me, girl?" he moaned.

"Because the motel is too far from town and because I'm the one with my ass hanging out here and it has to feel right – or as right as I can feel with just a handful of phony business cards as a cover."

"Didn't you get the hotel receipts? They were in the same package."

"You mean those slips of paper I'm supposed to leave conspicuously hidden in my room in case someone searches it?"

"Ok, they're not perfect, but they'll back up your story about being a travel representative."

"Except that if anyone is suspicious enough to search my room, I'm already toast."

"Well, I'm working on the EO Travel web page. It'll be up by tonight."

"Thank you," said Jude, not feeling terribly cheered. She hated to criticize CJ, the hardest worker in The Kinship. Confined to a wheelchair because of a childhood spine injury that left his legs paralyzed and contorted his body, he lived in a small apartment in the basement of the building where they had offices. He was accessible day or night, computers and phones within reach everywhere. Once, she tried to wrest him away from his work, threatening to take him on a vacation at her expense. He rudely rejected the idea and Jude's feelings were hurt until Gordon took her aside. "Don't force him to go out where people will pity him. He is needed and appreciated here. Let him be."

"What about a bed and breakfast?" asked Jude.

CJ clucked like a disapproving mother. "That's like living in somebody's house. A motel is more neutral."

She had to brake sharply when a gravel-spitting truck pulled out of a ramshackle diner in front of her. Outside the eatery was a message board with changeable letters that read FREE PIZZA FOR EVERY DEAD WOLF.

"We are a *long* way from neutral, CJ," she came back. "As soon as I crossed the Idaho border I started seeing gun racks on every car." Looking back at the diner in her rearview mirror, she asked, "CJ, do you think Finn could look like a wolf from far away? Like, through a rifle scope?"

"Finn? Nah. He looks like a cuddly grizzly."

"I'm serious."

"No, honey. He doesn't have big, standup ears like a wolf. He's got a skinny tail, and that cute Rottie-mix face."

"I probably shouldn't have brought him," said Jude, unhappily.

"They love dogs in Idaho. You'll be fine," CJ assured her. "I'll call you right back *avec les boutique hotels pour mademoiselle.*"

A few minutes later, Jude rattled over unused train tracks and into the town of Stanton. It was made up of one long main street where cars and trucks parked at an angle to the sidewalk. Sturdy brick buildings accommodated some of the mainstay services like banking and realty, while other storefronts with bright hand-painted signs advertised clothing shops, a bakery, a book store. Lisbet was right; Stanton catered to a tourist trade, and that would suit her cover.

After a brief drive-by of the places CJ had suggested, she settled on the Aspen Guesthouse not far from the main street. It was a sizeable clapboard house with red shutters and paned-glass windows edged in early Christmas lights. Jude cloaked herself in her new persona and rang the doorbell. A tall, rumpled man in his fifties let her in.

"Are you booked?' asked Jude.

"No, we have a couple of rooms. How long are you staying?" His hands had a slight tremor that belied his keen gaze.

"A few days. Do you take dogs?" she asked hopefully.

He nodded. "Dogs, cats, horses, mules, whatever you got."

"Well, I left my mule back home ... need him to take care of the cats. Hi, my name is Judy Harris." She thrust out her hand. The outgoing gesture and accompanying banter did not come easily to Jude, but an undercover role was to some degree a performance, and her new persona, Judy Harris, was in sales ... so people would expect an extrovert.

"Foster Dunne," he replied. He had on old sneakers and a sweater vest and wore a placid expression, reminding Jude of Mr. Rogers from the children's show. But as she shook his hand, she could feel the hard sinews of his fingers.

While Dunne loitered in the hall, she brought in her things, doling out bits and pieces of her reason for being in Stanton: she was a rep for a new company called EO Travel, scouting locations for nature and hunting tours that catered to Europeans. "A few Germans, Swiss, we're also signing up some groups from the UK," said Jude airily.

Dunne was quiet, his smile distracted. She waited for him to produce a sign-in sheet or discuss payment, but he did neither.

"And the Austrians are showing a lot of interest," she added, if only to get things moving again.

Finally he asked, "Is Glawischnig still around?"

"Excuse me?"

"Eva Glawischnig, the head of Austria's Green Party."

Jude reddened. Oh, hell. She and CJ had crafted a cover story they figured would pass muster in Idaho and right off the bat she'd run into an expert in European politics. Her heart sank as she conceded that CJ was probably right – she would've been better off at a motel.

"Oh, are you into politics, Mr. Dunne?" she asked, feigning curiosity.

"I'd like it if you called me Foster, and yes, I read a lot of history. But I'm a psychology professor."

"Where do you teach?"

"At the university in Saint Claire. We're on break now, though."

Saving Jude from further conversation, a stout woman with a no-nonsense expression marched into the hallway. Dunne introduced her to Mary Holt and asked Mary to show "Miz Harris and her handsome companion Finn" to the third floor. The housekeeper, or so Jude assumed, opened the door to a simple room with a queen bed covered in a thick, red and blue comforter. There was an old-fashioned braided rug on the floor and a crescent window that looked out over a pine-dotted ridge not too far from the back of the house.

"This is beautiful," exclaimed Jude, taking in the view.

"Yep."

"Can you hike up there?"

"There's a trail map on the front hall table."

"I appreciate the last minute accommodation and letting me bring my dog."

Mary shrugged. "We only have two other guests right now, a coupl'a hunters from Ohio." The way she said 'Ohio' made it sound like an undesirable foreign country. "Breakfast is from seven to nine. You need earlier, let me know. Front door's open til midnight. If you think you'll be out later than that, take a key from the table with the maps. But please return it."

"Thank you," said Jude.

"By the by," said Mary at the door. "I heard Mr. Dunne tell you he's a psychology professor? He tells that to everybody. I mean, he used to be, but he doesn't teach any more. Sometimes he forgets."

"I'm sorry. Is it ... Alzheimer's? He doesn't look that old."

"No, he had a snowmobile accident a while back. Left him with some brain damage. His memory comes and goes, and sometimes things just fly out his mouth – can't tell if it's real or imagined. But on good days, he's sharp as a tack." She gave a last look around the room. "There's extra blankets in the cupboard. And if you do go up in the hills, take a GPS with you. It's real easy to get lost."

Given the terse welcome she'd gotten from Mary, Jude wasn't sure if her parting statement was a warning or a wish.

Chapter 5

Jude set out after loading her backpack with a few essentials like water, dry socks, and phone. She was looking forward to some exercise and escaping Judy Harris before having to dive into the role full time. That was the most difficult part of working undercover – having to play the character every moment, even when she thought she was alone. Because she never really knew who might be watching and listening. Of course there was no reason anyone should anticipate her appearance in Stanton, but all it took was one slip, and she knew from hard experience that people didn't like finding out they'd been scammed. Some of them took it very personally.

The morning had begun bright, but now accumulating clouds dimmed the sun and left the air damp with a sense of impending snow. Finn's nails clicked on the hardwood floor as he paced with anticipation. She spread out the map and saw there was a trail that ascended the hill outside her window then wound around the Saint Claire Lake. The total mileage was not noted, but it was marked "easy to moderate."

Two miles later, Jude was glad she hadn't chosen a "difficult" one. She thought she was fit; she ran some with Finn and went to a gym at home. But by the time she got to the southernmost tip of the lake, she had to stop and catch her breath. She removed her nylon windbreaker, balled it up, and exchanged it for the thermos of water in her backpack. She took off her hat for good measure, shook her hair free, and drank deeply.

Jude drew in a deep breath, able to taste the sweet, pure air. Far beyond the blanket of pines on the other side of the lake, a mountain ridge jutted into the sky. Below the path, the icy cold lake sparkled and seemed to dance to a tune that a warbler was singing nearby. Although every so often she heard the drone of a small airplane in the distance, she hadn't encountered a soul. For the first time in days, she felt a sense of peace.

For Jude, peace was hard to come by. She was a fighter and animals were at the center, always had been. The spark had been ignited in her second foster home, where she'd been a serious and guarded ten-year-old whose gangly legs hadn't yet found their gait. She chewed her nails and gnawed on her chapped lips incessantly. Her foster parents had a dog named Buster, a stocky white and brown pit bull mix with a damaged eye. Jude adored him, and he adored her. He'd wait patiently for her to return from school when she fed him what was left of her bologna sandwich. At night, he'd climb on her bed, giving her short, raspy licks of love.

One day in a funk – she couldn't remember now why – her vigilance abandoned her and she mouthed off to her foster dad. At the time it only felt like the equivalent of baring her teeth at him the way Buster sometimes did. But he slapped the ten-year-old across the face. Buster came to her rescue, digging his teeth into her attacker's leg just above the knee. Enraged, the man hauled the dog outside and tied him to the fence. The next morning he was gone, and Jude knew better than to ask why. She scoured the streets looking for him, she visited the local shelters and left food out in the alleyway behind the house. But Buster never returned, leaving an empty place in her heart that she still felt.

She was self-aware enough to know his loss had left a mark and that she probably identified with him and the other animals abandoned on the street or whipped into submission. But she had little desire to psychoanalyze the feelings away. Maybe someday. For now she drew strength from the anger and defiance that burned inside. Who would fight for the animals if she let the fire die out?

Jude hoisted her backpack and continued. Finn bounded ahead, ignoring his slight limp, and every so often he darted back to make sure she was near. Another half mile and the trail veered away from the lake. Finn galloped down to a rocky stream littered with downed timber. He wagged his tail happily when he saw her, then leapt across and up the other bank, daring her to follow.

Something had captured his attention. Jude raced after him, finding him on the top of the next hill at the tree line. He was standing rigid, his nostrils quivering with a new scent. Ahead of them lay a snow covered meadow, and from out of a dense thatch of trees on the other side trotted a wolf. She reached down to hold Finn by his collar and quietly warned him to stay. He twitched with an urge to give chase.

The wolf's small size suggested a female. Her heavy winter coat was a light brown with darker shading, easy to see against the white open space. She appeared to be tracking something along the ground. The sound of the plane didn't reach Jude's consciousness until she saw it come over the trees and scoop low over the field as if it intended to land.

The wolf had heard it, though. She darted to her right, sprinting toward the trees. The plane swung around, its engine sputtering, and cut her off. The wolf wheeled and dashed in the opposite direction. A man in a safety harness opened the passenger door of the plane and leaned out with a rifle in his hand. He fired. The pop, pop, pop sounded hollow in the damp air. Panic stricken, the wolf ran one way then the other as the plane gave chase.

The aircraft banked once more and this time, when the man fired he hit his target and the wolf dropped. The engine coughed as if in protest and the pilot pulled up the nose and flew off, disappearing over another ridge. Jude's eyes stayed glued to the wolf, who was trying to get up and run. She'd gain some traction with her front paws, but then her hind legs would collapse under her. A moment later, she fell over and lay still.

Jude's feet seemed to carry her of their own accord as she raced down the slope, stumbling over buried branches and roots. Finn ran ahead of her, a mewling sound coming from his throat that she had never heard. Or was it coming from her own throat? The wolf was still alive, but barely. She lay on her side, her flank shuddering, her lips pulled back from her teeth. Blood oozed into the foam at her mouth and more poured from a gaping hole in her haunches. Jude could do nothing but stand with her hands clamped against her head and watch helplessly as the wolf took her last breaths. Her amber eyes stayed fixed on the human, first alight with terror, then darkening in glassy surrender. Jude dropped to her knees and reached out to the wolf's neck where a thick black radio collar had been affixed. She stroked the blood-flecked fur of the wolf's flank, her palm feeling the life drain beneath her fingers.

The drone of the plane broke the silence. "Let's go, Finn," she said. They ran back to the ridge and crouched in the shadows of the trees as the single engine plane came into sight. It circled once and then landed in the field, skis sending up sprays of snow. Two men got out: the pilot, still wearing his headsets, and the man with the rifle. He walked over to where the wolf lay and poked her with his gun to make sure she was dead. Satisfied, he grinned at the pilot and they high-fived each other in congratulations.

They retrieved a hank of rope, then dragged the wolf by her legs to the plane, threw her body over one of the wing struts, and tied her there. The pilot cranked up the engine and the front propeller began to whir. His partner went back to the site where he felled the wolf. He examined the ground for a moment, then looked up in Jude's direction. She held her breath. After a moment, he kicked some snow over the mass of blood, then jumped into the passenger seat, and the plane took off.

Jude watched it climb into the sky, the wolf hanging precariously on the wing strut. She watched until the plane disappeared and Finn came up to lick the tears from her face.

Chapter 6

CJ was doing an internet search while Jude fired questions at him. "Slow down," he said. "First, it sounds like the number is an FAA registration ID that has to be visible on the plane itself, like a license plate on a car. I'll see if I can find out who it belongs to."

During the long walk back to the guesthouse, Jude's sadness was replaced by fury at the men who had killed a collared wolf in such a cold-blooded way. She resolved to find out who they were.

"Second, it's not legal," said CJ. "I'm on the Idaho Fish and Game site now, and according to them, it's unlawful to hunt or even *locate* game from an airplane. Sounds like the men did both. Unfortunately, shooting a collared wolf *is* legal. It says here that hunters are only 'discouraged from harvesting' wolves wearing radio-collars, but they're supposed to report it and return the collar."

"*Harvesting*, CJ? Harvesting is what you do to corn. What I saw was chasing down a defenseless animal with a plane and slaughtering her with a high-powered rifle. Someone put a radio collar on this wolf in order to *learn* about her."

"I hear you."

The more Jude thought about it, the more irate she became. "It was horrible. I can't get the image of that poor wolf out of my head. What did she ever do to deserve that? She was part of a pack ... a family. Maybe she was trying to find food for her pups. Do you know that a wolf pack has incredibly strong emotional and physical bonds? Their whole lives are about being part of a pack. What will they do now? They didn't just kill a wolf today – they broke up an entire family."

Her friend and coworker remained silent at the other end of the line, allowing Jude to talk. "And after she was shot she kept trying to get up and run, but she didn't have a chance. How could she? There's no way to escape that kind of brutality."

"What do you want me to do?" CJ asked gently.

"Find out who owns the plane. If they're supposed to report killing a collared wolf to the state agency, I'm going to follow up and see that they do. If not, I'll get them arrested or fined. It's the least I can do."

"Go get 'em, girl."

"The bastards who shot her? They high-fived each other like they'd won some kind of video game. But they killed an animal ... a beautiful, intelligent wolf, minding her own business." Jude clenched her teeth. "I don't understand people, CJ, sometimes I just don't understand."

* * *

The main street of Stanton acted like a tunnel through which the sharp wind whistled. It whipped her scarf against her face and made her squint to keep grit from blowing into her eyes. So it was with more than a little relief that Jude finally stepped into the Tripp Creek Café. Some would have called it a family restaurant with its plain wood tables and ruffled valance curtains. All in all quite folksy, except for the overwhelming wall décor, every inch covered with hunting photos, beer decals, pictures of high school football teams, and posters romanticizing the Old West. Jude tried to put a name to the haphazard design so she could describe it to CJ, finally settling on "Saddle Blanket Revivalism."

She took a small table by the front window and shrugged off her jacket, welcoming the warmth. Soon, a waitress wearing support hose and thick, brown shoes sashayed over.

"Evenin'. You waiting for someone or you want to see a menu?" she asked cheerfully.

"Just me tonight," replied Jude.

As if to underline this unfortunate state, the waitress gathered up the second, unnecessary paper placemat and silverware. Jude hated to eat out by herself. It wasn't so much the consumption of food – she spent many a dinner in the quiet of her apartment with a book propped open. But when she sat alone in a crowded restaurant it always felt like there was a spotlight illuminating her aloneness and inviting silent speculation about the flaw in her character that had left her bereft of a dinner companion.

The waitress rattled off a few specials, all of which included meat. That was problematic. Jude was a vegan, but in most undercover situations she could hardly advertise it. There were things you had to do to fit in, and even questioning whether a vegetarian dish was made with eggs or cheese could send up a red flag.

Sensing her hesitation, the waitress said, "I'll come back in a minute after you've had a chance to look at the menu. By the way, my name's Abby if you need anything."

Jude examined the menu, finally settling for the pasta marinara and a large green salad – a meal that could easily pass as "normal." She put the menu aside and glanced around the busy café. A few tables were occupied by families, but most were taken up by workmen wearing flannel and heavy leather boots. In the middle of the room Jude caught the eye of one who looked to be in his early thirties. Not unattractive, he'd been laughing at something his tablemate had said. When he locked eyes with Jude, his grin remained unchanged and he dipped his chin in a gesture that reminded her of a cowboy tipping his hat.

Damn! She quickly averted her eyes, hoping he hadn't seen the shock that she felt. He was the one who had shot the wolf, and he was sitting with the pilot. She was sure of it. Anger coursed through her and she bit down hard to keep it from escaping.

She managed to order and wait for her food without making eye contact again, but she snuck a peek once in awhile as the two men ate with gusto. Over her own dinner, Jude put her head down and pretended to study her paper placemat, which was printed with a map of Stanton and an abbreviated history of the town. It had once been called Tripp Creek, but it had been changed to Stanton in 1928 after William Bois Stanton and the Union Pacific Railroad decided to lay tracks through the town. The railway no longer operated here, but on the map, highlighted by a red star, was a place called the Tripp Sheep Ranch, a few miles outside of the town center. She'd seen the name before on lawn signs and bumper stickers left over from November promoting John Tripp for Idaho State Senator. Jude glanced up to find the wolf shooter looking in her direction. The history of Stanton on her placemat became her refuge.

"How was that?" asked Abby, returning to collect Jude's empty plates. She was a sturdy woman with a broad smile, and from the way she chatted with the other diners, it was clear that she'd been working here a while.

"Hit the spot, thanks. The folks over at the Aspen Guesthouse recommended you."

Abby balanced the plates on one arm. "Bless ole Foster's heart. You here to hunt?"

"No, I work for a company that's putting together hiking and hunting tours, so I'm in the neighborhood checking it out."

Abby's face brightened at the prospect of more customers. "For sure," she gushed. "There's lots of visitors come through here. We're not far from Yellowstone and Sun Valley, but not nearly so touristy. If your people want something more authentic, this is the place to be."

Jude forced a smile. "So far I'm liking Stanton."

"Can I get you anything else? Coffee? Dessert?"

"No, thank you. Just the check."

A male voice came from behind Abby's shoulder. "No one leaves here without tasting the fruit cobbler. It's the best in the county." The wolf killer ambled over, presumptuously pulling out the chair across from Jude and taking a seat.

Abby used a free hand to swat him on the shoulder. "What is that? Some kind of pick-up line, Cash?" she scoffed. "You can't come up with better 'n that?"

"I'm just telling the truth," he said innocently. Up close, he had the look of someone who spent his life outdoors; his light blue eyes stood out against sunburned skin, weathered beyond his true age. He flashed an exuberant grin, revealing white teeth behind his thick, brown mustache.

"This lady ... I don't know your name," said Abby.

"Judy Harris."

"She works for a travel agent, putting together huntin' tours,"

Abby continued. She tilted her head to an older, heavier man who had remained standing – the pilot. "This here is Roland Pike. He's an airplane pilot. Why don't you take her up, Pike? Show her around."

He tried to smile, but his fleshy jowls dragged down the corners of his mouth, turning his expression into one of discomfort. "It's not my plane," he said.

Taking back the conversation, Cash turned on the charm. "Hello, Judy Harris. My name's Orin Cashman, but everybody calls me Cash."

Jude consciously tried to soften the hostility in her gaze. *You're Judy Harris*, she cautioned herself sharply, *you're a travel rep who helps people hunt animals. This is an opportunity. Do your job.*

She extended her hand. "Howdy, Cash," she said with as much friendliness as she could muster.

"You be careful of this boy," warned Abby.

Cash clapped his hand over his heart as if wounded. "Me? This gal's a nat'ral redhead and knows how to speak western. It's me who needs the caution."

"That'll be the day," huffed Abby. She leaned in to Jude with a conspiratorial whisper, "Cash works for the *government*."

This time it was Jude who poured it on, pretending to be shocked. "The government? Are you a spy or a politician?"

"Which one would get me a date?" asked Cash, his eyes sparkling.

Abby looked disgusted. "I'm going back to work," she said.

Roland Pike echoed her sentiment, telling Cash, "I'll be outside."

When they were out of earshot, Jude replied, "Neither. But I wouldn't mind someone showing me around. Do you really work for the government?"

"Yeah." He was still grinning. "Wildlife Services."

Jude's jaw muscles twitched in an effort to keep her face impassive. The information was coming too fast for her to digest. *Wildlife Services? He works for the U.S. government? And he mowed down a collared wolf from an effin' airplane!*

"And what exactly do you do in Wildlife Services?" she asked.

"Predator control. You're in wolf territory, ma'am." He put his elbows on the table and leaned in flirtatiously. "Coyotes, bears, wildcats. We protect the good folks of Stanton from bloodthirsty beasts."

"Mmm, in that case, I definitely need a guide," said Jude coyly. She felt nauseous flirting back, but it wasn't just the occasional meat and dairy she had to stomach to get information. "How about tomorrow?"

"Aw, gee. Tomorrow I gotta work," he said. "Maybe this weekend?"

"Sure. Do you think your friend Roland Pike would take me up in his plane?"

"He's workin' tomorrow, too. He doubles as a hunting guide. Got a date with a couple of he-man hunters from Ohio," he said, tingeing 'Ohio' with the same disdain that Mary had. "They gonna shoot themselves a big ole elk at The Mountain Elk Ranch."

The name sounded familiar and Jude found it on her placemat. "Oh, sure. Here it is starred on the map. What is the Mountain Elk Ranch?"

"Private land hunt," he replied and when she looked at him quizzically, added, "It's owned by the Tripp family."

"Any relation to the man who ran for state senator?"

"One and the same. John Tripp. He won by a landslide, too. He has the biggest sheep ranch in the area, but also operates 'bout ten thousand acres where they farm bull elk and bison. It's like a theme park for limp-dick hunters ... excuse the language. But that ain't real hunting.

These guys fly in with their brand new camouflage outfits and a check for ten grand. For that, they get a ride from the airport, snacks, and a guide who takes them to the right spot – usually because Pike's already been in the air to get the elk coordinates – and then tells them what great tracking skills they've got. It's a joke because the animals are raised from babies, they'll eat right out of your hand. They're not afraid of people." As he spoke, he fidgeted constantly in his seat like a hyperactive five-year-old. "Don't get me started on private ranch hunts."

"I've heard of them," said Jude truthfully. "And we have clients who might be interested. Is ten thousand really the going rate?"

"Depends on what you want to shoot. If you just want a cow, it's two grand. But everybody wants to score on the big elk and that costs a lot more. We had a guy took down a monster bull last year, cost him thirteen-five. And that didn't include field dressing, skinning, and shipping the whole freakin' head and rack to Fort Lauderdale, or wherever the hell he lives."

"Sounds like you don't approve."

"I don't care for it, they're as far from real hunters as you're gonna get." He shrugged. "But it's a business."

"I guess I'm on my own then," said Jude, reaching for her wallet.

Cash fingered his mustache. "Well, I'm going to take you out, no doubt about that. But until I do, I wouldn't be trekking around by my lonesome. A lot of strange goings on out there. Don't know if you heard, but there was a man killed the other day."

"Oh?" Jude hoped he couldn't see her heart beating through her fleece vest.

"Damn good trapper, Craig Eberhardt. I learned most everything I know 'bout trapping from him. They haven't caught whoever done it, but there's a group of animal rights terrorists doing some illegal stuff around here and they're real high on my list. They hate our way of life."

"As in government employees?"

"As in trappers and hunters." Putting a period on it, Cash rapped once on the table before getting up. "I'm serious. If you do go backpacking the hills up there, stick to the marked trails and watch out for ice."

She looked up and said in her best western accent, "Well, thank you kindly, mister. I'll see you around."

He laughed. "Yes, you will." Then he did tip an imaginary hat before strolling out the door.

A few minutes later, Jude paid her bill and followed in Cash's footsteps. As she was leaving, she passed a gaunt man in his sixties coming into the café. He held the door and she murmured her thanks, but neither paid the other much mind.

* * *

Ben McIntyre walked in and sat at a table near the kitchen without removing his coat or winter cap. Abby spotted him and after delivering full plates to a nearby table, took the chair across from him.

"Hi, Mr. McIntyre. How're you doin' this evening?"

"Just fine, Abigail, just fine."

"You want the usual? We have a really nice beef barley soup." When he hesitated, she seemed to read his mind and added, "But maybe that's a bit heavy. The other is potato leek. I haven't tried it, but I was told they slaved all day in the kitchen over that pot."

"Sounds unlikely. Nobody slaves over anything in the kitchen these days," said Ben. "But I'll take it.

"Sold," Abby said emphatically. "You want a sandwich, too?"

Ben shook his head. "I don't think so, I'm not that hungry."

"I'm going to have Jimmy make you a turkey sandwich for later. In case you get hungry ... later."

“Sounds like a plan.” Ben gave her arm a gentle pat. “You’re a good girl, Abigail.”

She clasped his cold hand in hers. She wanted to say more, but couldn’t seem to come up with the words, so she gave him an encouraging smile and got up to put in the order.

Chapter 7

The vintage GMC truck seesawed from side to side as it rattled up the uneven dirt driveway. Ben McIntyre grasped the wheel in one hand, steadying his take-out container with the other. He pulled into his usual place, turned off the ignition, and sat for a moment to collect his strength. Not for the first time he considered throwing the pills away. They only made him feel sicker ... and tired all the time. Or was that the cancer? The oncologist wasn't sure about anything; it could be the medication, it could be the white blood cells, it could be this, it could be that, we'll just have to wait and see. She was a nice lady who wanted him to stay hopeful. Ben didn't have the heart to tell her it was too late for that.

He opened the truck door and it groaned in protest, reminding him that he ought to take some oil to the hinges ... tomorrow morning when he was rested. He grabbed his supper, then picked his way over the frozen path to the house he and his brother had built nearly thirty-five years ago. It had started small, but Ben had added on something or other every few years so that now it was a bear to heat. First was the deck so he could look out over the pond, then an addition when the second child was born. Finally, he'd redone the kitchen for Joan. Tried to make it a surprise while she was visiting her cousin in California. But they were late delivering the counter tops, so that when he brought her back from the airport, the whole place was a disaster – a big hole where the sink ought to be, sawdust on the floor, and pots and pans spread out everywhere. Still, his wife's eyes lit up like he'd handed her a diamond necklace. He didn't use the kitchen much anymore.

The light over the front door threw its beam across the walk and over the covered woodpile nestled against the house. Somewhere down by the pond a coyote yipped and another one answered.

He was opening the door when he heard leaves rustle by the edge of the woodpile. Ben turned half expecting to see the swish of a coyote tail or a startled raccoon. But a figure appeared at the edge of the light. Apprehensive, but not frightened, Ben waited. A young man stepped into the full light. He had an entrenched stubble of beard and his wary eyes were drawn in an expression of perpetual opposition.

Ben stared, trying to fast forward the years so he could make sense of this moment. "Hello, Colin," he finally said.

"Hello, Dad."

* * *

As Jude came through the door of the Aspen Guesthouse, she heard the scrabble of canine nails on the wood floor, and Finn trotted happily around the corner to greet her. Behind him was Foster Dunne.

"Good evening," he said. "How was your dinner?"

"Um, very nice, thanks," Jude replied uneasily. "What is Finn doing down here?"

"I invited him," replied Dunne amiably. "Heard him pacing up in the room and thought he could use a change of scenery."

On the tip of Jude's tongue was an irked, "What were you doing in my room?" But she'd just retrieved her laptop which she had left locked in the car, and other than that, there was nothing he could have found to give her away. She also remembered Mary's admonition about his brain injury and decided to let it go for the present.

"Would you like some herbal tea?" he asked.

"You're kind, but I should turn in."

"Come on to the kitchen," Dunne pressed. "I've got a kettle on." He went back the way he had come, and Finn followed as though he had found his new best friend.

Jude rolled her eyes and trailed after them.

The professor was pouring steaming water into a large mug and began dunking a tea bag. "Chamomile or Lemon Ginger?" he asked.

Jude relented. "Lemon Ginger is fine."

Finn thumped his tail against the lower cabinets hard enough to rattle the kettle on the stove. "This is a good dog," said Dunne, bending down to take Finn's head in his hands. "He's been through a lot."

"Yes, he has, as a matter of fact." Jude was taken aback. "How do you know?"

"He told me."

"He did, did he?"

"Didn't tell me how he came by that limp, though."

"He broke his leg when he was a pup," said Jude.

She was glad that Dunne didn't quiz her on the details because she didn't want to have to invent a story; it was always best when maintaining a cover to stick as close to the truth as possible. Jude had rescued Finn during an investigation into a puppy mill. He was only a few weeks old and nearly dead when she found him, suffering from hypothermia and a broken leg. The property owner had dumped the sick and lame puppies – dogs he couldn't sell – in a metal cage, to be disposed of when he got around to it. Jude contacted the local sheriff and the ASPCA, and while they were tending to the breeding females in the squalid sheds, she found the cage out back. Some of the puppies were already dead. But the tiny black and brown mixed breed struggled to reach her. Jude picked him up and warmed him underneath her coat, next to her heart – a place he continued to occupy.

Dunne handed Jude her tea and motioned for her to sit at the table. Above them the floorboards creaked each time one of the infamous "hunters from Ohio" walked across the room.

"Stanton seems like a lively town," commented Jude, blowing on her tea to cool it. As long as she was here, she might as well dig a little. "Certainly if you go by the placemat at the café."

Dunne chuckled, "I think their tableware might be overstating it."

"You have a state senator from Stanton I hear."

Silence.

"And, well ... someone at the café told me that there was a murder recently. That's got to be big news."

"Seems so." Foster took off his glasses and peered through them at the overhead light looking for smudges.

"It sounds as though he was a popular guy," said Jude, probing a little more.

Foster put his hands on the table and used them to push himself into a standing position. "I wouldn't believe everything you hear," he said dully. He brought his cup over to the sink, poured out its contents, and walked out of the kitchen.

For a moment Jude stayed where she was, trying to regain her equilibrium after his abrupt exit. Then she got up and did the same.

Back in her room, Jude double-checked to make sure nothing had been disturbed. It didn't appear so. Maybe Foster Dunne was just lonely and needed Finn's company. Nevertheless, when she got on the phone with CJ, she spoke in hushed tones.

"I got the impression that I'd hit a nerve when I said that Craig Eberhardt was popular," Jude informed CJ. "But he's had some kind of brain injury, so I don't know what to make of it."

"Well, in all actuality, my dear girl, your host may not be totally off his rocker."

"What do you mean?" Jude pulled the comforter closer around her shoulders. She had changed into thick acrylic socks, sweatpants, and a long-sleeved Washington Wizards jersey to fend off the chill in the room; the guesthouse wasn't going bankrupt from heating bills, that was for sure.

"I just sent you a link."

Jude opened her laptop, went into her mail, and clicked on the link. It directed her to a Facebook page, the profile picture displaying a white wolf hanging by a back leg, blood smeared along the side of his head. The page belonged to "Thrill-to-Kill."

"What is this?" asked Jude in disgust.

"It's a page managed by Craig Eberhardt."

"How in the world did you find it?" Jude asked in awe. "And how did you get access to the page?"

"Ve hef our vays."

Scrolling down the page, she saw similar images: coyotes caught in foothold traps, hunters proudly lifting the heads of animals they'd shot–a veritable parade of killings. Each photo was more repellent than the last. Below one of them, a man stated, *Felt good to bring that sum bitch down*. Thrill-to-Kill concurred, *Yeah, hope to see a lot more!* Others had equally hostile observations. *Big dog down, keep up the good work; Like to put a bullet in some pregnant bitch and kill the whole pack!*

CJ said, "You know, last year before wolf season began, the state counted 659 wolves. Then they killed over seventy percent of them during hunting and trapping season. There's probably been some new pups born, but since this year's season began, the count is already 75 wolves killed."

"You've got to be kidding. Are they trying to wipe out the entire species?"

"Go down to a picture of several wolves dumped in the back of a pick-up."

Jude followed his instructions and soon found the photo with the caption, *Half a pack, whacked and stacked.*

"Mr. Kill gets some real pushback here. Check it out."

A person named Shawn had written, *You wolf haters are sick bastards*. Eberhardt responded, *Shawn, you're a liberal, tree-hugging pussy*. Then followed a childish exchange about who was more ignorant. Other posts and gruesome photographs of dead and maimed wolves spurred equally vile antagonism. Facebook fist fights. Eberhardt and allies lashed out at anyone who found fault with hunting, vowing to kill every wolf they could find. Some even claimed to ignore quotas and hunting regulations in their quest to get rid of them all. This drew bitter responses from a number of people. A person named Kylie H. threatened to shoot anyone who tried to kill a wolf on her property. Another, Tom Ryan, posted that he wouldn't mind *gutting every hunter in Idaho*. And then one that read, *I find out who you are Thrill to Kill and I'll skin you and mount your head on my wall.*

"So I'm looking at this stuff," CJ was saying, "and I'm thinking it could just be the ravings of your basic social media lunatics, but I'm going to see if I can track down some of these folks. Maybe we'll find one in Eberhardt's back yard. Just maybe one who found out Thrill-to-Kill's identity and made good on a promise."

"You think the cops have seen this?" asked Jude.

"I doubt it. They might have my computer skills, but they don't have the imagination. Who would expect a Wildlife Services agent to have a public Facebook page like this?"

"Speaking of, tonight I met the guy who shot the collared wolf. He *works* for Wildlife Services. Fancies himself some kind of cowboy. He actually had the nerve to come on to me."

CJ grunted. "Does the name John Tripp mean anything to you?"

"Sure. He owns the big sheep ranch here and he just won a seat in the Idaho legislature. Why?"

"The FAA registration on that plane goes to John Tripp in Stanton."

"The same person?"

"Him or a son, or father, I suppose."

"What is he doing letting Wildlife Services use his plane? I thought it was illegal to hunt from a plane."

"Well, apparently that doesn't apply to Wildlife Services."

"Is that true? They don't have to follow state regulations?"

"It's not entirely clear. Their policy directives say that they do have to comply unless it 'conflicts with their statutory authority.' Sounds like double-speak to me. Everyone I've talked to says it's very hard to get information out of Wildlife Services. There are a couple of senators who have been trying for years, but haven't had any luck."

"They shouldn't have to rely on *luck*! Wildlife Services is a federal agency, funded by taxpayers. Something very weird is going on around here."

"Then you just watch your step, missy. Especially with your new cowboy, wolf-killer friend."

Sometime later Jude woke from a nightmare. She was looking at Eberhardt's Facebook page and the photo of the grinning hunter holding up the lifeless body of a wolf. Only as she looked closer she saw that it wasn't a wolf, it was Finn. His eyes were blank, his tongue hung limp, and blood was spattered on the rocky ground at the hunter's feet. Jude cried out in the dark, and Finn padded over to the side of the bed. He put his cool nose into her outstretched hand and stayed until he felt her heartbeat return to normal.

* * *

They stood a few feet apart, tension crackling in the misty puffs of breath that encircled their faces. Ben gripped the paper bag containing his dinner so tightly it started to rip. Finally, he looked away from his son and said gruffly, "Best come in then." He shouldered through the front door of the cabin, switched on a light, and nodded in the direction of the wood burning stove in the corner. "Remember how to start a fire?" he asked.

"Of course," said Colin. He found what he needed next to the cast iron stove and sat on his haunches to set up the kindling and newspaper. It had been eight years, but the box of wooden matches hadn't moved from its spot on the windowsill. Aware of his father opening cabinets slowly and deliberately in the kitchen, he put a match to the wood and waited while it took. When the flames steadied, he carefully added a couple of logs and stood up to face what came next.

Ben had put the sandwich still wrapped in wax paper on the counter that separated the kitchen from the living room. "You want something to eat?" he asked Colin.

Colin shook his head.

"Suit yourself." He came into the living room with his container of soup and sat in a worn armchair by the stove.

"Place looks good," said Colin. "You did the kitchen." He ran his hand along the countertop as if to reacquaint himself with his old house.

"You never saw it?"

"No."

"That's right," concurred Ben with an acid edge to his voice. "You didn't come back for your mother's funeral."

Colin looked down. "You know I couldn't."

"Oh, now I remember ... you were in jail."

"I was," said Colin. He remained standing, unsure whether or not he wanted to sit and make himself a more permanent target.

"Your brother stayed with me for a time."

"That was nice."

"And he had a family to take care of."

"David is the good son."

"You don't have to be snide."

"And you don't have to drive it home that I've disappointed you. That's always been my understanding."

Ben had a few spoonfuls of his soup which by this time had turned lukewarm. He set it on the table next to him. "Why'd you come back?" he finally asked.

"I heard you were ill."

"Who told you?"

"It's not important. What is it?"

Ben waved his hand wearily. "Some kind of cancer."

"Are they doing anything?"

"I've got some chemo pills."

"What does the doctor say?"

"She says take the chemo pills."

The corners of Colin's mouth twitched to cover a wry smile. "And are you listening to her?"

Refusing to be drawn in to his familiarity, Ben exploded, "What do you care? Just what is it you want from me?"

His father's indictment fueled Colin's guilt, like the logs feeding the fire a few feet away. He'd been in federal prison when his mother died and they wouldn't let him out to attend her funeral. It still ate him up inside, less because it made him such a fuck-up in his father's mind, but because he wanted to be there for his mom. Yes, he'd been a lousy son and he had to live with that. What did he want from his father? Colin had no idea. There was too much anger on both sides to answer that question.

Ben gestured irritably to the chair across from him. "Sit," he said. "Have a sandwich."

Glancing over at the counter, Colin asked, "What kind is it?"

"Turkey."

Colin ran a hand through his wavy hair, brushing it off his brow and buying a moment to keep his temper in check. "I don't eat meat, Dad, you know that."

"Oh, yeah." His father pretended to remember. "What did they feed you in jail?"

"Crap mostly. But I managed. I traded food a lot."

"So when did you get out?"

"Eighteen months ago. But I only recently heard about your illness." He could see his father trying to assess whether he was telling the truth.

"You got a job?"

After a pause, Colin said, "I'm doing some carpentry here and there. Making do."

The fire had begun to warm the room, yet Colin kept his jacket zipped. In a compromise, he removed his thick work gloves, stuffed them into his pocket, then perched tentatively on the arm of a love seat across from his father. The knuckles of his right hand were scraped and two fingertips were wrapped in bandaids. He searched for something to fill the silence. "The place looks good. I see you took old Marvin down," he added, referring to the elk head mounted over the front door ever since he could remember. Then noticing the absence of all the hunting trophies on the walls, he said, "Wow, you took them all down."

"I'm sure that sits well with you," remarked Ben. He adjusted himself in his chair, suppressing the moan that begged escape at the stab of pain in his lower back.

"You were so proud of them."

Ben stared warily at his son. "If it's all the same to you, I'm not up for a fight."

"I'm not either."

Colin held his breath, afraid that if he let go, he'd say something he'd regret. Speaking his mind rarely had a peaceful ending with his dad. Finally, he asked, "Are you using the hunting cabin at Freedom Lake?"

"Why do you want to know?" Ben looked at him through narrowed eyes, and then it dawned on him. "It's you, right? Holy Crap, you're back at it. Lord a'mighty, when will you learn?"

"I need a place to stay, Dad. Just for a few days. Then I'm gone."

Ben stared at the wood burning stove, his mouth making unconscious chewing motions.

"I'm not in any trouble, if that's what you're worried about. Please, Dad. Just for a few days."

With some effort, Ben got to his feet and went into the kitchen where he retrieved a key from one of the drawers. He handed it to his son and their rough fingers touched.

"I'll bring it back and you won't have to see me again," said Colin. "Take care of yourself, Dad, okay?" He turned to put two more logs in the wood burning stove, then slipped out into the night.

Ben pressed his palms to his eyes and then to his mouth to keep from calling his son back.

Chapter 8

Jude hurried past the Tripp Creek Café on her way to the state's local Fish and Game office. Gordon's mission for her in Stanton was quite specific, but she wanted to find out what the connection was between Wildlife Services and the rancher John Tripp. With any luck, she might also get more of a bead on Craig Eberhardt as a Services employee.

The office was located in the back of Fielding's Outfitters. She was told to ask for Sal. At nearly eight thousand square feet, Fielding's was the biggest hunting and trapping retail outlet within miles. It was crowded for a weekday morning, a central station for burly, canvas-vested and flannel-jacketed men as busy shooting the breeze with one another as buying merchandise. Jude decided to take a look around.

She wasn't a complete novice to the hunting culture, but the array of products left her slack-jawed. Guns and rifles occupied only a corner of the store. There were entire shelves filled with scents and "critter" decoys – electronic devices with speakers and remote controls to lure animals into the hunters' gun sights. One was a battery-operated fake squirrel that vibrated and squeaked like an animal in distress. Jude walked past flashlights, knives, GPS systems, binoculars, and laser scopes, nearly every item offered in a camouflage pattern. Above her head, models of hunting tree stands, from single-man chairs to more elaborate mini-tree houses, were assembled in the rafters. One of them was festooned with a banner proclaiming it "Your Home Away from Home." She wandered down another aisle where bow sets were displayed. Many resembled assault rifles fitted with wheels and pulleys and came with sizeable price tags and names such as "Bear Mauler" and "Sinister Compound Bow." Jude picked up an arrow shaft and felt its cold, steel heft in her hand. The packaging on the box promised "more penetration and shorter blood trails ... more bone-crushing power for deeper penetration." Beyond the shafts were the arrow heads – fist-sized steel missiles as sharp as razor blades.

The unmistakable clash of metal on metal drew her attention to the traps. Here were a multitude of ways to capture an unsuspecting animal: cage traps, body-gripping traps, coil-spring traps, rolls of wire cable for creating snares designed to tighten around an animal's neck. A store clerk was demonstrating the operation of a steel-jawed coil spring trap.

"Now this is your number nine Bridger Wolf Trap," he explained to the customer, pointing to a large, square-jawed contraption with heavy springs. "The nine inch spread snaps higher on the leg for a better hold. This'll take coyote, wolf, or even bigger."

Jude wondered if it was the same type that had slammed onto Eberhardt's leg.

"How much?" asked the customer.

"One nineteen, but I can cut you a break on six or more."

"No can do. Need cheaper."

"Not a problem. How about this MB 730, absolutely affordable, will do the trick every time," the clerk moved on. "Heavy duty laminated jaws. Like I said, very affordable. I can sell you a half a dozen for under two hundred. What are you looking to take?"

"Coyotes. Dirty sons-of-bitches. One got into my chicken coop and tore up half my flock."

"Put a few of these around, you won't have any more problems. Let me show you the action."

The clerk set the trap on the floor and opened the jaws by stepping on levers, one on each side. With his feet in place, he set the "dog," a latch that held them open. He looked around to make sure no one was in close proximity, then stepped off gingerly. He retrieved a scarred axe handle from behind the counter, then lightly touched the pan between the jaws. Like a gunshot the jaws clanged shut, creating another set of deep gouges in the wood.

Further down the counter, a man examining wire cables threw over his shoulder, "I've used those and they're not as good as the Bridgers."

"No?" queried the customer.

The man shook his head. "The Bridgers will break the coyote's leg on impact, which is what you want. Takes the fight out of them. You get less wring-off."

The novice trapper cocked his head.

"Wring-off, you know, where the animal chews his leg off to get out of the trap."

"Oh, I don't care about the pelt. I just want to kill the damn varmints."

"Yeah, well, if it chews its foot off, it gets away. See what I'm saying?"

Jude was unaware that she was staring dumbfounded at the exchange before her. The store clerk looked over and asked, "Can I help you, Miss?"

"Oh, yes," she tried to say brightly, as if the discussion she'd just heard was nothing more than the merits of one toaster over another. "I'm looking for the Fish and Game office?"

The clerk indicated the rear of the shop. "Go through that door to the restrooms, keep on going straight and you'll see it."

She followed his directions, relieved to get away from this supermarket of death and suffering for animals. She felt physically sick and her hands shook with anger. Was this the hunter's idea of "fair chase" – the code that supposedly made killing animals ethical if done in a manner that does not give the hunter an improper advantage? What was *fair* about state-of-the-art lures, night scopes, GPS systems, and high tech weapons? They made a mockery of fair chase.

After taking a moment to pull herself together, Jude walked down the corridor and knocked on the last door where a sign on a piece of paper scotch-taped to the door identified the office as belonging to the Idaho Department of Fish and Game.

"Open!" a deep voice called out.

Inside, a long-limbed woman with short brown hair sat behind a desk, squinting at a computer screen. She wore khaki cargo pants and a black zip jacket. "I'll be right with you," she said holding up a finger. Then she typed a sentence and used her mouse to save the document.

Jude took stock of the disheveled space. Pamphlets were heaped in uneven piles on top of file cabinets and books were stacked on the floor. A coat tree in the corner held a mountain of outdoor gear, including a pair of rubberized overalls and a down jacket. Two pairs of boots had been kicked off, landing a few inches away from a rubber mat meant to collect the melting ice and mud.

"Sorry, I just had to input something while it was fresh in my mind," said the woman. "Hope it's decipherable, I can't seem to find my reading glasses." She patted various pockets in her uniform, but couldn't locate them. "Oh, well, what can I do ya for?"

"I'm looking for Sal."

"You found her." She looked to be in her mid to late forties, and her rangy physique seemed perfect for a Fish and Game warden.

"My name is Judy Harris."

"Ah, you must be the gal that Foster told me about."

"Word spreads fast in Stanton," said Jude, making a mental note to take CJ's hotel recommendations more seriously in the future.

"Foster Dunne is my brother. He tells me you have a big dog that doesn't drool and is very well mannered."

"My better half," said Jude with a smile.

"Sal Mayhill," the warden stuck out her hand.

Jude launched into her story of working for EO Travel and her reasons for visiting Stanton. "Thought as long as I was here, I'd pick up a copy of hunting and trapping regs and maybe a trail map if you have one."

"Sure," replied Sal, getting up to rummage through some materials on a bookshelf. She was a couple of inches taller than Jude and in her squared-off shoulders, it was easy to see the resemblance to her brother. "You can find pretty much all the information you need on our website. Just have to know what zone you're in to tell what you can hunt and when," she cautioned. "Here you go. You plan to use guides?"

"We do. I'll be looking for some local people when we start to finalize our packages. In fact, I ran into a couple of guys yesterday from Wildlife Services–"

A buzzer sounded over the office door. "'Scuse me," said Sal. "I have someone outside."

With a rhythm that attested to routine, she climbed into the rubberized overalls and a pair of heavy boots. Then she grabbed a clipboard from her desk. "You can come out if you want to," she said.

Jude didn't have to be asked twice.

The Fish and Game officer greeted a man at the bed of his pick-up truck. With barely a glance at Jude, he threw back a tarp, exposing a jumble of rough fur and bone. Out of the mess, Jude detected the heads of three small wolves or coyotes in various stages of decomposition. There was also a more recent kill – a male wolf lay stretched on his side. A magnificent animal, he was black and gray, with a graze of silver fur on his underbelly and muzzle. Jude held herself back; he looked much like the charcoal pair of juveniles she had seen in Yellowstone. She remembered what CJ had told her about the number of wolves killed since the season began and like a counter inside her mind, the number ticked upwards from 75 to 76.

"He's a monster, ain't he?" asked the trapper proudly.

Wordlessly, Sal pulled on gloves and turned her attention to the other animals, pulling their carcasses to her where she could examine them.

"Thems is coyotes," he said to Jude, pronouncing it *kai-yotes*.

She nodded in return. "You don't say."

Sal was looking closely at one of the skulls still covered with gristle and fur. Her eyes narrowed suspiciously as she asked, "When did you take this one, Curt?"

The portly trapper with a full beard pulled off his cap and returned it to his head with the brim backward. He squinted up at the clouds, stalling for time.

"She looks at least a week to ten days before you even got her into the freezer," Sal scolded. "The other two don't look a whole lot newer. You checking your traps regular?"

"Yeah, of course."

"I see a lot of tooth damage and necrosis." The state rule mandated that traps had to be checked every seventy-two hours, and in that time, a panicked animal could do fearsome damage to their teeth trying to chew through the steel trap. But Sal was looking at the kind of breakage that indicated an even longer period.

"I check my traps. Sometimes ... sometimes you miss one or two," he responded defensively.

Sal turned her attention to the wolf, making sure the trapper had affixed a tag from his allotment as required by law. The trapper tried to distract Sal as she worked. "As I was coming over, guess who stopped me?"

"Couldn't begin," murmured Sal, measuring a broken canine.

"Two federal agents from the F. B. of I.," he said. "Thought they might be spies for Barack Hussein Obama, what with their city suits and all. But they come on account of Eberhardt. Didn't say so, but I know." He threw a wink in Jude's direction.

Sal never looked up.

"They're going around asking about sprung traps. I told 'em some asshole messed with a couple of mine and Walt Beale got hit for even more, all busted up with a sledge hammer. He's spittin' nails. I asked the 'feebies' if they're after Craig Eberhardt's killer. Oh, they like to play it cagey, like they're in the movies, so they didn't say nothin'. Must think I'm dumb as stone. But make no mistake, they're looking for who killed Eberhardt. Freakin' eco-terrorists is who. Animal activist scum. Sick fuckers, the way they killed him. I don't go anywhere without my shotgun. One of them comes near me and he's looking at– "

"Alright, you're done," broke in Sal. "You've met your quota, though. No more wolves."

"Ah, Jeez," he whined. "You siding with the tree huggers now? Wolves are evil. If we don't kill 'em, they're gonna kill us."

Sal gave a weary sigh, having heard it before. Squaring up to him, she said sternly, "It's my job, trapper. No tags, no wolves."

"Shoot," he said, turning away. "Just like a woman to ruin my fun."

With a barely disguised glare, Sal stripped off her gloves and pulled a notebook from her back pocket. "Put him on the scale and let's get him weighed. Then you can go." She went over to wash up in the outdoor sink. The ice cold water made her chapped hands worse, but the predators she had just inspected, long since dead, were host to massive bacteria and gloves weren't enough to protect her.

Jude took the opportunity to engage the trapper. "I heard about the man who was killed," she said. "That's horrible. Do they know who did it?"

"Oh, they got their ideas, alright," he assured her. "Wouldn't tell me his name, but they showed me a picture of the guy they're looking for. Young man, but old enough to know better, dark hair tied back in a ponytail like a damn hippie."

Jude stood planted, trying to rein in her emotions. This was exactly why she hadn't wanted to come to Stanton in the first place. It sounded like Colin. She suspected it might be after she'd seen how close Stanton was to his childhood home in Saint Claire. Of course she'd thought about him ... a hundred times. But the memories had been worn threadbare over the years. Now, the trapper's general description matching Colin brought them all back with a piercing clarity.

She was in her final year at the university and had stood at the fringe of some student protests to stop the school's testing on animals. At one of them, a tall, lean young man approached her and asked if she cared about animals and if she knew what was happening to them in the labs. When Jude nodded, he thrust a protest sign into her hand and said, "Then if you don't speak out, you're complicit." He pulled her into the center of the rally where she was welcomed. Jude had known what it was to be marginalized, treated as a something rather than a someone, and she quickly fell in with the small group of animal activists living near the university. There, in a run-down section of the city, she finally found a home, part of a band of comrades who shared the same passion to speak up for the voiceless. They protested and chanted, handed out leaflets, got handcuffed and dragged to jail, then released, only to do it again. Living off the grid, they were a zealous troupe of fighters, sleeping on couches in the basement, cooking vegan meals, vigilantly composting, talking late into the night about the best ways to expose animal cruelty.

There, too, she fell in love. Colin McIntyre was a grad student drop-out, not much older than Jude. Their number was loosely organized, but all of them looked to him as the leader, and she was captivated by his intensity. At the time, she was uncomfortable with some of risks they took, but she stayed for him. Colin became collaborator, lover, and her best friend. Jude couldn't imagine being anywhere else or with anyone else.

But soon, the edges of the tight knit group began to fray. One of the members tiring of the transitory life, accepted his parents' offer to pay for grad school. And then someone leaked plans for their sit-in at the university lab. Distrust seeped into the structure of the group like water permeating a wood foundation, rotting the framework. That last summer, Gordon appeared on the scene. He was ten years older, smart, strong-willed ... and he was making waves in the animal rights movement, releasing undercover videos of cruel practices inside factory farms and at circuses and rodeos. Gordon didn't engage in direct action. Instead, he fought for animals with attorneys and press releases. It was lawful, stable, and there was a job open for her if she wanted it.

The decision was excruciating, but Jude finally traded in a piece of her heart for the stability she'd never known. One night while the others were asleep, she threw her few belongings into a duffel and left, leaving just a note on the back of a crumpled anti-testing flyer.

She hadn't wanted to come to Stanton, fearful that she might see Colin after all this time, fearful that she wouldn't.

"The FBI is right, that trapper *is* dumber than stone," said Sal, interrupting Jude's train of thought. "'Just like a woman to ruin my fun'" she mimicked. "But not everybody in Stanton is like that. Just so you know." The trapper was gone and they began to walk back to her office.

"How much is a wolf tag?" asked Jude.

"Eleven-fifty. But that's if you're a resident. For your tour group you'd be paying the nonresident fee, and that's thirty-one dollars."

Jude swallowed her horror at the notion that one could kill such a magnificent animal for the price of a party pack of Budweiser. "Thanks, you've been really helpful. One last thing," she said as if she had just remembered. "I saw a program about biologists who put special tracking collars on wolves? Are those animals off limits?"

Sal began to strip off her overalls. "We discourage it," she said. "Radio collars are to keep tabs on them in the hope we can avoid conflict, but we can't stop folks from hunting them. Just have to return the collar."

"That goes for everybody?"

"Of course. The equipment is expensive. But it doesn't happen often. We had a few last year, but this year none so far."

None so far. That meant that Cash hadn't reported killing the wolf to the state authorities. This disregard for the regulations made Jude angry all over again. For her, the whole hunting and trapping culture was grotesque, but at least a misogynist, misguided trapper like Curt came in to get his "take" tagged and accounted for. As she stepped quickly back through Fielding's, away from the wolf carcasses and the smell that seemed to have attached itself to her clothes, away from the traps and the realities of a world where for many, killing animals amounted to a day's entertainment, Jude decided that she was going to find out if there were *any* rules constraining Wildlife Services.

Chapter 9

Jude's new task made it all the more imperative to find the ALF cell in town – if, in fact, there was such a group. Whoever was sabotaging traps would likely know a great deal about how Wildlife Services operated.

Stanton was nothing like the urban streets of her early protesting days, so she didn't expect to find a vegan restaurant where animal advocates might congregate. But using her EO Travel story to study menus, Jude canvassed the main street, searching for a place that might at least offer soy milk or a veggie burger. No such luck. But in the window of a craft shop, she spotted a flyer promoting an upcoming debate between John Tripp and Margaret Cunningham, a representative from his district. The issue was Stanton's Wolf and Coyote Derby. Jude had seen posters in town heralding the two-day shooting event, which offered trophies and a $1000 cash prize to whoever killed the largest wolf (length and weight) or the most coyotes. Children were encouraged to participate with "youth prizes" in the 10-14 age group. The flyer had been put out by Cunningham's camp and her position against the derby was clear. In this hotbed of hunting and trapping, an animal-friendly position was a place to start, and Jude asked the shop owner if she knew who was distributing Cunningham's material. The owner pointed down the block.

It was nearly four o'clock when Jude pushed through the door of a small bookstore called Eat, Sleep, Read. Their marketing plan looked simple: cram as many books into as small a space as possible along with a few comfortable chairs ... and keep a pot of coffee on hand. The aroma of a strong Italian roast led Jude to the back of the shop.

A young man came out through a beaded curtain carrying a tray of clean cups. His head was shaved and he had a nasty bruise under his left eye. But what caught her attention was his tattoo – a series of paw prints that ran from the back of his right hand up his arm and disappeared beneath his rolled up sleeve. She decided this was a place to linger.

"I'll have a black coffee, de-caf, please," she said. "Very cool place you have here."

He poured her a cup from a glass pot on a hotplate. "It's alright."

On the counter was a stack of Margaret Cunningham's flyers. "This looks interesting," said Jude, picking one up.

"Yeah, well, she's the only politician making any sense about the wolf issue."

"What is a Wolf Derby?"

"It's a contest to see how many wolves and coyotes you can kill – our town's equivalent of a county fair, only instead of rides and cotton candy, you get guns and blood."

Jude made a face and asked innocently, "Do you think wolves should go back on the endangered species list?"

"Of course." He took the opportunity to lecture. "The federal government is totally abdicating its responsibility to protect wolves and other wild species by letting states like Idaho do their own wildlife management. When your own state wildlife agency is funded by hunting fees, you think there will be *any* wolves left?"

He seemed ready to launch into further explanation when a woman came out from the back. "Oliver, I have to go into Saint Claire to–" She stopped midsentence when she saw Jude.

Recovering quickly, she turned her back, busying herself with housekeeping behind the counter. But she'd recognized Jude and vice versa. The same petite frame and straight back, the same forward thrust of her jaw. Her light brown hair was now cropped and she was a good deal older, but it was Laurel, of that Jude had no doubt. Was she the connection?

Jude pretended to browse for books until Oliver went into the back. She brought her now empty cup to the counter where Laurel was still tidying up and decided to test the waters rather than confront her directly.

"Great coffee," said Jude, "Hard to get good de-caf."

Laurel had recovered and looked Jude square in the eye. "Glad you liked it," she said with a quick, wary smile.

"I was just talking to Oliver about Margaret Cunningham."

"Yeah, should be interesting. Excuse me, I have to check something in the back." She disappeared through the beaded curtain.

Ten years sat well on Laurel Altman, thought Jude. Her teenage cheeks had filled out and she'd lost that hungry, count-me-in-whatever-you're-doing look. Of course, when they'd been activists together, Laurel was only seventeen. The last Jude had seen of her, she was being physically removed from the lobby of a university lab by two officers. Jude later heard that the teenager had become active in the ALF. She couldn't know for certain where Laurel's sympathies now lay, but she guessed from the girl's unwillingness to speak openly that she might still be involved.

Jude gave it a minute then poked her head through the curtain. Laurel was gone and there was no sign of Oliver. Dammit. There was only way she could have left. Jude trotted out to the sidewalk and down a narrow alley behind the bookstore.

Calling out Laurel's name softly, she walked tentatively to the back door of the neighboring shop, thinking Laurel might have gone in there. Jude had her hand on the doorknob when out of nowhere, she was shoved against the brick wall and her arm wrenched behind her back. Jude resisted, but her assailant increased the pressure.

"What are you doing here?" hissed Laurel in her ear.

"Christ, that hurts," gasped Jude.

"What are you doing here?" Laurel repeated.

"Would you ... Laurel, just let me go so we can talk, okay?"

Slowly, Laurel released her and stepped away. Jude wheeled around. "What the hell was that about?" she asked.

The girl's mouth was set in an unforgiving line and she breathed heavily through her nose, waiting for an explanation.

"I'd like to help if I can," said Jude.

"I don't know what you're talking about."

"No?" Jude rubbed her strained shoulder. "Pretty funny way of showing it."

Laurel glowered back.

"Look, I know about the traps," said Jude. "Everybody knows what you've been doing, including the FBI. I want to meet with whoever is running the operation." After a pause, she took a chance and asked, "It's Colin, isn't it?"

"Get the fuck out of here," said Laurel, lashing out.

Bingo.

"Listen to me, you folks are in trouble," Jude retorted impatiently. "You've been destroying government property and now they suspect you of murdering a government agent."

"We had nothing to do with that," Laurel blurted out, immediately regretting that she'd done so.

"Personally, I don't think you did, either. But I've got news for you – the FBI does, and two of them are already here in Stanton looking for Colin."

"Go away, we don't need you."

But Jude had seen a flash of alarm in Laurel's eyes, and she pressed, "I want to meet him face to face. I think we can help."

Laurel scoffed, "You and *Gordon Silverman*? *Help us*? That'll be the fucking day."

But Jude had made the contact. "I'm staying at the Aspen Guesthouse, but don't send word there. I'll come back to the bookstore." She brushed past Laurel and retreated up the alleyway, certain that despite Laurel's parting shot, she would go to Colin and he would make the decision. Jude hurried along the street, fighting the urge to look over her shoulder. A seed of doubt had begun to sprout, and it grew quickly, its vines choking her self-confidence. *Oh Jesus*, she thought, *what am I doing? I have just warned Laurel and Colin and whoever else about the FBI. I just crossed a line.* Her mouth went dry. *Could that make me an accessory? I don't think they killed Eberhardt, but ... but what if one of them did? What if it was Colin? Maybe he'd changed. Prison can do things to people.* The next thought came crashing through her jitters, even more unnerving. *What if he doesn't want to see me?*

Chapter 10

Silky layers of gold and orange streaked the horizon, as if an unseen hand had rolled out cosmic bolts of shimmering fabric. Oddly, its light gave the snow a lavender tinge. But as the sun fell, the colors faded. A young coyote trotted along a post and barbed wire fence, his nose to the ground tracking a mouse. His ears were almost too big for his head, like an awkward teenaged boy, and one of them was nicked from a rowdy play-fight with his brother. At eight months old, he was just shy of leaving his mother's side to make a life of his own, but his surging independence took him farther and farther from the safety of the pack every day. Too far today. The scent of the mouse and the vibration of his tiny mouse feet scurrying under the snow were tantalizing.

Then another smell stopped the coyote in his tracks. This one even more appealing. Sweet with decay, it promised a satisfying meal. His hunger drove him forward and he hopped over a black cottonwood tree that had fallen and taken the fence with it. He opened his nostrils to drink in the robust new scent in the prairie grass. The prey was not running – it was there for the taking.

Suddenly, his paw touched a hard object and heavy jaws slammed into his leg like the vicious bite of a larger predator. The coyote yelped in pain and he tried to flee. But he was jerked back by a chain affixed to the trap. The motion dug the steel teeth into his lower leg even deeper, but he tried again, and again was tripped up and yanked backwards. He had never encountered this. What was this thing that kept him from running, that kept him from escaping the pain? It hurt so much. Fear rose up in his throat; he made a sound that started as a bark, then careened into a screeching howl. *My pack, my pack! Come find me. I want to come to you, but I cannot.*

He howled again, throwing his head back and erupting with the cry that was to sail over the tree tops and across the streams to the far away place where his pack gathered. He waited for the return call, but none came. Only the sound of the wind whispering across ice ponds.

The young one panicked. He bucked. He lurched from side to side, trying to shake the bad thing from his leg. He bit down on the metal, but it wouldn't let go. As the darkness descended, he fought the trap and the pain until he had no more fight left.

Chapter 11

"Stop the killing!" cried the woman. "Real people wear fake fur!" She was camped out in front of a clothing store across from the Tripp Creek Café, handing out flyers to anyone who would take them. Most would not. A man burst angrily from the store, and Jude could hear them from where she stood.

"Move on, Harrington," he told her. They obviously knew each other. "Nobody gives a rat's ass about you and your fur."

Clutching the stack of leaflets to her chest, she turned her back dismissively and held one out to a woman passing by. "Don't buy fur. Cruelty is not a fashion statement," she urged. The woman took the piece of paper, but shoved it unread into her pocketbook as she walked on.

"Not in front of my store," insisted the owner, taking Harrington by the elbow. "Come on, get outta here."

She wrenched her arm from his grasp and marched across the street in Jude's direction. She was a large-boned woman with long braided hair and high Slavic cheekbones; immediately she spotted Jude as a potential target. "Please don't buy fur. Animals need their skin," she announced, thrusting out a flyer.

Jude glanced at it quickly, half expecting to see a scrawled note from Colin, but saw only a computer-generated handout featuring a photograph of a wild fox juxtaposed with a picture of pelts at an auction. An older couple tried to pass by on the sidewalk unnoticed, drawing Harrington's attention. Jude took that moment to duck into the Tripp Creek Café. She couldn't afford to be seen with an anti-cruelty protester, much as she was tempted to offer a gesture of solidarity.

The breakfast crowd had cleared out, giving Jude an opportunity to linger over coffee at a corner table. She missed Finn snoozing at her feet, but the Wi-Fi connection at the guesthouse was decent only on the main floor where Foster Dunne kept showing up at inopportune moments. Jude had resigned herself to keeping her laptop with her at all times, especially knowing Dunne had been in her room. She ordered coffee and a bagel and booted up. *Who or what was Wildlife Services?*

Right away a red flag went up. Wildlife Services was a program of the U.S. Department of Agriculture's Animal and Plant Health Inspection Services (APHIS).

Jude had some experience with APHIS, an agency charged with establishing standards for the care and treatment of certain animals bred for and used in medical and product research. The standards weren't high and enforcement was sporadic at best; animal protection groups were forever hammering away at the agency to do its job. She was puzzled. What did the APHIS have to do with *Wildlife Services*? Wolves weren't used in laboratory research. The public face of Wildlife Services on the web didn't offer much of an explanation. They claimed to focus on dispersing bird populations at airports to prevent airplane strikes. Jude had to dig deep into the site to find any information about wolves. Even then, the brief text stated only that they worked with state agencies to investigate livestock depredation and to engage in the "direct removal of depredating wolves to resolve conflicts." Infuriatingly vague and benign language.

She turned her attention to John Tripp, who owned one of the largest sheep ranches in Idaho with a herd of 20,000 rams and ewes. He was a fourth generation sheep rancher and held leadership positions in several livestock industry groups: Idaho Sheep Ranchers, National Lamb Feeders, U.S. Wool Growers, and Rangeland Resource Commission. Jude had to wonder with all these duties and running a ranch, how he had time to serve in the state senate.

She came upon an interview in an Idaho news magazine that offered some insight into why his private plane might have been used to gun down a gray wolf. He was quoted as saying:

I lost 85 sheep last year to predators. We have to get rid of these wolves. And I mean kill 'em. There should be an open season on wolf hunting, just like we have for coyotes. And we have to be allowed to use any weapon at our disposal, including ATV's, night scopes, aerial hunting, and live bait. Folks around here understand this. Without active management, these wolves will eat the sheep farmer out of operation. We need simple, common sense laws, not more government constraints and regulations.

Question: The government has removed gray wolves from the endangered species list here in Idaho, haven't they?

Yes, it's about time the federal government understood what we're going through. They made a big mistake in the first place. They didn't listen to us, they bowed to the liberals and the environmentalists. Now maybe they understand the ramifications of what they've done. Wolves are multiplying like vermin and they're running rampant, killing our livestock.

Question: Aren't there ways to protect livestock without eradicating all the wolves?

Not unless you want to pay double for your beef, lamb, and wool. But it's more than that. You've got to understand – wolves kill for fun. They slaughter the sheep and don't even eat them. The people promoting non-lethal options don't get this business. These environmental activists from Yale or Harvard are clueless about how to run a ranch. What they promote as non-lethal methods cost more than the loss of sheep. And here we let our sheep out on the range. It's a beautiful thing and lets the animals do what nature intended. My lamb is as organic as you're going to get.

From the corner of her eye, Jude saw the check appear on the table. But so engrossed in the article, she didn't look up. A minute later, taking the hint, she closed her laptop, dug for her wallet, and picked up the slip of paper to see how much she owed. Below the circled total, it read: *3pm Albertsons*. Jude quickly scanned the cafe, but the waitress was nowhere in sight. Her rational mind told her that it could be some note the waitress jotted to herself, it could be someone else's check, it could be any kind of accidental notation. But she knew it wasn't. Her racing heart told her it was a message – Colin would see her.

* * *

Jude pushed her cart down the cereal aisle and tossed in a box of Cheerios, adding it to the few items that would make her look like a legitimate shopper. This was her second trip down the same row and she was beginning to wonder if she'd interpreted the message correctly; it was already 3:20 and she hadn't seen any sign of Colin or Laurel. It *had* to be the place, though. This outlet of Albertson's chain of grocery stores had shoppers going through all day long and would be a good neutral ground to make contact. She turned the corner and nearly ran into Laurel standing on tiptoes reaching for something on the top shelf.

Without making eye contact, Jude steered her cart around her and meandered a few feet down the aisle, intent on finding just the right bag of flour. She was examining one product when she heard Laurel's hushed voice behind her. "Go outside and look for a brown Taurus wagon with a dent in the rear fender."

Jude hesitated, a hundred questions playing on her lips, but a woman with two small children in tow was striding toward them, perhaps trying to escape one of her whining toddlers.

Laurel said with hushed urgency, "Go now. Leave everything here." And without a hitch, she took over Jude's shopping cart and walked away.

As instructed, Jude left through the automatic doors and looked over the parking lot. A puff of exhaust came from one of the cars in the last lane to her right – a mud brown Taurus with a badly dented bumper. She went up to the passenger side and knocked on the lightly tinted window. The door opened and she got in.

The first thing she noticed was the paw print tattoo on the driver's arm. "Hullo, Oliver," she said.

This, however, was an entirely different young man than the one she'd met at the bookstore. That one seemed distant, but at least cordial – this one barely looked at her. His wore a baseball cap pulled low over his eyes and a sulky expression.

"I appreciate this," said Jude, trying to break the ice.

He said nothing and gave away nothing with either a look or gesture until they had driven about a mile and turned onto a side road. Then he reached into his pocket and tossed her a black bandana.

"Tie this over your eyes," he said flatly.

"Aw, come on, Oliver," Jude pleaded. "We're on the same side."

"Put it on."

She thought he was overplaying the security, but understood where he was coming from. The Animal Liberation Front was perceived as an extremist group, trademarked by a black-hooded figure and scrawled graffiti. And although it had no centrally co-ordinated operation, federal officials labeled groups of activists as "cells" to bolster the perception that they were organized terrorists on the scale of Al Qaida. Indeed, despite the fact that no one had ever been killed or even hurt in any ALF operation, the FBI called them the "top domestic terrorist threat," leaving white supremacists and anti-government reactionaries with their arsenal of weapons and portfolio of deadly crimes further down the list. Whether or not law enforcement really believed the ALF to be a threat was irrelevant. The business sector lobbies were powerful – particularly in agriculture and pharmaceuticals. They had pushed through the Animal Enterprise Terrorism Act, which was driving law enforcement's heavy-handed response to proponents of animal rights.

Jude saw that there was no negotiating with Oliver, and she started to wonder if his paranoia was justified. If he needed to keep Colin's location secret, even to her, then maybe Colin had a lot to lose should the wrong people find out where he was. Doubt about his innocence clenched her stomach as she tied the bandana over her eyes.

"Laurel told you who I am, right?" she asked.

He didn't answer.

"How far is it?"

Oliver didn't answer that either, leaving Jude to ride the rest of the way in silence. After a few miles, she gave up trying to remember the turns. The farther they went, the rougher the road, and by the end it was all she could do to hang on and keep from hitting her head on the roof when they hit big potholes.

Some time later, the car came to a halt. Oliver got out, and Jude heard his footsteps retreat, crunching over dried leaves. She waited a moment, then removed her blindfold. They were deep in the woods at the end of a poorly maintained dirt road. It took her eyes a moment to adjust to the wan light of dusk, but she made out a plain log cabin about a hundred feet away. She got out of the car and walked tentatively closer. As she neared, the door opened and Colin stood framed in the doorway.

She willed her feet to keep moving, her mouth to say something, but they refused to obey. She stood frozen while an unseen hawk's screech pierced the immeasurable space between them.

Colin made the first move, casually trotting down the two step landing and giving her a cursory embrace. "Your hair got so long," he said, pulling away and looking at her. "I like it."

She had prepared herself for how awkward this moment would be, how nervous she might feel at seeing him, how remorseful, how lonely. But now, matching his crooked smile and meeting his gaze under the furrowed brow she knew so well came as naturally to her as breathing. She reached out and touched his stubbled cheek. "You look good," she said.

They grinned at one another like shy teenagers.

"You still with Gordon?" he asked.

"With The Kinship, yeah. But not like with ... Gordon. No, not that way."

He gave her a look that she couldn't decipher, then asked, "How is that old fart?"

Jude laughed. "He's fine. He sends his regards."

"Bull*shit*," guffawed Colin. They both knew it wasn't true. "Come on in. We'll talk. Uh ... sorry, though. Mind if we check for a recording device?"

All at once the good feeling Jude had at seeing him vanished.

But she lifted her arms and let him respectfully pat her down, looking for a telltale wire or microphone. She reminded herself that this was a business meeting.

* * *

Logs sizzled and popped in the fireplace as Jude poked at them from her cross-legged seat on the floor. Colin was heating some black bean soup on a Coleman stove. There was an undercurrent of strain in the room, not the least of which came from Oliver. He lounged indifferently on the sofa, one leg thrown over the armrest and a beer in hand, but resentment radiated like heat from his body.

Jude had had enough of his silent temper tantrum. "I'm not your enemy, Oliver," she said.

"You're not my friend, either," he retorted.

"You think I'm going to rat you out to the FBI?"

"If I thought that, I wouldn't have brought you here."

"Then what's your problem?"

"I don't trust you."

Colin ambled between them and handed Jude a beer. "Oliver doesn't trust anybody," he said, taking a swig from his own.

"Well, what the fuck is she doing here the exact same time as the feds?" asked Oliver petulantly.

"Bro, chill," said Colin. He took a seat on the other side of the fireplace, leaning his back against the wall and stretching out his legs. He smiled at Jude, but his eyes bored into hers. "So what gives? The timing is a little odd, yeah?"

Jude had to tread carefully. She explained about being at Yellowstone and Gordon's sudden arrival upon hearing about Craig Eberhardt. "A contact in Boise told him that because of the trap interference, the FBI was getting on board."

Colin looked bemused. "The FBI thinks *we* killed that lunatic?"

"Apparently."

He shook his head in disbelief. "Wow, they are some radical ideologues. What happened to a regular homicide investigation? By real cops?"

"Why do that when you can pin it on the ALF?" added Oliver, his voice dripping with sarcasm. "Eberhardt was a major a-hole. There's probably a dozen people who would've liked to take him out."

"Like who?" Jude pressed.

Oliver backed off. "I don't know. Why don't you ask around?"

"I can't. Not directly, anyway. I'm here as a travel representative named Judy Harris."

"So Gordon sent you ... to do what?" asked Colin.

"Find out who's interfering with the traps and if there's a connection to the murder."

"And what is Gordon's interest?"

Jude looked down, scratching at the label on the beer bottle. "He's testifying at a hearing on the AETA and wants to be proactive about any bad publicity for the animal movement."

"Screw Gordon Silverman and his friggin' *publicity*," exclaimed Oliver.

Affronted, Jude looked up. "And what's wrong with publicity?" she challenged. "Maybe you guys ought to think about your image a little more."

Oliver waved her off derisively. "Double fuck *image*! We're trying to save animals, not get ourselves on Oprah."

The sounds of a motorcycle outside halted the confrontation. Jude glanced at Colin, but he appeared unruffled by the cycle's arrival. A moment later, Laurel came through the door, holding a sack of groceries. She looked at Colin and then at Jude, her body language speaking volumes about her feelings for the trio's leader. The tension in the cabin immediately ratcheted up a few degrees and Colin stepped in.

"Can I have a word outside with you two?" he asked, nodding to Oliver and Laurel. Peeling himself from the sofa, Oliver complied. Laurel did as well, but not before setting down the grocery bag with more force than seemed necessary.

It felt a very long two minutes to wait out the hushed argument that took place in the driveway, but Jude knew they were being careful. Oliver didn't know her at all, and Laurel was just a youngster when they'd been activists together. Only Colin knew her – she hoped well enough to know that despite their differences she would never betray him. And he must have said something along those lines because when they returned, Laurel and Oliver seemed somewhat chastened.

Colin got everyone up and working on putting dinner together, and soon after, the four sat around the hand-hewn coffee table, savoring black bean soup and fresh bread, and drinking red wine out of chipped mugs. Full stomachs and wine seemed to lighten the mood, and for awhile Jude was lulled into the comfortable fellowship of old times.

"How long have you been here?" Jude asked Colin.

"Few weeks, maybe."

"Here, in this cabin?"

"No, I was hanging with Oliver for a while, but decided to get my own place for a bit. This is my dad's hunting cabin. Ironic, right?"

Laurel got up from the sofa to pour herself more wine, and Oliver took the opportunity to point out that she had dog hair on the seat of her pants. She calmly brushed some of it off, saying, "Black pants, white dog, what can you do?"

"What white dog?" asked Colin.

"Your father's dog," Laurel replied, surprised that he didn't know. "Her name's Oona. She goes everywhere with him."

"Hunh, I saw him the other day, but I didn't see any dog." Colin looked into the smoldering fire. "We always had one, as far back as I remember. Sometimes more than one. My father used to hunt with them, which I hated. But he was very attached to them..."

The conversation went from dogs to wolves, and Jude described the aerial gunning she had witnessed. "I keep thinking I should have done something," she finished. "Scared her off or run out in the field and kept them from shooting her."

"And you're sure it was Tripp's plane?" Colin wanted to know.

"According to the registration. I was reading about him this morning. He claims that he lost 85 sheep to wolves, so I guess he'd want Wildlife Services to come in and help manage that situation. But the hypocrisy is stunning. In the interview I read, he goes all conservative and complains bitterly about government regulations and interference in peoples' lives, but he's sure happy about a U.S. agency killing wolves to protect his business interests."

"That doesn't begin to cover the hypocrisy," said Colin. "First of all, the ranchers get reimbursed by the federal government for confirmed wolf attacks that result in the death of a sheep or cow. And guess who's charged with confirming whether or not a predator is responsible? Wildlife Services. Second, John Tripp and all the other ranchers are grazing their livestock on public lands for less than one-tenth of what it would cost to put them out on their own property. Then, the money the government does collect in grazing fees goes right back into a fund that pays for shit like fencing and water development to support *more* livestock grazing."

"So, the ranchers use public land essentially for free," offered Jude.

"While the rest of us pay the environmental cost," Oliver added.

"I hate them," Laurel asserted. "The public trust doctrine says that all wildlife, including wolves, belongs to all Americans. And behind our backs, the government is decimating wildlife in the most horrible ways to appease the ranchers. They do whatever they want," she added bitterly. "They shoot wolves and coyotes from the air, they trap them, and they do something called 'denning,' which I can't even talk about without wanting to go out and whack somebody."

But Jude wanted to know.

"Okay, *denning*. It's when they kill wolf or coyote pups right in the den. They go after the babies. Sometimes they throw burning cartridges of sodium nitrate and charcoal in the dens. It's supposed to suffocate the pups, but it's more likely to burn them alive. Or if it succeeds in flushing them out, the men break their necks or shoot them execution style. I've even heard they chop their heads off with a shovel." Laurel stared belligerently at Jude, as if furious that she'd been made to describe the most heinous of Wildlife Services' activities.

Her indictment had once again fouled the air inside the cabin, but this time with a shared sense of anger at the brutality toward animals. Jude stared at the floor while the others silently wandered the room, unable to shake the images. Jude finally got to her feet and went outside.

Colin found her on the front porch, her forehead pressed against one of the posts, her arms wrapped tightly across her chest. He put his hands on her shoulders and gently pulled her back to lean on him.

"How can human beings be that cruel?" asked Jude softly. "I wonder all the time and never get close to an answer."

She sounded so lost that Colin couldn't help himself. He

wrapped his arms around her and pulled her close. Jude not only let him, but felt her body melt into his. The way it used to be. They stayed in their gentle embrace listening to the night sounds. But then she had to know. "Did you do it?" she asked.

"Do what?"

"Did you kill Craig Eberhardt?"

He turned her around roughly and grasped her shoulders. "How could you even think that?" he demanded, his scowl deepening.

"Just tell me you didn't do it."

"Christ, Jude. I *didn't do it.*"

"Then why does the FBI think you did?"

"I don't know," he said angrily. "I'm an easy target – I'm Animal Liberation Front – I'm everything corporate America hates and fears."

"But you have been messing with traps?"

"I'm not answering that."

"It's illegal, Colin. You're asking for trouble."

He moved away from her and put his hands on the porch overhang, leaning out and staring up into the dark sky, flushed with messy, brilliant stars. "Not anymore. I'm done asking," he said thickly. "We used to *ask* for a lot of things, didn't we? Like good boys and girls, we wrote our congressmen, we drafted petitions, we drew signs and marched and protested, and we played by their rules. Shit, we did everything we could, screaming at the top of our lungs about what the world was doing to animals, how human beings were raping the earth and the oceans. No one is fucking listening, Jude."

Laurel poked her head out the door and they quickly turned. "It's nearly seven," said Laurel. "I thought, Jude, you couldn't stay long because of your dog and all."

"Yeah, thanks."

When Laurel retreated inside, they stood without touching, but close enough to hear each other breathe.

"Oliver will take you back," he finally said.

"Bet he loves being my chauffeur," responded Jude lightly.

"Don't mind him. He's still angry about spending six months in jail on some crap misdemeanor in Wyoming."

"What happened?"

"He got caught freeing a marten from a snare."

"Good Lord, don't prosecutors have anything better to do?"

"The right to hunt and trap is taken very seriously around these parts," Colin said wearily.

"Was it bad for you?" They both knew she was talking about his two years in federal prison.

"Some day I'll tell you about it."

Oliver tromped out of the cabin and went straight to the Taurus to start it.

"But not now," said Jude sadly.

"Not now."

"Will I see you–"

He put his finger to her lips to stop her from asking. "Don't," he said. "Don't do this to me."

Jude finally saw the hurt in his eyes – the hurt that had been there since he'd opened the cabin door, the hurt that might have been there since she'd walked out on him years ago.

She tugged gently at the collar of his shirt. "Take care of yourself," she said.

This time it was Jude who fell silent in the car and Oliver who wanted to talk. With the bandana prohibiting sight again, all she could do was listen to his tirade at Wildlife Services and their indiscriminate trapping practices. They didn't post notices. They didn't check their traps regularly. "I've seen animals that have been dead for days in those things," he said. "At least the fur trappers have some incentive to check their leg holds and snares – they want the pelt before rot sets in. Not Wildlife Services. They're getting a goddamn *salary*. And we're paying for it."

"So I guess you weren't too unhappy to hear about Craig Eberhardt."

"Are you kidding? I am beyond gratified that he suffered the same pain that he put countless animals through. I heard he was *alive* when he got put in his own trap. And just like the animals, he tried to claw his way out. His fingers were all torn up. That's what I call justice."

She turned her head in Oliver's direction, and in her mind's eye she saw again the bruise on his left cheekbone. It looked to be about a week old, and she wondered what kind of accident or fight caused it. And now he was saying that he *heard* Eberhardt had been alive in the trap? Jude had read a few newspaper articles about the homicide, but that detail had never been mentioned. How the hell did Oliver know that?

Chapter 12

The town hall was a tinderbox. At least it felt that way to Jude, who had come to the much-anticipated debate on the Coyote and Wolf Derby. The parking lot was full a good half hour before it was to start, so she left her car down the street and joined the stream of people heading to the hall. A sign posted on the front door announced "no firearms," but there seemed to be no police presence to enforce the mandate. She found a spot against one wall with the others who were too late to get a seat. And now, crammed into the claustrophobic, ochre-painted room fitted with industrial carpeting and vinyl ceiling panels, Jude took stock of the crowd. She and CJ had figured this might be a good place to put faces on one or two of the voices expressing rage at the Thrill-to-Kill Facebook posts. Moreover, she wanted to see John Tripp in person.

At the front of the room, two tables were set up on either side of a lectern. Tripp hadn't yet arrived, but Margaret Cunningham was seated at the far table. She had a stoic, determined look about her as she reviewed her notes. Much to Jude's surprise, next to her sat Lisbet Hammond. Their eyes met, and Lisbet's face lit up. Jude quickly looked away, hoping the Yellowstone biologist knew better than to initiate contact with someone working undercover.

The room was clearly divided along party lines. On the side nearest Jude, if camouflage caps and work dungarees were indicators, sat the anti-government, gun-enthusiast, pro-Derby contingent – hunters, trappers, and ranchers. Across the center aisle congregated anther group wearing t-shirts that read "Guns DO Kill People" and "Protect Our Wildlife."

Jude was not surprised to see Cash and Roland Pike standing in the back. Cash appeared uncomfortable in the crowded room, shifting his feet and looking this way and that. Trying to stay out of sight, she tucked herself behind a burly man to her right. As she searched the sea of faces, she landed on two men that she immediately made as FBI. Short hair, one in his early forties, the other about ten years younger, neither one had taken pains to hide his affiliation. Only missing were their Ray-Bans and flak jackets. Like Jude, they were casually scanning the crowd.

A murmur from the back announced John Tripp's entrance. He stopped to shake hands and exchange a few words with friends as he made his way toward the lectern. Tripp looked every inch the celebrity statesman, Jude thought. He was square-jawed and clean-shaven with just enough gray around his temples to engender confidence in his experience. Although he was just over six feet, his cowboy boots and Stetson added a couple of inches; a bolo tie with a silver and turquoise slide completed the western look. Tripp went over to Cunningham and took her hand in both of his, greeting his female opponent in true politician style.

She had won the toss and elected to speak first. Cunningham stepped up to the lectern as the pro-derby posse settled back in their folding chairs and crossed their arms defiantly. "We have a proud tradition in Idaho," she said. *So far, so good.* "In 1893, the historian Frederick Jackson Turner wrote that the expansion of the western frontier shaped our history, infusing practicality, energy and individualism into the American character. And with the new century came a growing appreciation of the beauty in our wilderness and the need to protect it. As Idahoans, we must carry that tradition forward. It is incumbent upon all of us to protect that which makes our state so magnificent – including our wildlife, and particularly the iconic wolf."

Her opening remarks had been received quietly, but now the mention of "wolf" drew some hisses and boos. Cunningham smoothly launched into the economics of wildlife watching, arguing that wolf recovery was predicted to bring in seven to ten million dollars annually.

"Wolves are good for our state. Of course I understand the ranching community's concern about loss of livestock," she continued. "But there are some forward thinking ranch owners who are willing to consider non-lethal methods of predator control, such as increasing guard dogs and herders, lighting, and electrified fences."

"Too expensive," someone called out.

"Expensive as well are the paychecks our counties hand over to Wildlife Services, as is the national perception that here in Idaho we want to kill all the wolves – a perception that negatively affects our tourism. There is a vast expanse of publicly owned land here in the west, and almost three-quarters of it is currently grazed by privately owned livestock. But it doesn't belong to the ranchers – it belongs to all the taxpayers of the United States and it belongs to all Idahoans." Cunningham directed her next remarks to her supporters. "Most of us do not benefit from the subsidies that go to just a wealthy few. Shopkeepers, plumbers, waitresses, all rely on tourist dollars. You often hear ranchers and hunters say that they are the stewards of the land. But I say, we are all stewards of the land. What do we tell people visiting Idaho when they see us slaughtering coyotes and wolves in a so-called *sporting event*? What will we tell our children when there are no wolves left? It's time to find an economically stable and environmentally sound balance that that will accommodate the ranching and hunting industries along with our precious wildlife."

Cunningham's supporters erupted in applause and cries of "That's right!"

One man yelled out, "Well, I pay taxes and the wolves are killin' off all the deer and elk in the whole damn state. How am I gonna eat?"

A woman on Cunningham's side rose from her seat. Jude recognized her as the anti-fur leafleter named Harrington. "Hey, Winston," she hollered. "I see you at Albertson's every week buying a case of beer. Why don't ya use that money to buy groceries instead."

"Meat is too expensive. I have to feed my family," he retorted.

"Give me a break," scoffed someone. "By the time you pay for bullets, gas, license and hunting fees, your venison costs like $22 a pound."

"And don't forget to add in the value of Winston's *time*," added Harrington, rolling her eyes, "which makes the whole thing add up to ... $22 a pound."

Winston shot her the finger and she launched a mirthless laugh in his direction. As she sat back down, a couple behind her patted her on the back, "Nice, Kylie."

Something pinged inside Jude's head, feeling like the vibration her cell phone made to notify her of incoming email. But she brushed it aside; John Tripp was getting ready to speak.

Idaho's biggest sheep rancher had no interest in trying to counter Cunningham's arguments. He had no need to. Not when he could capitalize on the fear and resentment that so many residents already harbored. Big government wanted to take away their guns. Hunting and teaching your kids to hunt was the great American tradition – just another fundamental right that the environmentalists wanted to strip away. The reintroduction of the "most deadly predator on the planet" represented Washington's treason against civilization itself. He finished with as phony an emotional plea as Jude had ever witnessed. "Just two days ago, one of my ewes was attacked and killed by wolves," he said. "I care deeply about each and every one of my animals. Do you know what it's like to see one of them tore up like that?"

His false sentimentality made Jude sick. Tripp was in the lambing business – every year he sent thousands of baby sheep to the slaughterhouse. Nonetheless, he seemed to be winning over many in the crowd who nodded in sympathetic agreement.

"Damn right!" shouted a man. "They kill for the fun of it."

Another called out, "I say gut-shoot the sons-of-bitches. Make 'em suffer!"

Margaret Cunningham held up her hands to try and stave off the disorder that Tripp seemed happy to instigate. "We must look at wolves in a reasonable way," she said. "Let's hear from someone who knows more about them than anyone." She introduced Lisbet as a wolf biologist from Yellowstone and posed the question, "Is it true that wolves kill for *fun?*"

"Not at all," replied Lisbet. "Like many carnivores, wolves are opportunistic hunters. Their attacks actually have a very low yield in the wild, only between four and eight percent of their attempts are successful. And when they do attack, they're often themselves wounded by the hooves of an elk or moose. So if wolves come across unprotected sheep, they will take more than they can immediately consume. But they're not wasteful. They'll come back and eat everything they've killed."

Tripp twisted his mouth into a smile. "Then why is it last month I found three of my sheep ripped up and lying around on the hillside?"

"What did you do when you found them?"

"I brought my men in to move the rest of the herd and I called the authorities to come take a look."

"There's your answer," said Lisbet evenly. "With people combing the hill, the wolves likely left the area. I would also add that many times hunting and killing wolves actually increases attacks on livestock. When a pack is disrupted with the death of one or two, the juveniles without a family are much more likely to go after livestock because the pack can no longer teach them how to hunt other prey, such as elk or deer."

A heavy-set man in the third row stood up, his face beet red with anger. "You enviros are all the same," he burst out. "You're not even from around here. You love the cute little puppy pictures of wolves and you want to keep 'em out there, by golly, so you can take a picture with yer expensive camera. Woohoo, you saw a freakin' wolf!"

Lisbet pressed her lips together. "Every one you kill makes it that much more unlikely that anyone *will* see a wolf."

"That's the way we want it," insisted the man. "We ought to make the derby twice as long."

This brought the anti-derby folks into the mix and sparks flew as each side slung accusations at the other. The woman named Kylie stood and railed against involving children in the derby. "You're gonna teach these kids to kill? You're gonna give them cash prizes for destroying a life? What is *wrong* with you people?"

On the other side, a woman took a step forward to get in her face. "Listen here, Harrington, hunting is the American way of life! I want my kid to hunt, and I'll be damned if a bunch of big city know-it-alls are going to tell me how to run my family."

"So you put a gun in your kid's hand at age ten?" sneered Kylie. "Then wonder what the fuck happened when he mows down a bunch of shoppers in a Boise mall?"

"Oh, get off it! You don't know the first thing about guns."

"Wanna bet?" challenged Kylie. "Step foot on my property with your traps and your goddamn bow and arrows and I'll show you what I know about guns!"

A lone police officer finally appeared and hurried to the front of the room. In the commotion, Jude made eye contact with Lisbet, then began to push her way to the double doors in the back. Outside in the chilly night air, she trotted toward the parking lot, hoping that Lisbet had taken the cue. She had, because she appeared a few minutes later and joined Jude, who steered her away from the glare of a streetlamp.

"You begin to see what we're up against," said Lisbet after a quick embrace.

"I do. Listen, where are you parked?" she asked.

"Just over there."

"I can't talk long," said Jude in a hushed voice, as they walked to Lisbet's car. "Is there someplace we could meet tomorrow?"

"Did you find out anything about Eberhardt?"

"Not yet. I need to find out more about Wildlife Services first."

Footsteps drummed on the pavement and Jude felt an object whizz close to her ear. Then the explosion of a brick rocketing through Lisbet's windshield. Both women leapt back as the car alarm sounded, and over the noise a man shouted, "Hey, Wolf Lady, you're next!" A side door in the town hall swung open and light streamed into the parking lot framing the police officer in the doorway.

"Where can we meet tomorrow morning?" asked Jude hurriedly. "Not in Stanton."

"There's a coffee shop in Saint Claire, just past the fire station. Can you get there by 9:00?"

"Okay." Jude squeezed her arm then slipped into the darkness, leaving Lisbet, pale and strained, shaking broken glass from her coat. She'd have to file a report and deal with the curious onlookers by herself.

When Jude got back to her car, she sat with the keys in her hand, trying to make sense of what had just happened. Someone had finally managed to turn off Lisbet's car alarm. But it wasn't the only warning that had gone off for Jude. She was shaken by the level of hostility toward wolves. In her investigations, she'd seen many animals treated badly, but it was usually out of ignorance or apathy, born of a belief that animals were things to be used, then discarded. But there were people here who *loathed* wolves, who wanted to see them suffer. It was an ugliness that she had rarely encountered. And the verbal attacks from the animal defenders were scary as well. Jude thought particularly about the woman named Kylie, red-faced and belligerent, the same anti-fur protester that the shop owner had addressed as *Harrington*. Or *Kylie H* ... the person who'd posted threatening messages on Thrill-to-Kill's Facebook page. Jude was certain when she heard her name that they were one and the same. Had Kylie figured out that Craig Eberhardt ran the Thrill-to-Kill page? If so, what might he have done to push Kylie too far?

Jude entered the town hall troubled by Oliver's fury at Wildlife Services and his knowledge of unreported details about Eberhardt's death. But after seeing some of the anti-derby folks, especially Kylie Harrington, her doubts about Oliver had some company.

Chapter 13

"Damndest thing," Charlie Ferrow went on, "you'd a thought with a thirty-thirty load, they coulda killed him outright, even from a hunnert yards."

Ben gazed out the passenger window of the car while his friend drove and kept talking. "That's what I heard, anyhow. You know Gary Powell at the Post Office? His brother-in-law works at the hospital where they brought Eberhardt. A thirty-thirty. The bullet blew a hole right through his shoulder. Then while he's down, they snap a big ole coil spring on his leg. Poor bastard. No way he could get that thing off, not when he couldn't move his arm. Christ! I'm still having nightmares 'bout it. Those animal activists are a bunch of sicko's, I'll tell you that much. Can you imagine? Left to die in a twelve-inch steel jaw? If the cops catch whoever did this, they better lock him up the hell away from here 'cause everybody I know would like to take a crack at this guy before they give him the death penalty. Oh, and get this ... two FBI agents come to my house to hear the story from me direct, and whiles they're at it, they're perusing my collection. They see my Marlin 336 and ask me what kind of ammo I use. Oh, shit. Can't lie about it, I gotta tell 'em it takes a thirty-thirty load. But I says there ain't a hunter around here who *don't* have a rifle like that. I mean, hell, you got a Marlin, right? Or a Winchester?"

Ferrow drove up the dirt driveway and Ben winced every time the wheels hit a rut. The pain in his back had spread to his abdomen, and the news from his doctor this morning hadn't helped.

"Listen, uh, you want me stick around?" asked Charlie, hoping the answer was no. His discomfort about "the cancer" was unmistakable. They'd been pals for years, but he hadn't even asked what the doctor said. Ben understood; he didn't want to hear it either.

"Nah, Charlie," said Ben. "You've done enough. I appreciate the lift. I would have canceled today, but my doctor gets peeved at me when I do that."

"A lady doctor, yeah? That'd be all I need – another woman touching my private parts and bossing me around."

Ben chuckled weakly and opened his door. The sound of a power saw came from the back of the house. He hesitated.

"You got some work goin' on?" Ferrow asked.

There was no contractor van anywhere to be seen.

"Yeah," Ben lied reluctantly. "Um ... just some little things."

"Sure you don't want me to stay? You need help getting inside?"

"No, I'm good."

Ben got out and walked slowly toward the front door. He paused long enough to watch Ferrow turn his car around and drive off. The saw whined as it cut through another board.

Colin was in the back adjusting a three-foot board into the space where he'd removed one of the rotting planks on the back deck. A pencil clenched between his teeth, he held the board in place, nailed in one side, and then the other. He turned to cut the next and saw his father standing at the edge of the driveway above him.

"Mornin', Dad."

Ben stared at him.

"I borrowed your saw. Hope that's okay." Colin was shaken at how pale and thin his father appeared.

"I thought you would have left by now," said Ben.

"Yeah, soon. I just ... when I was here before, I noticed that some of the boards were looking pretty weathered. You don't want to let that go, you know? And you had a little bit of this red oak left, so I thought..."

Ben walked away.

"Thanks, son," Colin finished under his breath. He stood for a moment, corralling his emotions, then went into the house after his father.

Ben had dropped into his favorite chair and was leaning back, eyes closed.

"Are you alright?" Colin asked.

His father answered coldly, "You bring the key?"

"A couple more days."

"I want you out of there."

"Like I said, just a couple more days–"

"Leave!" Ben barked harshly. It cost him, and he winced in pain. "Agents from the FBI – they came looking for you."

Colin licked his lips, which had suddenly gone dry. "What did you tell them?"

"I didn't tell them anything ... not this time. But they'll be back, you know it. The Eberhardt thing is serious business, son."

"Jesus, Dad, you can't think I had anything to do with that, do you?"

"I'm not saying you did, but they must think you know something."

"They can't prove anything."

"And what did they prove to put you in jail for two years? You had *tools* in your car? You were in the *vicinity* of the mink farm? They had nothing," said Ben bitterly.

"The judge thought they had enough. And I wasn't innocent."

"But they cannot bend the rules just because..."

"I'm an unrepentant animal activist?"

"Among other things." Ben started to cough which turned into agonizing spasms in his gut that doubled him over.

Colin ran to get a glass of water for his father, who was pushing his hands against his knees, trying to breathe through the pain. "What can I do, Dad?"

Ben surrendered. "There are some pain pills in the drawer next to my bed."

Colin went to the bedroom, relieved for the few moments alone to digest what he had learned. He knew the FBI would come looking for him, but he didn't know they'd already visited Ben. More surprising, though, he never thought that his father had followed his case. All this time, every day of the trial and every hour in prison, he believed his father didn't know and didn't care. The conflicting emotions and the memory of life inside suddenly took his knees out from under him; he sat on the side of the bed and put his head in his hands.

It all came back – the interminable stretches of time, the boredom so thick it could suffocate a man. The constant noise, no escape from the cacophony twenty-four-seven. Shouting, steel doors clanking, bolts screeching. It was even worse in solitary where he'd spent weeks, all for refusing to wear their leather shoes. Guys going nuts, cackling, screaming, pounding and kicking on the doors and unbreakable windows. On the day of his release he checked into a motel in the middle of nowhere and stayed for a week, drinking beer and eating junk food, watching TV. At the time he thought it was just the quiet he was after, but as the days passed he knew it was more – he wasn't quite ready for what came next. From the moment they slapped the handcuffs on him, all he wanted was to go home. But when the jail doors were open there was no home to go home to.

His father's cough put Colin back in motion. He rummaged through the drawer and found several bottles of pills. Some of the names of the medications were new to him, but he did recognize Fentanyl. A convicted stock broker two cells down had gotten some smuggled in and was blissed out for a week until a guard found the drugs. Something jingled in the back of the drawer and Colin pulled out a handful of dog collars. Along with the pain pills he scooped them up – a possible bridge over the enormous gulf that separated father and son.

"How come you named him Far Away?" asked Colin, fingering one of the frayed leather collars. He had one ear tuned to the gravel driveway in case the agents showed up again.

The meds had started to kick in and Ben's face had taken on the same absent, glassy-eyed look as the guard who'd confiscated the Fentanyl.

"I didn't. I named him Farley, but your brother couldn't say it. He called him Far Away and it stuck."

Colin picked up a thick red nylon collar and looked at one of the tags. "Hooper. Oh man, Hoop. What a great dog. Do you remember when we drove to Saint Claire and he followed us?"

"Sure. Probably ran five miles."

"He got into a couple of fights, didn't he?"

"He could be testy."

"Hoop was a good dog, though."

"They were *all* good dogs."

"You kept their collars," noted Colin sadly.

"Sure, I wasn't much for taking pictures."

Colin gathered up the old keepsakes and recalled something Laurel had said. "Where's your dog now?" he asked. "Don't you have a dog named Oona?"

"Used to. She got hit by a car."

"Oh, sorry, Dad. What happened?"

Ben shrugged. "She ran off. Went over to the main road one day and got hit."

"There was no way to save her?"

Looking out the window at the ice-covered pond below, Ben shook his head. "She was dead. I buried her down by the pond. She liked it down there."

"Didn't the driver stop at least? I mean, did they explain how it happened?"

Ben closed his eyes and didn't answer for awhile. Finally he said, "Think I'll just rest here for a bit. Those pills make me sleepy."

"Okay. I'll go finish the deck."

Waving his hand weakly in the air, Ben retreated from his son once again. "I wish you wouldn't, Colin. All that hammering. I just want some peace and quiet."

It was forever the way with Ben, thought Colin. His youngest son had always been too vocal, too loud and abrasive. Ben, like the other dads, wanted to share the weekend hunting parties with his two boys. But Colin wouldn't even look at a rifle. As a youngster, he wept inconsolably at the sight of a deer carcass being dragged home. Then as a teenager, he argued for the sentience of animals and proclaimed his rejection of meat at the dinner table. He pounded away at his father's closed mind and his mother's bowed head until he left for good, slamming the door behind him. But it was just all noise to Ben, and it seemed as though nothing had changed. His father would choose to live a mute life even as the last remnants of it were falling down around him.

Colin put away the saw and locked the shed. He retrieved his motorcycle from behind the bushes. As he was strapping on his helmet, a familiar ache of longing constricted his chest. It wasn't that he expected his father to see things the way he did, it was that he felt so invisible to him. There were no photographs of his childhood on the walls. No, that space had been reserved for deer antlers ... until recently, apparently. Hell, he kept souvenirs of his dogs instead of his children, and even then he kept them hidden away in a drawer – all the memories in a place where they would never remind him of anything. To hell with him. Colin kick-started the cycle forcibly and roared away.

Chapter 14

Saint Claire was three times the size of Stanton. Still, Jude was wary about being seen with Lisbet so she slid into a booth at the back of the coffee shop and kept her head down. A few minutes later Lisbet bustled in and sat across from her, unwrapping a long scarf from around her neck. She looked decidedly unhappy.

"I had to rent a car to get back to work," she said. "It's going to take them a week to get the windshield replaced."

"I'm glad you weren't hurt," said Jude.

"Well, one of these days they're going to aim the brick right at my head," complained Lisbet.

Jude leaned forward and asked intently, "What is going on? I've never seen anything like the venom that runs through this wolf debate. And John Tripp was deliberately adding kindling to the fire. I was up half the night trying to figure out what's at stake for him." She pulled out a spiral notebook from her backpack to review some of her notes. "According to the USDA's own stats, three quarters of all livestock loss last year was non-predator related: disease, birth complications, weather. And wolves are only a small fraction of the predators who do kill livestock. Heck, I found a USDA report that showed feral dogs take down more sheep than wolves. So why is there so much animosity toward them?"

Lisbet took a huge breath before attempting to answer. "Historically, cows and sheep were never on the menu. But as far back as the Middle Ages, when huge tracts of forest were cleared for farmland, deprived of their habitat and the prey that naturally lived there, wolves were forced to kill livestock. Back then it was all small farms, so it pissed off a lot of people and made it easy to demonize the wolves. For centuries in myths and stories, they've been associated with great strength and ferocity. I honestly think that hatred of wolves is ingrained in our culture, especially out here where they do still take livestock."

"There were hunters at the town hall last night," said Jude. "Are they in the same camp? Angry that wolves will take all the elk and deer that they want to shoot?"

"That's part of it. But I have this theory that because we have imbued wolves with an aura of mythical strength and cunning, hunters particularly enjoy the challenge of killing them. And it's a vicious cycle. Hunters kill wolves because they are so 'bad' and continually manufacture evidence that they are 'bad' to justify killing them."

"And a rancher like John Tripp gets votes by telling people what they want to hear, which is why he stirs up the pot."

"Exactly right."

Although there were only a few people at tables too far away to overhear, Jude lowered her voice. "A couple of days ago I saw a wolf gunned down from the air by Wildlife Services. She was wearing a radio collar."

"So that's what happened," said Lisbet, hanging her head. "I have a colleague who's been tracking a small pack in the north.

They lost the signal on one of them just about two days ago. I wish we had some proof."

Jude added, "They were using John Tripp's plane."

"Well, ain't that a sweet deal," said Lisbet caustically. "Wildlife Services budgets about a thousand dollars for each lift-off to go after coyotes and wolves, so they're probably paying Tripp to lease his plane while they're taking care of his 'predator' problem."

Jude doodled in her notebook for a moment before telling Lisbet, "You know, everyone in Stanton is under the impression that Eberhardt was killed by animal activists. But he was no Eagle Scout, I can tell you that. He got a real kick out of killing animals."

"All the more reason to think that sticking his leg in a coil spring was a statement of some kind. Like an animal rights thing, yeah?"

"Unless that's exactly what the killer wants people to think."

"You mean to throw the cops off track?"

Jude shrugged. "Maybe. Let's not forget, too, that Eberhardt worked for Wildlife Services, and the stuff I'm starting to learn about them stinks to high heaven."

"You got that right. What are you going to do?"

"Pay a visit to John Tripp," replied Jude grimly.

* * *

The old Subaru clattered over a cattle grate; the marquee overhead was intended to look rustic and unassuming, but the letters spelling out TRIPP RANCH, fashioned from twisted barbed wire, sent out a more foreboding message. Showing up uninvited was risky, but to Jude, the practices of Wildlife Services seemed nothing more than industrialized animal abuse, which in her experience was driven by money and power. In Stanton, that money and power belonged to John Tripp.

The dirt road continued for a mile with little else but flatlands and utility poles on either side. Then it split and she stayed to her left, where sheep began to dot the fenced-in pastures. The outline of a large warehouse-like building came into view, and Jude pulled up behind a piece of farm machinery parked along one side.

She wandered into the building where a handful of men were repairing the rails on rows of empty stalls in preparation for winter shed lambing. To protect them from the cold temperatures and predators, the ewes were moved inside to give birth, then they were herded with their lambs into larger pens until they were ready to join the rest of the flock to graze on the open range. Come spring, the lambs and ewes were separated, the ewes and rams shorn of their wool, then bred again for the next cycle. At about three months, lambs were herded into trucks and shipped to a slaughterhouse. Prices for their young flesh were higher in the spring, especially for Easter dinners.

"Can I help you?" a dark-skinned man asked in accented English. In addition to reading up on sheep farming, Jude learned that Tripp hired scores of Peruvian workers to tend to his herd. He was proud of the fact that after staying on for a few years, working hard and sleeping in tents on the range, his immigrant employees could come away with nearly twenty-thousand dollars apiece. "Not bad money to send home when all is said and done," Tripp was quoted as saying. "A lot of them even put on weight here."

Jude said, "I'm looking for John Tripp."

"He's up at the house." The man told Jude to keep heading up the road. "'Bout a quarter of a mile. You can't miss it."

Indeed, no one could. The Tripp home was a grand stone and redwood manor with sparkling floor-to-ceiling windows. Set on a hill with views of a pristine snow-topped mountain range, it was part of a complex that included a garage and barn and behind the house an airplane hangar and landing strip. As she drew near the house, several cars and trucks passed her in the opposite direction. Names painted on the sides of a few, such as C&B Ranch, T Bar Farm, and Williams Dairy, told Jude that a gathering of ranchers had just ended. She parked behind a dark sedan out front and checked herself in the rearview mirror. She'd let her hair down and put on a hint of blush; it couldn't hurt. Leaving her jacket in the car, she walked up a series of steps and rang the bell.

A moment later, a young woman who could have been the daughter of the worker at the lambing sheds answered the door. She wasn't wearing a traditional maid's uniform, but her white button-down shirt and black slacks were close enough.

Jude handed her a phony EO Travel business card. "I'm afraid I don't have an appointment, but I wondered if I might have a word with Mr. Tripp," said Jude, putting on her most winsome smile.

The solemn young woman let her into the foyer and said she'd see if he was available. Silently she stepped across the polished wood floor and knocked on a pair of sliding doors. When they opened, Jude caught a glimpse of a cathedral ceiling and a roaring fire in a wide stone fireplace.

"He'll be with you in a minute," said the woman when she returned.

Left alone, Jude took stock of her surroundings. A suitcase embossed with the initials JRT sat by the front door. Hanging from the handle was an airport tag, and she made a mental note to find out what IAH stood for. She wandered into the open room across the way, pretending to admire the décor. It wasn't easy. Part bar, part sitting area, the space was decorated with so many dead animal parts that she lost track in her quick survey: chandeliers made of antlers, an enormous elk head mounted over another fireplace, rabbit skin covers on the bar stools.

"Miss Harris," came a voice behind her.

Jude turned to see John Tripp striding forward. "I'm afraid I only have a minute. What can I do for you?"

Tripp drew from his politician's well of practiced charm, summoning forth a broad smile, though the tightness around his eyes revealed a much steelier core. He grasped her hand the way he had with Margaret Cunningham, as though they were old friends.

"Thank you for seeing me. I'm sure you're busy so I'll try to be brief," said Jude, then glanced toward the front hall. "I wouldn't want to make you late for your trip."

"Not to worry. I'm just returning, actually."

"I hope it was a successful venture," said Jude.

"It was indeed."

She let it go at that and launched into a short version of her cover story and her interest in his elk farm. "I spoke to your foreman who was very helpful about group accommodations. With our European contacts we're envisioning some pretty large groups and I thought if I could personally meet you, that would lend some additional credence to my recommendations."

He was cautiously curious, but maintained a fixed cordial expression. "Not sure how much more I can tell you. We can only accommodate a certain number of hunters at any given time."

"Of course. That's precisely why I was drawn to your ranch ... the personalized service. You offer a unique experience in the American way of life. I'm certain you know just about everyone in the hunting world and can recommend others for any overflow. Would be a great way to bring some revenue to the area." She could see a spark of interest and decided to skip ahead. "And if you'll forgive me, on a personal note, I have to tell you how impressed I am at how in tune you are with your constituents. I'm talking about the debate at the town hall meeting."

"I gather you were there?"

"Yes, and I admire your forthrightness. Our clients are from Europe, but I'm a proud American and so many people don't understand that it's ranchers like you who are the real guardians of these lands."

"I'm glad that you see it that way."

"You have to worry about an overpopulation of predators." Pressing on, Jude said, "You would think that the state and federal governments would have an interest in managing wildlife in a way that doesn't cause the kind of animosity we saw at the town hall." Tripp glanced over his shoulder, then graciously began to steer her back toward the front door as Jude continued, "I mean, can't the federal government provide some help? What about Wildlife Services?"

He eyed her keenly for a moment, then clasped her hand again. "Wish we could discuss this further, my dear. But I must get back to my guest. It's been delightful to meet you, and I hope we can do some business together." His smile vanished before he'd turned away, telling Jude that despite what she thought had been a passably charming performance, his mind was elsewhere – either that, or she'd hit a nerve.

Outside, the corrugated aluminum dome of the airplane hangar gleamed in the late afternoon sun, drawing Jude like a beacon. With Tripp busy, she decided to chance a look. She drew aside the heavy tarp of green plastic hung over the front and saw Tripp's plane. No one was around, so she slid through the opening.

Light filtered through the steel trusses supporting the roof. She spotted a storage cabinet where a clipboard hung from a nail hammered into the frame. Jude examined the notations, guessing they logged flight times and fuel allocations. She tried the cabinet itself. It wasn't locked.

Inside were shelves crammed with a variety of airplane parts: clamps, air hoses, rivets. Among them Jude noticed one particular piece of equipment. It looked like a three-pronged antenna with a hand grip. A wire ran from the antenna to a scuffed canvas bag. She lifted one of its flaps to find a black box receiver. Next to it was stuffed a leather collar with a matchbox-sized transmitter. She knew this collar. It belonged to the wolf who had taken her last breath underneath her trembling hand. Bits of hair and grime were embedded in the shearling underside.

For a moment, she thought about taking it, then reconsidered. If it went missing she'd be an immediate suspect. Instead, she took out her phone, snapped a few photos, and put the collar back. The purpose of the radio antenna and the receiver had come to her with soul-crushing clarity. They had used it to track the wolf – the very equipment designed to monitor and protect her and her pack had led the killers right to her. Of all the hunting technology Jude had seen the last few days, this seemed the cruelest.

A voice inside her head insisted that it was time to go. But she was in the belly of the beast and itched to find out more. She moved over to the Piper Cub. On the body of the plane someone had pasted rows of decals. Decals of wolf heads. The way cowboys notched their guns and soldiers marked their helmets in a gruesome tally of their victims, here was the body count. Jude grit her teeth and examined the wing strut where the wolf had been strapped. There were traces of dried blood.

From her shoulder bag she took a pen knife and a small notepad. She tore off a piece of paper and began to scrape some of the blood onto it. Hard to know if the blood belonged to the same or another wolf, but Lisbet and her colleague might have a way of finding a match. God, the fight for animals felt like such a Herculean task. At that moment an oppressive weariness overcame Jude, so much so that when she heard a sound at the hangar's entrance and saw a man's figure appear in the opening, she almost lifted her hands in surrender.

"Hoo-ee, if it ain't my cowgirl," said Cash, but his tone was not friendly.

Jude casually slipped the pen knife into her back pocket and palmed the folded paper, her heart racing.

"What are you doing here?" he asked.

"Oh, hi." She hoped her voice remained steady. "I came by earlier to talk about my travel company with Mr. Tripp. And I remembered he had a plane–"

"How'd you know that?"

"Abby at the Café told me. Don't you remember? She said that you and your friend should take me up sometime. Well, I didn't want to say at the time, but I'm terrified of flying, every time I have to go abroad, oh my God ..." Jude was verbally scrambling, sounding to her own ears like what she was – a guilty, inept burglar. "And I just thought that if I actually could see a plane up close, which I've never done, it might help me get over my fears."

"Kinda like picking up a rattlesnake if you're scared of snakes, hunh?" Cash didn't sound convinced.

"A little like that, I guess," laughed Jude lightly. "Only I hope this plane doesn't bite."

"It don't, but Roland Pike will, he finds you sneakin' in here."

Recovering, Jude sauntered in his direction. "Hey, I saw you at the town hall last night. I waved, but I guess you didn't see me."

"I saw you all right." Cash grinned, and she returned it, hoping his attraction would trump suspicion. "You still up for a guided tour?"

"Absolutely."

"Great," he nodded. "How 'bout day after tomorrow?"

"Sure, that'll work."

"Done," said Cash as though they'd just completed a business deal. "I'll pick you up at the Aspen House. Nine o'clock sharp."

An icy finger of fear traced itself down Jude's back; she couldn't interpret the way he was looking at her. *How did he know she was staying at the Aspen House? How much did he suspect? Was he merely playing along, just as she was, hoping to learn what she was up to?* She lifted her chin in acknowledgement and walked out of the hangar, leaving Cash staring at her back. The wind had quickened and she thrust her hands deep into her pockets, tightening her shoulders against the cold, but more important to protect the blood sample. She had the sensation that at any moment he would lasso her with a rope from behind and drag her to the ground. *What in hell had she gotten herself into?*

"Judy!" Cash called out after her.

She turned. *This was it. He hadn't believed a word she said.*

"Dress warm, ya hear?"

Chapter 15

Working undercover, Jude thought, was like walking a high wire. At the slightest misstep you windmill your arms into the air, looking to grab something solid to stop the fall. But there is only nothingness around you. Nothing familiar, nothing comforting, nothing but pretense, thin and fragile as a wren's egg.

This morning, the further she got from Stanton, the more she could feel sensation coming back into her fingers, as though her very hands had been asleep. She could feel herself re-aligning, Judy Harris mutating back into Jude Brannock. She could ask for soy milk with her coffee again. Granted, no one in Idaho had it, but at least she could ask. And that made her feel more ... real. Even Finn, in the back seat of the Subaru seemed to relax in a way he hadn't for days.

Her phone began to chirp, and when she saw who was trying to reach her, she eased onto the side of the road and picked up.

"Walt Kincaid," stated the gruff male voice.

"Thank you for calling me back," said Jude. Before they left the coffee shop, Lisbet had given her Kincaid's number, thinking he could answer some of her questions about Wildlife Services. But she'd warned Jude that Kincaid didn't talk to just anybody. "You spoke to Lisbet?"

"She vouches for you. So you're in Stanton, Idaho, is that right?"

"Yes, and Lisbet suggested I call you because I'm seeing some weird stuff go down with Wildlife Services."

He chortled at the other end of the line, a hoarse, smoker's laugh. "Is that so?"

"She said you used to work with Wildlife Services in Montana," prompted Jude. "Why did you leave?"

"Principles."

"Uh ... can you be a little more specific?"

"I got sick and tired of killing animals for no reason," he replied. "How much do you know about the agency?"

Jude told him about seeing the aerial gunning on public lands and the use of a private rancher's plane.

"Well, then you're seeing them in action," said Kincaid. "They may be leasing Tripp's plane because something happened to one of their own. The agency has had a lot of accidents, crashes because they're flying too low or the gunner shoots the damn plane up. But aerial gunning is only the tip of the iceberg."

"Go on."

"Well, start with the fact that Wildlife Services killed almost four million animals last year."

"I'm sorry," said Jude. "How many did you say?"

"About four million."

"How is that possible?" she asked incredulously.

"Most of 'em are birds. But they exterminate a lot of mammals ... any kind you can think of: black bears, raccoons, badgers, fox, beavers, coyotes. A lot of coyotes. They probably shoot, trap and poison over 200 coyotes every day."

Jude's mind was reeling, trying to process what Kincaid was telling her.

"They like to say that they mostly *disperse* animals," he went on. "But that doesn't apply to predators – wolves and bears and such. Those ... they kill ... just about all of them."

"Is there some kind of documentation for all this?" asked Jude haltingly.

"Well, they put out a report every year. But like I said, Wildlife Services is an iceberg. What you see is only the tip – most of it's below the surface. For instance, the extermination of four million a year is what they admit to," said Kincaid. "I worked as a trapper for them, and for every target animal I caught, there were two trapped by accident. That's pretty run-of-the-mill. Happens all the time."

Her voice cracking with outrage, Jude exclaimed, "Why aren't those reported? Two-to-one is not an accident, it's recklessness ... it's ... crazy!"

"That's why I left. The agency will hire anybody who can set a trap and keep their mouth shut. These guys catch a whole lot of animals they're not supposed to – anything that's attracted to the bait. The animals don't know any better. Fishers, bobcats, deer, rabbits, mountain lions, you name it. I've seen federally protected species like golden eagles caught in the traps. But Wildlife Services only reports within their own agency, so it's covered up."

"And no one calls out their incompetence?"

"Not many people know what all is going on. These boys like to stay under the radar."

"They must be answerable to Congress for funding," insisted Jude.

"The folks in Washington aren't that bright. Last year there was a reporter in California that wrote up a big expose on Wildlife Services, and for a while it looked as though the politicians might take notice. But then the head of the APHIS grabs the mic and says, 'don't listen to what you hear about Wildlife Services because it's not true.' He actually stated that the agency's unintentional lethal take – that's the animals killed by accident – is *one-tenth of one percent.*" Kincaid let out a guffaw. "I mean, come on! Even if the traps had signs on 'em that said 'coyotes only' and all the animals could read, you'd get way more than that. The traps are baited, for Christ sake. Hundreds of animals are attracted to the bait. Like I said, Congress ain't too bright."

"Or they don't want to hear."

"There's a couple of senators that are listening and I'll talk with anyone who's interested, but I keep a low profile now. Ever since I talked to that reporter they've been puttin' the squeeze on me. I got audited for the first time in my life, and even though I've got a lot of experience, I'm not having much luck getting a job."

"Do you think Wildlife Services is behind it?"

"Dunno. Could be I'm having a string of bad luck."

* * *

She pulled into the parking lot of the Hampton Inn at the Boise Airport, put Finn on a leash, and found Gordon in the conference room.

"I couldn't leave him in the car," said Jude, as Finn galloped across the carpeting to Gordon.

Reaching down to scratch the big dog on his hindquarters, Gordon said, "Of course not. If anyone complains, we'll tell them he's a service dog and keeps your anxiety disorder under control."

"That wouldn't be far from the truth," said Jude with a wry smile. What she had learned about Wildlife Services in the past twenty-four hours burned like acid in her gut and she was eager to get Gordon on board. "Thanks for coming. Hope this isn't too much out of your way."

Gordon shrugged. "Slightly. I have to be in Wisconsin this afternoon."

"What's going on there?"

"The University in Madison has resumed their maternal deprivation studies on infant monkeys."

Jude let out an involuntary moan. "No, they're doing it again?"

The studies, purportedly conducted to shed light on human attachment disorders, dated back fifty years. Infant monkeys were taken from their mothers and exposed to conditions that created intense fear. After tests were conducted on their blood and spinal fluid, they were killed to study their brains. Many psychologists had since condemned the studies as cruel and irrelevant, but it hadn't seemed to stop a few scientists from seeking a half a million dollars in grant money from the National Institute of Mental Health to continue the experiments.

"They're doing it again," Gordon affirmed ruefully. "And this time, they're not euthanizing the babies when they're done, they're sending them to Tulane for more testing. But let's get to the task at hand. I'm on a tight schedule."

"I do appreciate you coming. I really needed to see you in person." She took a deep breath. "Colin had nothing to do with Eberhardt."

"How do you know? Because he *told* you he didn't do it?"

"Yes, I believe him. Why are you skeptical?" Jude asked, taken aback. "You know that violence is not the ALF way."

"Colin is very strong-minded, and I've seen him get angry. Craig Eberhardt might have been in the wrong place at the wrong time."

"Well, that's not what happened."

Gordon let it rest for a moment before asking, "But he and his crew are dismantling traps, yes?"

"Probably, but I didn't push and Colin wouldn't admit to it. Does it matter?"

"You'd think a couple of years in prison would have changed his ways," noted Gordon disapprovingly.

"I can't speak for him," Jude responded, studying her hands.

"And what about Oliver Neeland? He has a criminal record, you know."

"I know. But it was only a misdemeanor for freeing an animal from a trap."

Gordon lifted an eyebrow. "Is that what they told you?"

"What do you mean?"

"Before becoming an activist, Oliver Neeland did four years for assault with a deadly weapon. He nearly killed a guy. Maybe he didn't mention that."

Jude flushed. "Colin told me about the lesser charge. I don't think he knows about the other."

"He knows," Gordon assured her.

Perhaps because it rankled that Gordon seemed so sure he had Colin's number or her belief that he was jumping to conclusions, but Jude didn't say anything about Oliver's verbal rampage against Wildlife Services. Or the bruise under his eye. Or the fact that he knew Eberhardt was alive when he was put in the trap. She told herself that there could be any number of explanations. Nonetheless, this new information about Oliver gnawed at her, as did her omissions to Gordon. He was her boss, he was her friend, he was The Kinship – she ought to be telling him everything. But she didn't.

"We'd better get you out of there," said Gordon. "The cops will find out about Oliver on their own and the chips will fall where they will. But we can't afford to have you in the mix."

"But–"

Gordon held up his hand. "The subcommittee has already gotten wind of the Eberhardt killing. I have no doubt they're going to bring it up at the hearing, whether or not there's been an arrest. What am I supposed to say if one of my people is found to have engaged with an ALF cell in Stanton?"

"Gordon, hear me out, please. There is something much bigger going on – Wildlife Services, the agency that Eberhardt worked with."

"Ah, Jude, I've got enough on my plate without taking on another government agency," he objected.

"Aren't we supposed to be helping animals?" she wanted to know, her sense of justice wounded. "As far as I can see, Wildlife Services is just another form of industrialized animal cruelty. They're a renegade operation, killing at least four million animals every year – probably far more than that – and no one knows about it."

Gordon frowned and leaned back in his chair. "I'm listening."

"I guess CJ has filled you in on John Tripp and his connection to Wildlife Services." At Gordon's nod, Jude continued. "Yesterday, just as I was coming up to the Tripp ranch, a whole bunch of other ranchers were leaving. I think there had been some kind of meeting. That wasn't so surprising. As an Idaho legislator, Tripp is a spokesman for the local agricultural interests. But ranchers weren't the only ones there. So was Bud Grimes, who's the regional director of Wildlife Services. I know because CJ backed out his license plate."

Gordon narrowed his eyes, intrigued.

"Okay. John Tripp has a relationship with Wildlife Services.

He's leasing his plane to them at probably a thousand bucks a pop and they serve as his personal paramilitary extermination service, paid for courtesy of the U.S. taxpayer. But why would the state director of the federal agency be making a personal appearance at his ranch?" Jude got up and began to pace the room. "On the way here, I spoke to a guy named Walt Kincaid, who used to work for Wildlife Services. In addition to telling me how careless their trapping practices are and the fact that the agency basically lies about it to the public and to Congress, he told me something else. Wildlife Services can't account for its spending. They work with what they call "cooperators," which are ranchers like Tripp and various state and city boards, who pay for some of their services. But the agency doesn't keep track of exactly where the money goes and where it comes from. It all just gets broken down into broad categories like livestock and crops. That's it. And last year, they lost twelve million dollars. Not lost as in gambled away, lost as in they can't account for it. You should have seen John Tripp's spread! Huge house, pool, airplane, servants, you name it. I'm just saying..."

"I didn't know it was that bad," sighed Gordon.

"Let me go back to Stanton and find out more about them," she pleaded. "I think it's connected to the Eberhardt murder. And if I can find out who did kill him, you can cross another problem off your list."

Gordon rubbed his temples. "The hearing is next week. I don't have time to gear up for another investigation that, as far as I can see, is shooting in the dark. Nor do I have the personnel to back you up. You'd be on your own."

"That's fine. Just give me a few days," she pleaded.

"Do you have a plan in mind?"

"Semi-plan. Believe it or not, I have a date tomorrow with Orin Cashman, the Wildlife Services agent who killed the wolf."

He thought for a moment before asking, "Is this about Colin? First you didn't want to go to Stanton, and now you don't want to stay away."

"No, it's not about Colin," she insisted, trying to convince herself.

"Because if you go back, I don't want you within ten miles of him, or Laurel or Oliver Neeland. I've got a bad feeling about Neeland, and our association with any of them at this point could hurt us badly. The House Republican Scott Olander on the Homeland Security panel just got back from a conference in Houston where I have no doubt that the power brokers lit an even bigger fire under him on this AETA thing." He looked at her sternly. "There are a lot of really good people working their butts off for animals. Don't make their job harder. Don't let them down."

On the drive back to Stanton, Gordon's words weighed heavily, as well as her guilt about not being honest with him. She had to wonder if she was even being honest with herself. This urgency she felt to expose the callous killing of animals by Wildlife Services ... was that reason she was heading back into "enemy" territory? Or was it really about Colin? She couldn't deny the pull she felt toward the tangible simplicity of what he was doing. Yes, they all shared an intense desire to help animals – all were devoting their lives to the cause. But Gordon's way was to work within the system, in the belief that his most effective tool was public pressure; if people knew what was really happening to animals across the spectrum they would demand change. Colin's way was to renounce the system entirely; compromise was a sell-out. The Kinship often embraced the smallest of improvements that impacted millions of animals. For Colin, the remedy had to be immediate, but it wasn't possible for more than a few. As the miles rushed by under her wheels, Jude was sure of only one thing: both sides carried a cost. Her thoughts turned to what was in front of her and she began once again to take on the role of Judy Harris. She could almost picture herself climbing the ladder to the high wire, the air getting thinner and thinner, her body feeling lighter and lighter, when all she wanted was to be connected to the earth.

Chapter 16

She stopped at the Tripp Creek Café where the lunchtime crowd had cleared out. Abby was working and Jude greeted her warmly. "I'll have a double salad and a bowl of the lentil soup," she said with some faint hope that it wasn't made with meat.

When the friendly waitress came back with her order, Jude noted, "For being slow, it sounds pretty busy back there in the kitchen."

"We're catering a Christmas party at the Tripp ranch in a couple of days. I'm only serving, but I can't wait to go. I heard they're having a band and everything."

"When is it?"

"Sunday night."

"Sounds like fun," said Jude.

"You should get Cash to invite you. He was in here a couple of times asking if you'd been in."

"Oh yeah, when?" asked Jude casually.

"This morning, for one."

"Well, I'm sure I'll run into him."

Left alone to finish her lunch, she fretted over why he'd go looking for her. She hoped it wasn't to cancel their date; right now he was her ticket to the inside workings of Wildlife Services. But neither did she like the idea that he was keeping tabs on her.

Kylie Harrington was back at it across the street, handing out leaflets. She thrust flyers at everyone walking by, and her appeals to reject fur could be heard through the paned window of the café. The woman was an enigma. Here she was, persistent in her open and earnest leafleting campaign, quite possibly convincing a few people to re-think the fur trim on a new jacket. Yet she kept her Facebook persona on Eberhardt's page obscure and often threatening. One particular comment hinted that she knew the identity of Thrill to Kill. Eberhardt had joked about a coyote caught in a snare, cracking, "Love to see coyotes hanging around!" Kylie had gone after him in a blistering harangue, writing, "You have to ridicule your kill? Haven't you done enough evil? You and your team."

Team? Jude had thought it an unusual word choice. But perhaps Wildlife Services trappers worked in teams. She would have liked to ask Kylie directly, but knew that approaching her in broad daylight would be a mistake. As Jude looked on, the clothing store owner once again stormed out to chase the unwanted protester away. Kylie stuffed the flyers into her coat, marched staunchly to the corner, and got in her car.

Jude didn't hesitate.

Kylie's pickup truck looked much like the other vehicles on Route 72, but the bright red "Save the Wolves" bumper sticker made it easy to keep her in sight. Jude stayed several car lengths behind as Kylie headed in the direction of Saint Claire. Soon after, she turned onto a side road, then another, and pulled into the driveway of a small, cedar-shingled house with a toy-littered lawn. Jude drove by without glancing her way.

When the road curved, she made a u-turn and drove to within a decent visual of Kylie's house. She eased over to the side and pretended to read a map. A few cars went by, but the road was not well traveled and no one stopped to offer assistance, which was just fine. Jude waited.

Twenty minutes later, a yellow school bus stopped in front of Kylie's house. A boy, probably eight or nine, shambled down the bus steps, dragging his backpack behind him. The bus gave a short honk, pulled in its stop sign, and continued along. Figuring the driver had honked to let mom know her son was home, Jude drove slowly down the street. She was rewarded when Kylie stepped out of the house to greet her boy, two brown terriers yapping at her feet.

Jude rolled down her window as she drew next to the mailbox. "Excuse me," she called out. "I am so lost!"

Wrapped in a thick cardigan, Kylie came down the driveway to give her directions. Her son mumbled a greeting and dropped his backpack in favor of a half-deflated soccer ball in the yard. The two terriers took turns barking at Finn and at the soccer ball.

"I think I'm driving in circles," said Jude.

"Where you headed?" asked Kylie.

"Stanton."

"Oh, that's easy." In the yard, her son was kicking the soccer ball, letting out his pent up school energy. He coughed once or twice.

"Hey, didn't I see you at the town hall meeting the other night?" exclaimed Jude, feigning recognition. "Boy, you sure took a few of them on!" When Kylie bent down uncertainly to peer through the window, Jude knew that she had to tread a fine line between keeping her cover intact and trying to draw Kylie out. "I'm just in town for a few days and dropped by that meeting. It's totally nuts the division over wolves around here. But I gotta say, I really admire your passion."

"Yeah." Kylie still didn't sound comfortable, and after what Jude had seen at the town hall, she couldn't blame her.

"Oh, sorry. My name's Judy Harris. I work for a company that's putting together tourist-type visits in this area. I think I might have seen you outside the Tripp Creek Café. That's where I've been eating most of the time."

Kylie's leeriness seemed to fall away. "Right, right. Now I recognize you."

"Like I said," Jude prattled on, "I'm not from around here, and to be honest with you, some of our clients like to hunt. But I couldn't believe my ears at what some of those folks said about wolves. I mean, that one guy talked about *wanting* them to suffer. I don't get it."

"They're ignorant a-holes," Kylie spat out. "But they're not the worst of them."

"What could be worse than that?"

Kylie hesitated. "I'm sorry, I didn't catch your name."

"Judy Harris." She rummaged in her bag for an EO Travel business card and passed it through the passenger window. While Kylie studied it, Jude asked, "Would it be okay if I let my dog out to pee? He's been cooped in here for the last hour while I've been getting myself lost. He's really good with other dogs."

When Kylie nodded, Jude got out and opened the door for Finn. The terriers yapped at his heels in excitement. Secure in his size, Finn stood still, politely letting them sniff every part of him until they had taken his measure, then he strolled off into their yard.

Jude leaned against the car. "I really like wolves," she said truthfully. "Maybe because I love dogs so much."

"They don't deserve the treatment they get," agreed Kylie. She turned to call to her son who was coughing more persistently.

"Derrick, go inside. Your inhaler's on the kitchen table." Her attention back on Jude, she said, "Sorry, what was your question?"

"Why does John Tripp hate wolves so much?" asked Jude.

"For John Tripp? It's politics," announced Kylie, color coming up into her cheeks. "Wolves aren't really a huge problem for him. What he wants are votes, and he gets them by taking on the big bad wolf. You gotta understand, most folks around here honestly believe that God created all wildlife for the taking. And when the federal government reintroduced wolves ... well, that just makes it worse. You'd have better luck if the government started building affordable housing for Muslims in Stanton ... at least *they* wouldn't be killing the elk."

Jude chuckled. "Ok, that's John Tripp. What about the others?"

"Some of them have been brainwashed into thinking that the wolves will decimate all the ungulates – deer, elk and the like. And some of them..."

After a moment, Jude encouraged her to go on. "Some of them?"

"Well, some of them just like to kill. Period." Kylie's face turned hard.

"And you have a few in Stanton, I gather?"

"Yup." Kylie glanced back at the house to make sure Derrick had gone inside. "Ever heard of Wildlife Services?"

"Think I have," said Jude vaguely, although she felt a sudden burst of adrenaline quickening her pulse.

"There's a lot of them that make a business out of killing, racking up the numbers, and they don't care who gets in the way."

The pain and distress in her face was so clear, Jude guessed at something personal. "What happened to you?" she asked softly.

"Not to me, my son. A few months ago, our oldest dog Shadow bit into one of their M-44's. Derrick was with him. He tried to help, but he breathed in some of the cyanide. He was real sick for a while, and he still has breathing problems and headaches. Monster headaches."

All pretense gone, Jude wasn't sure she'd hear Kylie right. "Cyanide? I don't understand."

"You don't know about the M-44's? Wildlife Services uses them, mostly for coyotes." To Jude's horror, Kylie described the traps: small tubes loaded with a sodium cyanide capsule. Driven part way into the ground, the exposed top was baited to attract canids. When a wolf or coyote bit down on it, a spring ejected sodium cyanide into the animal's mouth and face. The force of the ejector could spray cyanide granules up to five feet. Wildlife Services claimed the cyanide kills within forty-five seconds, but Kylie and her son knew better.

"Shadow started to go into convulsions. I could hear Derrick screaming and I came running. Shadow was gasping and foaming at the mouth, struggling for air. I sent Derrick back to the house to call 911 while I stayed with my poor Shadow. My God," said Kylie, the memory dulling her eyes, "he was in such agony. It seemed to go on forever, but I guess it was only ten or fifteen minutes. Every once in a while he would thrash his legs and moan. There was nothing I could do but stroke him and talk to him. I saw the trap and knew what it was."

"But Derrick didn't?"

"No, he thought Shadow was choking on something and he tried to get whatever it was out of his mouth. That's when he inhaled the cyanide. By the time I got back to the house, Derrick was vomiting and could barely stand up. He nearly didn't make it."

Jude was aghast. "How are these traps legal?"

"They're not. Not for regular hunters or trappers. But Wildlife Services doesn't have to follow any state rules. Shit, they don't even follow their own rules. They're supposed to post warning signs, but they don't. No one ever notified me that the M-44's were there."

"Did you confront them?"

"Damn right. I knew there was a team working the area, but not a single one of them admitted to having placed that trap. And they claimed that in places where they do set the M-44's, they put up warning signs. But we're down in that hollow all the time – there were no signs. Besides, no one could have seen the trap, not in the high grass. Basically it was their word against mine."

"I am so sorry," said Jude. "Will your son be okay?"

"We hope so. Sometimes he gets all wobbly for no reason, but the headaches don't come on as much they used to, and the doctors are optimistic." She tightened her sweater around her shoulders. "Look at me, here I've been chewing your ear off when all you wanted was directions."

"You've been through a lot," said Jude sympathetically. Feeling as though her time had run out, she prepared to leave and was fastening her seatbelt when Kylie leaned in toward the passenger window.

"You know what the worst part was?" asked Kylie, looking bewildered, as though she didn't quite know the answer herself. "No one from Wildlife Services ever took responsibility for what they did to Derrick. No one ever apologized about my son or our Shadow. They never do."

Jude let the car keys drop into her lap. "Are you telling me this has happened before?"

"Oh, yeah," replied Kylie. "A family dog up in North Salmon was poisoned, and another one a few miles from here."

"Have you notified the state authorities?"

"Of course. But the IDFG don't do squat, and besides, they have no control over Wildlife Services."

"That's incredible! Three family pets killed and no one is doing anything about it?"

"There's plenty more than three, I can guarantee that – and not all from the cyanide traps. Quite a few dogs and cats have gone missing. Folks'll tell you that coyotes got them, and maybe that's true for some. But this past summer, a farmer over in Saint Claire uncovered a grave where the bodies of different animals were dumped. There were four dogs, three of them purebreds, so you know they were pets, not feral dogs. All of them showed signs that they'd been caught in a snare or a leg hold trap. Whoever put them there had removed their collars, so they couldn't be identified. They even found a lynx in the pile and they're a threatened species around here."

"That's so sad," Jude exclaimed. "They don't get federal protection?"

"Not if your federal protection is Wildlife Services," said Kylie with a bitter smile.

All the way back to the guesthouse, Jude kept envisioning the helplessness and terror that Kylie must have experienced watching her beloved dog suffer. And she could easily understand Kylie's rage over the damage done to her child. So wanton. Worse than negligent – even if Wildlife Services had posted warning signs, they would have to know that small children wouldn't be able to read them. She believed Kylie in any event. What mother would let her child play where there were cyanide traps? It could happen to anyone. For a moment, a vision of Finn swam before her eyes – her dog, wild-eyed, desperately gasping for breath, and nothing she could do but watch his slow and painful death. What would she feel knowing who had set the trap, that he lied to her face about it, that he went out and did it again? How would she respond? As if from a bubbling cauldron, she could feel a dark part of herself rise up through the toxic brew. *I would want to kill him.*

* * *

"By her own account she knows how to use a gun and she looks strong enough to get him into a coil spring trap," Jude admitted to CJ.

"The means and the motive," he concluded.

"All true, except I'm not convinced."

"Why not?"

"I think she might have connected Craig Eberhardt to his Thrill-to-Kill Facebook page, but it's less clear that she connected him to the particular cyanide trap that injured her boy and killed her dog," cautioned Jude.

"I wouldn't admit to making the connection if I'd killed him."

"I don't know, CJ. She's got a sick child to take care of. As angry as she is – and she has a right to be – I find it hard to believe she'd risk going to jail for the rest of her life."

"I have news for you ... most people aren't weighing the risks of going to jail at the moment they pull the trigger."

"Perhaps not," conceded Jude. "But from what Kylie said, there are other people who have lost family pets because of an M-44. And cyanide is only one of the many poisons they use. Wildlife Services freely admits to using Rozol, Strychnine, and something called Kaput-D, which is a blood-thinning drug they use on prairie dogs and squirrels that causes them to slowly bleed to death through various orifices, including eventually their skin. *Four million animals*, CJ. And you take what Walt Kincaid told me about non-target animals ... it's nothing more than mass slaughter."

"Sort of makes you want to kill somebody, eh?" CJ mused. "How could a government agency keep this so hidden?"

"You ever heard of the 3-S's?"

"Educate me."

"It stands for Shoot, Shovel and Shut-up – shorthand for

poaching wolves, burying them and keeping quiet about it. They think it's such a catchy phrase, the hunters and trappers put it on bumper stickers around here."

"So Wildlife Services is regularly disposing of their non-target animals and not reporting them?"

"Walt Kincaid told me as much. And it's supported by what Kylie said about the mass grave where they found so many dogs ... all the identifying collars had been removed. An animal that they think will give them bad publicity, like a family pet? Just dig a hole, get rid of the evidence."

CJ was silent – a rarity for him.

"Hey, quick question for you," said Jude, trying to bring her friend back. "What airport uses the identifying code IAH?"

"That's the George Bush International Airport in Houston," he answered.

"Very interesting." Pieces of information were flying around Jude's brain like atomic particles. "You know, Gordon mentioned to me that this congressman on the Homeland Security subcommittee, Scott Olander, was at a conference in Houston recently. Do you happen to know what that was?" She was picturing John Tripp's suitcase in the front hall.

"It was the annual ALEC conference."

"ALEC, hunh?" Jude's stomach tightened. The American Legislative Exchange Council was a corporate funded group that crafted pro-business bills for state and federal legislators. The council was stacked with agribusiness lobbyists trying to protect their supply chain from oversight and regulation. ALEC was behind the state ag-gag laws under which animal activists were being prosecuted for filming the abuse of farm animals in factory farms and slaughterhouses. "I think John Tripp may have been at that conference. Can you find out if he was there?"

"Can do. So, what now?"

"I want to dig into these abuses of Wildlife Services. For all we know, there may be a lot more Kylie Harringtons out there. Maybe one of them killed Craig Eberhardt."

"And just how do you plan to unravel this government conspiracy?"

"I have a date with Cashman in the morning and will use my charms, such as they are, to get him to open up about his activities on the job."

"What is he planning for this *date*?"

"I don't know," Jude said lightly. "He's giving me a tour of the area. We'll probably ride around in his truck or something."

"Ok," said CJ, not sounding confident. "But I wish you'd bring Finn. After what you told me about the 3-S's, wouldn't want to see you end up a shovelee."

Chapter 17

Bringing Finn was out of the question. Cash was an experienced hunter and trapper, and Jude had witnessed him examining both hers and Finn's footprints next to the fallen wolf. He'd surely be able to guess Finn's size and weight from his paw prints. No, she couldn't even let on to Cash that she had a dog.

Jude zipped up her jacket and gave Finn a hug before she left the room. "I'll be back soon, big guy. Man the fort, okay?"

He pricked his ears forward and tilted his head in confused anticipation. Her energy was saying "walk," but then he heard the dreaded "stay" word. He padded to the foot of the bed and lay down with a sigh.

Jude trotted down the stairs and ran headlong into the two FBI agents she'd seen at the town hall. They were talking to Foster Dunne. She nodded at them and busied herself with the muddy boots she'd left in the coat closet.

"This is Miz Harris, one of our guests," explained Dunne.

The older of the two acknowledged her with a brief "ma'am,"

and turned back to the bed and breakfast owner. "We'd like to see your guest registrations for the last three weeks," he said, a tinge of Michigan or Illinois in his accent.

"Why?" Dunne wanted to know.

The other agent who possessed more swagger answered. "As I'm sure you know, a federal employee was murdered in Stanton several days ago. It's possible that whoever is responsible was passing through and stayed here."

"It's just routine," reassured the first. "We're asking all the hotels in this area."

A prickle of sweat broke out on Jude's upper lip. Were they going to check out everyone on Dunne's guest list? EO Travel wouldn't stand up to scrutiny and they'd be tracking down an elusive Judy Harris. She tried to calm her anxiety by reminding herself that there were a lot of hotels in the area; it would take awhile.

"Don't you need a warrant?" asked Dunne affably.

Jude couldn't help but smile as she bent down to tighten her laces. *Way to go, Professor*. Dunne was a strange guy, but he was growing on her.

"It would be more helpful if you would just let us take a look," said the senior.

His partner added, "Unless you have something to hide."

"I have nothing to hide," said Dunne.

"Good. First, a couple of questions. Have you lived in Stanton long?"

"You could say that. 'Bout thirty years."

"Do you happen to know Ben McIntyre?"

Jude caught her breath and remained in a crouch, re-doing her boot laces.

"Why?"

"Not at liberty to say, sir."

"Sure, I know Ben. He lives up Saint Claire way. Retired now, I think."

"How well do you know him?"

A pause. *Dunne trying to see behind the questions?* "We're acquaintances. We say hello in town occasionally."

"He lives alone?"

"Yes, his wife died a couple of years ago."

"He has two sons."

"I believe that's true.

"Do you know them?"

"Not well. I knew his older boy David. He attended the university where I teach."

"And what about the younger son Colin?"

"Saw him around sometimes."

"Seen him recently?"

"Colin? No, not in years. Has he done something wrong?" There was something a little too innocent in the way he asked that made Jude think Dunne knew more than he was letting on.

The senior FBI agent must also have picked up on it because his voice took on an edge when he asked, "When was the last time you saw him?"

"Golly, I don't know. Probably his last year of high school."

"Mr. Dunne, we heard that Colin and his father were estranged. Do you know anything about that?"

"Gentlemen, you're asking questions I have no way of knowing," he replied. "Why don't you ask Ben?"

The senior agent didn't respond except to say, "Let's have a look at your register."

Jude tugged on her gloves and went outside to meet Cash.

* * *

"Where we headed?" asked Jude.

"You'll see," Cash said. He revved his jeep up a steep hill, a trailer carrying an ATV clattering behind them. "You wanted to see hiking trails, right? That's where we're goin' then." He waved to a 4x4 racing by from the other direction.

"How did you know who that was?" asked Jude. "All I see in Stanton are pick-up trucks and they all look the same to me."

"I know everyone in Stanton."

"Clearly. Have you always lived here?" she asked breezily.

Cash seemed happy to talk about himself. Just an all-around American boy with a lifelong love of the outdoors. "The worst year of my life was when my mom made me go to college," he said.

"Why is that?"

"Jeez, sittin' in a classroom all day, thought I'd go crazy."

"And is Wildlife Services the dream job?"

"Yup."

"How come?"

"I'll show you," he said, pulling the truck over to the side of the road at the head of a steel beam bridge.

When they got out, he led her to the middle of the bridge. Below them rushed a frothy river, water tumbling over ice-crusted stones as if trying to get somewhere in a hurry. Hills rose on either side, one bright in the sun with young pine trees bending toward the light, the other dark blue in the shade. Further down the river on a sandy bank, a small herd of whitetail deer were drinking, occasionally lifting their heads to scan for danger.

Cash spoke quietly, even though the deer were upwind. "I could never give this up."

"It's beautiful," agreed Jude.

"More than that, it's ... the wildness of this place. It feeds something in me."

Jude could see it. The change in his body language was noticeable. At the café that first day, at the town hall, and even driving his truck, he was restless and jittery. Now, surrounded by trees, river, and clouds, he seemed to relax; his hands were steady, his speech slower. But embarrassed at having opened up to her, he tried to conceal his vulnerability by playfully pushing his shoulder into hers. "I mean, look at those deer, the does are so perfect with their long legs and deep brown eyes. Kinda like you."

"My eyes are hazel," replied Jude.

"Whatever. Come on, we're ditching the truck."

He pulled down a ramp at the back of his truck and unloaded the ATV. It was packed with all kinds of gear, including a rifle, storage boxes, and an extra can of gas. The oversized tires gave it a high clearance for snow, Cash explained. This is how you get around in the back country.

Jude looked at everything and asked, "So where do I sit?"

"Right behind me, cowgirl," he grinned, handing her a helmet. "Hop on."

She climbed aboard, adjusting the helmet over her hair which she had plaited in a single braid, and grabbed onto the hand holds, grateful that she didn't have to strap her arms motorcycle-style around Cash's waist. He drove across the bridge and then veered onto a dirt road. For the next hour they traveled narrow tracks and trails, rumbling the ATV through shallow streams and up hills, each one leading to a higher elevation. He pointed out the places where elk had bedded in the protection of downed trees, where once he had seen two male black bears fighting, where he'd kicked over a log and startled a rattlesnake. It lunged, but luckily the snake's fangs only hit his boot. After awhile, getting accustomed to the diesel smell of the vehicle, Jude began to pick out others: the earthiness of damp leaves and the astringent aroma of pine bark. When they'd dip into a hollow or traverse the darkened side of a hill, the air was sharp and cold. But then they'd come up into the sun which felt blissfully warm on her shoulders and cheeks.

Finally, they reached the pinnacle of a wide ridge. Cash stopped the ATV and walked to the edge. Removing her helmet, Jude followed. The sight from the bridge had been lovely, but this was breathtaking. A mile below lay an indigo blue lake, nestled at the base of several peaks, as if they held the water in cupped palms. Beyond the lake was another row of peaks dusted with snow and hardy evergreens, and beyond them more mountains – and more and more. Each range grew lighter in color, from a dark teal to robin's egg blue, finally fading so that there was no difference between mountain and sky.

Cash said, "Would you give this up if you didn't have to?"

"This is one of the most amazing sights I've ever seen," said Jude, quite in awe.

"That over there," said Cash, pointing to the tallest mountain, "borders the Payette National Forest, from here about twenty miles. But you can see at least a hundred miles."

Jude hungrily scanned the horizon, trying to capture the vista in mental snapshots. She felt a kind of spiritual vertigo, as though she were standing above the earth and yet entirely within it. So big. So damned magnificently immense. Like looking into the beating heart of the universe.

Cash took her reverence as an opportunity to seize a kiss. After all, he'd given her this incredible gift, she owed him that much. He leaned in for his reward.

Jude recoiled, affronted as much by his advances as by the very contradiction of this man who'd used a high-powered rifle and an airplane to kill a wolf minding her own business. "Hey, tell me something," she blurted out. "If you love the wildness so much, how can you do what you do?" As soon as the words popped out of her mouth, she winced. Stupid, stupid mistake – to let her outrage get in the way.

"You mean, control predators? Where you from, girl? If you don't control them, nobody could live here," said Cash, leaning in again."

But she twisted away, wagging her finger. "You don't control *me*, cowboy."

He found this quite amusing, and at once Jude understood that part of what he liked about hunting was the chase. Animals, girls, it was all the same. *Okay, Mr. Wilderness Lover*, she thought, *but you're not going to catch this one.*

They moved on, but now Jude adopted a new strategy. First she would draw him in, divulging details of a fictional childhood, just enough to let him believe she was warming to him. Then she pushed him away, becoming aloof, more interested in the panorama than in the man. And all the while, she tried to get him to talk about his job.

"Tell me again about this elk ranch of Mr. Tripp's," she said. They were sitting sideways on the ATV, sharing a thermos of coffee. "I might put something like that in our program for the hunters, especially for those that don't have a lot of hunting experience."

Cash shrugged. "Whatever."

"I know you don't approve," Jude noted.

"Each to his own. The hunting ranches serve a purpose, I suppose. But real hunters don't go in for that stuff."

Jude smiled. "Not honest enough for you, is it?"

"No, ma'am. I hear people call hunting a *recreational sport*, and that's just an affront to me. Football is a recreational sport. Hunting is ... a way of life. At least when it's done right."

"And it's your way of life?"

"Oh, I enjoy a good hunt. But if you ask me who I really am, I'd have to say a trapper. It's pure and keeps me close to the land. You've got to know your animals, where they'll go for food and water, you got to know how to track them, you've got to think like them. And of course, there's an art to setting a trap right."

"I'll bet it takes a lot of skill. I'd love to see what you do sometime."

"Really?" he asked.

"Absolutely."

"Some people find it tough to watch," he cautioned.

"I'm a big girl. And I used to do some hunting with my dad." It wasn't a total lie. One of her foster fathers had been into shooting squirrels.

"So you're not all lovey-dovey about animals and that crap?"

"Who, me? Come on, cowboy."

He started up the ATV and fifteen minutes later, they came to a stretch of road that ran parallel to a stream. Cash pulled up next to a wide thatch of tall, wheat-like grass growing by the water. He got off and began combing through his gear.

"We'll check some traps," he said. From one of the containers he took out a bucket filled with tools that included an odd-looking hammer, a long-handled trowel, and plastic jars labeled with different scented baits. He pulled on a pair of gloves and with bucket in hand, walked down the road a few feet, sighting a particular tree to his left, a rock to his right. Satisfied that he'd found the spot, he stepped carefully toward the stream, looking for tracks. "Follow exactly in my footsteps," he warned. "And stop when I tell you to."

Jude's stomach turned over. She'd asked for this, but the prospect of finding a trapped animal was unnerving. No other way, though, to get him to trust her and possibly learn something new.

After a few feet Cash motioned for her to halt. She peered over his shoulder, but didn't see anything.

"This is called a Double Dirthole Set," he explained. "I put a little beaver meat or gland lure into each hole and bed my trap right here." He carefully brushed away some leaves to reveal a coil spring trap. "I've got a couple more a little further down. No one's been over here, yet. But they'll come."

"How do you know?" asked Jude.

"This is a good corridor. You've got tracks and scat along the ditch here, tracks coming over from the field." Straightening up and surveying the scene, he added confidently. "Oh yeah, they're a' coming."

He threw a handful of dirt over the trap and moved on to the nearby sets to make sure they hadn't been triggered or moved. Jude breathed a sigh of relief as they backtracked to the vehicle. Before putting his tools away, Cash withdrew a small notebook with lined paper, flipped to the current date and made a few notations.

"What's that?" asked Jude.

"A field diary. A good trapper records where he sets his traps, how often he checks them, and what you catch."

"How very organized you are."

"We have to keep them, especially now."

"Why now?"

"There's some kind of animal rights crazies running around busting up traps." He shook his head at the wrongness of it. "We use government issue traps that have serial numbers on 'em, and I have to account for any that go missing or get destroyed. That's the part of working for Uncle Sam I could do without – the paperwork."

Sensing an opening, Jude commiserated, "I don't envy you there. I hate paperwork. Gee, you have to write down *everything*? Including *who* you take on your field trips?"

Cash winked at her. "Well, there are a few things we don't make note of."

"Like girls," she said coyly.

"Like girls ... and other things."

"What other things?"

He snapped shut the lid on one of the storage boxes and looked up at her. "You've got real pretty hair, did anyone ever tell you that?"

"You're changing the subject," teased Jude. "How come? You don't want your boss to know how often you come up empty?"

"Listen, I have the best catch rate of anybody around here," responded Cash defensively. "No, we just keep the paperwork to intended targets."

"What are intended targets?" asked Jude, wide-eyed.

"I'm looking to trap coyote here, but sometimes some animal or other will go after the bait and wander into a set. It happens."

"And you don't have to record that?"

"Technically, yes, we're supposed to report the non-target takes ... trash catch. But hardly anyone does. It would look bad, a lot of people wouldn't understand."

"What do you do with the trash catch?"

"Throw it someplace where other predators will get it or bury the damn thing."

"And your supervisor doesn't find out?"

Cash scoffed, "Are you kidding? He's the one telling us to do it. I knew someone who actually got in trouble for *writin' down* the non-targets in his field diary."

"Get out of here," said Jude in mock disbelief.

"Yup."

Feeling as though she'd pushed enough for the moment, she donned her helmet and chimed, "Okay, where to now, cowboy? This is very intriguing."

They got back on the ATV and rumbled down the dirt road. This time, Jude clasped her hands around Cash's waist, hoping it would encourage him to keep talking. "So what happened to the guy?" she called over the engine noise.

"What guy?" asked Cash over his shoulder.

"The guy who got in trouble?"

"They told him that if he liked to do paperwork so much, they'd find a nice place for him in the Boise office."

"A fate worse than death, right?"

"For me it would be, yeah."

Jude laughed. "Where is he now?"

"Dead," shouted Cash. "I told you about him. He's the guy who was murdered."

"Oh, shit. I didn't know being a perfectionist was so dangerous."

"Perfect had nothing to do with it, darlin'. Eberhardt wrote everything down. It was some kind of obsession with him. Maybe because he was so damn proud of himself or thought he was a better trapper than everyone else and he wanted the numbers to prove it. It's like if he didn't write it down, it didn't happen. Guy was an asshole like that. He could have lost all of us our jobs."

The wheels in Jude's head began to whirr. Cash had just confirmed what Walt Kincaid told her was happening back when he worked for Wildlife Services. Agents were not reporting the non-target animals they caught. Moreover, they were being *directed* by their supervisors to Shoot, Shovel and Shut-up. But Eberhardt had been the renegade. For whatever twisted reason, he insisted on recording everything he trapped. Did that obsession have anything to do with his death? Clearly, the brass at Wildlife Services had every reason to keep lawmakers and the public from learning of this callous disregard for wildlife. A more immediate question came to mind: where was Eberhardt's field diary now?

Cash had stopped the ATV and gotten off to check more sets. Jude became aware of him waving to her from a field across the way. He wanted to show her something. A sense of impending dread washed over her. She closed her eyes, wanting to make it all go away – the role-playing with Cash and the miserable, rusted-out traps waiting for an unsuspecting paw.

He called her over, a wide grin on his face. And Jude steeled herself, trying to paste a cheery expression on her own as she made her way into the field.

"Don't get too close," he warned.

When she saw why, Jude's worst fear was realized. On the other side of a downed cottonwood tree, a coyote was caught in a leg-hold trap, and he was alive. At the sight of humans, he tried to pull back, his eyes wild and frightened. But the trap held his right front leg immobile in its vice-like grip. Jude saw it had cut down to bone, and the flesh around the wound was ripped raw. Blood was smeared across his snout from trying to chew off the trap.

"Wait here, I'll be right back," said Cash. "And don't get any closer 'cause he'll bite you." He left Jude and the coyote staring at one another.

The coyote was small and looked entirely spent, his ribs showed through his gray and white coat. His big ears, one of them minus a chunk in its pointy tip, were twitching with nervousness. Why did Jude think he was just a young one? He tried to flee again, but buckled immediately and collapsed on the ground, his front leg stretched out as far as it would go. His fur was matted with mud, saliva and blood. The prairie grass around him was worn down to the dirt from his thrashing and was littered with pieces of bone and gristle. Jude remembered something that Lisbet had told her: often the pack would rally around their injured member. They couldn't free him, but they could bring him food. The pack was gone now.

"I'm so sorry, little one," whispered Jude, her heart breaking. "I'm so sorry for what they've done to you."

The coyote glared back at her, and she kept silently repeating, "I'm so sorry, I'm so sorry." She wasn't aware that her lips were moving until Cash was beside her.

He carried a thick, heavy bat in one hand and had a revolver tucked into his belt.

"What are you going to do?" asked Jude.

"I'm going to dispatch him. Stand back."

Before Jude could open her mouth, he had struck the coyote on the snout with the bat. The animal fell over on his side, stunned. Then Cash set his boot on the coyote's throat.

"Stop!" Jude screamed.

Cash hesitated.

"Stop! What are you doing?"

"This is how it goes, girl," he said over his shoulder. "Might be able to save the pelt."

The coyote's back legs twitched. He was still alive. "Please, can't you just shoot him?" she asked, trying to rein in her hysteria. "Don't let him suffer any more!"

Eyeing her distrustfully, Cash stepped away. "What's the matter with you?" he asked. "I thought you were all into learning about traps."

Jude swallowed. "Well, I ... this isn't right."

"Fine," said Cash. "You do it."

There was a glint of more than challenge in his eyes. She'd seen the same look when he'd found her in the hangar at Tripp's ranch. He was questioning who she was. He held out his .22 revolver. "You do know how to shoot, right? I imagine your dad taught you."

"Yes." Her voice cracked.

"Then go ahead."

She did in fact know how to shoot, but wished she didn't. He was testing her, and the coyote was suffering terribly. Taking the revolver by the grip, she leveled it and drew back the hammer.

"Go closer," said Cash with some irritation. "Get him through the eye or put a bullet in his ear. It won't make such a big mess."

Jude stepped toward the coyote as he was regaining consciousness. He didn't have much left, but he lifted his head weakly. Her hand began to shake and she could feel ice cold sweat dripping down the back of her neck. Inside she was howling, *I can't do this. Help me somebody! Don't make me do this!* Cash's stare was like a laser, opening up a red hot hole in her cover, in all she had worked for. He was waiting. She looked one last time into the coyote's eyes. He was waiting for her, too.

Jude squeezed the trigger.

Chapter 18

John Tripp pulled up the collar of his leather jacket to stave off the wind at the back of his neck. His companion Bud Grimes, state director of Wildlife Services, unconsciously mirrored the gesture. The two men ambled along the fence that separated them from a herd of heavy-bellied ewes grazing on isolated patches of brown grass.

"How was Houston?" asked Grimes, glancing at the rancher for a telltale sign about whether his news was good or bad. "Did you get a chance to speak to Olander?"

"I did, as a matter of fact."

"What did he say?"

"He's still planning to hold up the transparency bill."

Grimes breathed a sigh of relief. After a series of articles in a California newspaper about the missing $12 million from Wildlife Services' operating budget, a member of the House Agriculture Committee had proposed a "transparency" bill aimed at making the agency more accountable for its spending. The bill had been sent to a subcommittee on livestock and rural development. Scott Olander was the chair and he wasn't letting it come up for a vote.

"I wouldn't get too comfortable, though," Tripp cautioned. "It's a political land mine and Olander is sticking his neck out trying to protect your agency. At the ALEC conference in Houston, a lot of members want to play up how badly the federal government manages our grazing lands, among other things. If more shit comes out about Wildlife Services, they'll throw you both to the wolves ... pun intended."

"You're telling me Olander would let the transparency bill go through just to make the federal government look bad?"

"What I'm saying is you better damn well find Eberhardt's field diary. If it lands in the wrong hands – Walt Kincaid or one of those animal activist types – you'll be swinging in the wind all on your lonesome."

Grimes removed his hat and ran a frustrated hand through his hair. "I'm working on it," he said.

"Did you speak directly with Chief Ramey?" grilled Tripp.

"Of course, twice. I even went to his office. It never surfaced," replied Grimes. There was a hint of defensiveness in his tone.

"What did you tell him?"

"I said it was protocol, for our record keeping."

"Go back and see him again," instructed Tripp. "Somebody must have found it."

"I can't do that, John. If I go back a third time to ask for one agent's field diary, Ramey's gonna start wondering why I want it so bad."

Tripp shoved his hands in his pockets and stepped closer to the fence to watch his sheep.

"What about the FBI?" asked Grimes, nervously fingering his thick handlebar mustache. "Maybe the local cops missed it when they went through Craig's apartment. The agents from Boise were in there after the cops. Maybe they have it."

"They would have come around by now," said Tripp brusquely. "Are you sure the cops even looked for the diary?"

"Of course. Ramey knows how our agents work. He thought it might have given them a timetable of Craig's activities before he was killed."

Tripp kept his back to Grimes. "You're in potential big trouble, my friend," he threw over his shoulder.

The Wildlife Services director quickly covered the distance between them. "You think I don't know that?" he challenged. "Maybe he hid the damn thing or got rid of it. That'd be the best thing ... we just let sleeping dogs lie."

Tripp pointed to one of his white, thick-coated dogs as large as any of the ewes. The Great Pyrenees was commonly used as a guard dog to keep predators away from the sheep, and now this one had come within a stone's throw of the fence to investigate the two visitors. "My dogs don't lie down or sleep while they're on the job," declared the rancher. "If they do, they might get themselves ripped to shreds by predators, along with my sheep."

"Is that a threat?" challenged Grimes.

"Nope. Just a fact."

"Glad to hear that 'cause I believed Craig when he told me that I'm not the only one named in his goddamn notes," said Grimes hotly. "You are, too, John."

"Hey, easy does it. This will all sort itself out," replied Tripp easily.

The Great Pyrenees eyed the men for a moment longer, then trotted off back to his job.

* * *

Colin took one look at Jude's ashen face and knew something was terribly wrong. "What's going on?" he demanded.

"Ask *her*," replied Oliver, who stood with his arms folded and legs planted in a wide stance, seemingly ready to cut off her retreat.

Seeing Colin's hesitation, Jude realized that he still didn't trust her. She hung her head and muttered, "Jesus, Colin, I only wanted ... to be with someone who understands. "Something happened and I needed a friend. You want to check me for a wire? Go ahead. On second thought, fuck it. Come on, Oliver, take me back." She wheeled around and began marching to the car.

"Jude, I'm sorry," called Colin. "Stay."

Oliver widened his eyes and gave Colin a look that did more than hint at his misgivings about Jude. "She's an undercover, dude," he reminded his friend. "Probably a good actress."

"Go to hell, Oliver," Jude shot back.

"It's okay," said Colin. "It's all okay. Jude, please stay." She stopped and shoved her hands in her pockets, staring at the ground.

Oliver motioned with his head at the Taurus. "She brought her dog. Not a smart move, if you ask me." Then he explained as if Jude wasn't there, "She found me at the bookstore and said she had to see you. I didn't want her making a scene, so I said to meet me at Albertson's like before, but I didn't know she was going to bring her dog."

"It's all right," Colin said.

"A big dog like that'll draw attention."

"I couldn't leave him," said Jude quietly.

"Where's Laurel?"

"In Saint Claire. She won't be back until tomorrow."

Colin straightened. "All right, go on back. I'll text you if I need you."

"But you've only got the cycle," Oliver objected. "How you gonna get her and the dog–"

"I'll handle it."

"Okaaay," murmured Oliver, looking between Colin and Jude.

"Goodbye, Oliver. And you can let the dog out now."

As soon as he'd gone, Colin walked up to Jude. "I apologize. Sometimes I get so paranoid, I can't see straight. I was wrong, okay?" When she refused to look at him, he bent down to greet Finn. "What's his name?"

"Finn."

"Think he's hungry?"

"He's always hungry," she said, her eyes brimming.

"Let's go in and get him something to eat. Then tell me what happened. You look like hell."

She told him everything. As daylight faded, Jude poured out the events of her outing with Cash and about shooting the coyote. "I don't even know who I am anymore," she said, her voice shaking. "I looked into that poor creature's eyes before I pulled the trigger, and I had this ... this picture in my mind of moving the barrel just a few feet to the right and shooting Orin Cashman instead. I could see it so clearly. But I shot the coyote. Oh God, there was so much blood."

"He was suffering, Jude. And Cashman was going to make him suffer even more. He was going to stand on his chest until he suffocated. That's the way the trappers do it, so they can keep the pelt intact."

"But I took his life. *I* did it, not anybody else. What does that *make* me?"

"It makes you an investigator who had to keep your cover. You were doing your job."

"Maybe I could have saved him."

"How? Even if Cashman wasn't there, from what you describe, the coyote was almost gone. His leg was probably fractured, his teeth destroyed. He wouldn't have lived a day in freedom – and he would've been in terrible pain."

"I think Finn knew what I'd done," Jude went on. "It was so weird. When I've been gone for a while, he always goes nuts greeting me, he's so happy. But when I came back to the hotel and walked in, he didn't get up, he didn't wag his tail. I think he feels ... betrayed. And I don't blame him." Jude buried her head in her hands, and before she knew it was heaving with the sobs she'd kept in for hours.

"Finn loves you, Jude. He knows who you are," Colin offered. But it only seemed to make her cry harder, so he stayed silent and waited until she was drained of emotion.

Finally, she blew her nose into the wad of tissues he'd pressed into her hand and sighed, "Guess it's my turn to apologize."

"What for?"

"I don't know ... running to you as though you can save me from myself."

"Maybe I can."

Jude looked up into his intense, dark gaze and smiled. "You're supposed to put on your own oxygen mask before you try to help someone else."

"I'm breathing just fine."

"Are you?"

He drew up, slightly piqued. "What is that supposed to mean?"

"Well, look at the way you're living," she said as gently as she could. "It must be hard to stay underground all the time and, you know, not be able to trust anybody."

Colin turned away brusquely. "Look, I'm sorry about before. But I don't think you ought to be talking about *trust.*" He retrieved another log to throw on the fire. "Eight years ago, you disappeared in the middle of the night, leaving just some bullshit note."

"Are we going to go back to all that? You got my letters, didn't you? I wrote you a bunch of times."

"I read the letters. I want to hear you say it."

Jude was silent for a moment, then said, "I'm sorry. I was young and scared."

"We were all young and scared. But I wasn't the one to run off with somebody else," he retorted.

Jude closed her eyes and white-knuckled the damp tissues in her hand. "Do we have to fight now?"

"Well, you never gave me a chance to fight then, so let's do it now. At least I might understand Gordon's particular appeal."

"You make it sound like I ran off with another man."

"Well, you did."

"It wasn't a romantic relationship. Not then, anyway," she finished weakly.

"Oh, that came later?" Colin asked, his voice etched with sarcasm. "When you were older and not so scared?"

"Please don't. Yes, I had an affair with Gordon, but it was brief and it's long over. We have a professional relationship, and he's my friend."

"So why did you leave?"

Jude lowered her head and picked at pieces of Kleenex, rolling them into little pill-sized balls. "I think you know the answer to that. I couldn't live the way we were living. We were getting closer and closer to the edge all the time. Our group was a mess. That last week, Seth was trying to convince us to break into the Penn State laboratory, for goodness sake."

"You should have talked to me about that."

"I did, but you didn't listen. You knew what was going on for me. You knew me better than anyone ever has. I didn't leave because I didn't love you."

"And love wasn't enough?"

"No, it wasn't." Jude flashed back. "You were barreling toward a life on the run or getting locked up, and I spent my entire childhood doing that – running from prison-like foster homes and from sour, overworked matrons at Social Services who didn't give a crap about me. I didn't want to run anymore, and Gordon offered the chance to stay put *and* do something good for animals." She took a deep breath. "How 'bout you? Was love enough for *you*? You knew where to find me. Heck, Gordon probably would have given you a job. But maybe you didn't really love me, you just loved the wide-eyed budding activist who would follow you into battle."

Colin poked aimlessly at the fire. "I guess if love was the only thing that mattered, we'd be living in the suburbs with a couple of kids, taking them to SeaWorld and serving turkey at Thanksgiving."

Jude snorted softly. "Nah, too extreme. How about an apartment in New York, rescuing street animals and raising little vegan activists."

"Hey, there you go. After school I could teach them how to build incendiary devices and dodge guard dogs at a mink farm."

"And I could take the kids on the road with me," added Jude brightly, "Show 'em the inside workings of a slaughterhouse. Like a science project."

Their attempt at humor danced between them, but only succeeded in underscoring the what-might-have-beens.

"Maybe not," said Jude.

And Colin echoed, "Maybe not."

Finally, Jude said, "I'm sorry I hurt you, Colin. If I could take it back, I would. I just didn't know what else to do. And I had to go in the middle of the night because I was afraid if I saw you I'd lose my nerve. I was crazy about you."

He came over to her, close enough that she could feel heat from the fire clinging to his shirt. "And now?" he asked, searching her eyes.

She evaded his gaze. "I don't know."

"I think you still feel something." He put his hand on the curve of her neck, sliding it underneath the braid that lay draped across her shoulder.

"Don't tell me what I feel," she protested, but made no move to shake off his hand.

Jude knew exactly how she felt, she just didn't know what to do with it. He slowly bent his head and touched her lips with his, gently. She responded in kind. As they kissed, his hands took her face, cradling it like a long lost treasure. Jude wrapped her arms around him, her fingers tracing the contours of his back muscles. She could feel her sensuality rising, seeking light as if from a deep, dark place in the ocean. When they finally separated, Colin looked directly in her eyes and brushed a few strands of hair away from her face.

"Hello, Jude," he said. At least that's what she thought he said. She wasn't sure. And she wasn't sure if she said anything back. All she knew for certain was that nothing could keep her from kissing him again, more urgently this time. She let herself go completely, as if her hunger could quiet the storms that loomed in each of their lonely lives.

Some time later, underneath the tangle of musty bedcovers, they lay spooned and warm. Jude suddenly woke, the image of the trapped coyote bursting into her dreamy state. She must have startled because Colin drew up the covers protectively around her. "Are you okay?" he whispered.

She was breathing fast, waiting out her frantically beating heart.

"What is it?" asked Colin.

"I understood something today," she murmured. "I think I've always known it, but today it really hit me. About us as humans on this planet. When I was with Cash, he took me to a place where you could look out and see miles and miles. There were mountains in the distance and other mountains behind them, even bigger, going on forever, and creeks and meadows, trees, and valleys. This vast expanse of earth and open space – the most magnificent thing I've ever seen. And I thought ... if not here, where are they supposed to live? Where do the wolves and coyotes and bears get to live? Don't they get *some*place?" She rolled onto her back, staring into the darkness. "In this boundless, wild territory, don't they get somewhere to raise their babies and roll in the snow and live out their already difficult lives? When I saw the coyote, it was so clear to me that as long as our own government works for the meat industry and people compete for the biggest antlers to mount on their walls and believe that fur coats are glamorous, these animals will never have their *some*place. Not even here where there's room enough for everyone." She turned her face to Colin and said with finality. "Humans want it all."

As much as he would have liked to ease her heavy heart, Colin sighed in tacit agreement. He settled for kissing her forehead and pulling her closer. Jude fit her body into his, but her eyes stayed wide open still seeing the young coyote lift his head to her.

Chapter 19

The sun was rising and getting to work on the frost that blanketed the gray and white landscape. Jude sat on the steps of the cabin's front porch, wrapped in an unzipped sleeping bag, her hands warming themselves around a cup of strong, black coffee. She watched Finn study an irate squirrel who was jabbering at him for coming too close to his tree.

The door behind her opened and Colin appeared carrying a toasted bagel and jam. He lowered himself to a spot next to her.

"How can you live here?" asked Jude. "I am freezing my ass off."

"I could warm it for you," he said with a grin.

"I'm sure you could," Jude laughed. "Actually it's my feet that are cold."

"Put 'em here." He handed her the bagel and took her feet in his lap. "Jesus, how many pairs of socks do you have on?"

"As many as I could find on the floor. I guess some things haven't changed."

"Well, for your information, this is mild for December," he replied, rubbing her feet vigorously. "It's going into the low thirties today."

Jude harrumphed and took a bite of the bagel. "A regular Caribbean holiday."

"What's he doing?" asked Colin of Finn.

"He's trying to make friends with that squirrel. So he can chase him."

"Somehow I don't think the desire is reciprocal."

"Oh, Finn can be very charming. We were staying at this sanctuary once, and he took a real shine to one particular goat. At first, she played cool, wary as any goat would be of such a handsome, debonair and worldly fellow. But he kept coming back and after a day or two, the goat was smitten." Jude sighed. "She followed him everywhere."

"What is he? A Rottweiler mix?"

"Something like that. I found him in a cage at a puppy mill. He was probably headed to a rendering plant, along with some other pups too weak or sick to sell at auction."

"He's a lucky fellow."

"*I'm* the lucky one."

They were silent for a minute, each wondering how to hold on to the morning, knowing it couldn't last. Jude was the first to acknowledge the inevitable and asked, "How long are you going to stay?"

"I don't know," said Colin. "My dad's pretty sick and I want to be around for him, but..."

"What's the matter with him?"

"Cancer."

"Oh, no. I'm sorry."

He looked at her, as if she had an answer. "I really don't know what to do. There's a lot of muddy water under whatever bridge still stands between my dad and me, and I don't even think he wants me around, but you see … I was locked up when my mom passed. I wasn't there for her when she needed me."

"And you're afraid the same thing will happen with your dad?"

"Yeah. I do have to live with myself. We've never been close, not that I recall anyway. But he is my father."

"Is he close to your brother David?"

"Kind of. David liked to do all the hunting things with him. But I'm not sure my dad was ever *close* to anyone. Except my mom and his dogs. God, he loved those dogs. He buried them all down by the pond in the back of the house. And do you know that he's kept all their collars? Well, not his last dog Oona. She was hit by a car. I don't know what happened to hers. But I found the other collars tucked away in his bedside table. No photos of us as kids, no basketball trophies, no old skateboards in the garage – but he keeps the dog collars."

"So you've seen your father?"

"A couple of times. This is his hunting cabin, you know."

"And he knows you're here?"

"Of course, he gave me the key."

"Maybe he's making an effort to connect with you." Then Jude suggested gently, "Guess you could stick around."

"There are obvious problems with that," pointed out Colin.

"Why don't you speak with the FBI," she said more urgently. "You have an alibi, right?" Even knowing how naïve she sounded, she finished, "They wouldn't arrest you for something you didn't do."

"Of course they would. And my alibi is Oliver. They'd try to pin the murder on me and use the prosecution as a threat to get him and Laurel to talk about the traps … can't do that."

"Are you protecting Oliver?"

Colin looked at her sharply. "What do you mean?"

"I just wonder about him and Eberhardt."

"You don't really suspect him of killing the guy. Are you nuts?"

Drawing her feet back, Jude said cautiously, "He's very angry, Colin."

"And for good reason."

"Where did he get that bruise under his eye?"

Colin hesitated, then said, "From me, as a matter of fact. I was breaking up some firewood and a piece flew off and hit him in the face. You think a black eye means he's a murderer?"

"Well, he said something pretty odd the other day when he was bringing me back to Stanton. He was going on about Wildlife Services and about Eberhardt getting what he deserved. And he said that Eberhardt was alive when someone put his leg into the trap and that he tried to claw his way out." She waited to see how Colin would respond, and when he didn't, pointed out, "How could Oliver possibly know that? I don't think that gruesome fact is public knowledge."

With eyes fixed on Finn at the edge of the trees, Colin shrugged. "I don't know how he knew. His uncle is a cop in Saint Claire. Maybe he heard it from him ... autopsy reports get around, I guess."

"Did you know about his felony conviction? You told me that he was jailed on a misdemeanor, but before that he was charged as a juvenile for assault with a deadly weapon."

"Who told you that?"

"Gordon."

Colin stood up and took the last two steps down the front porch. "Glad to know Gordon is on the job," he said curtly.

"Don't be angry at him, Colin," Jude pleaded. "I'm here undercover, he's just looking out for me. And we're trying to figure out who killed Eberhardt so you don't get blamed."

"But he's happy enough to finger Oliver."

"Gordon's not accusing anyone. He just has questions, and rightly so."

Turning back to Jude, Colin leveled his gaze at her. "Oliver did not kill Craig Eberhardt. I know him. He is keenly aware of what it would mean to the ALF if he engaged in that kind of violence."

"Okay."

"Okay," echoed Colin with finality.

After a moment, Jude said, "They're going to find you soon, you know. A couple of FBI agents were at the guesthouse yesterday asking the owner about you and your father."

Colin's frown deepened. "What owner?"

"His name is Foster Dunne. Apparently he was an acquaintance of your father's. I overheard the agents asking him about you."

"Foster Dunne. His name sounds familiar. What'd he tell them?"

"He said he hardly knew you, but he was being kind of cagey and I think they were suspicious. If they did their homework, though, they'd take whatever Dunne says with a grain of salt. He's got memory issues because of a brain injury."

"Well, the feds already paid my dad a visit. But he's not going to tell them anything. Besides, short term I'm leaving for a bit. I've got something I have to take care of."

Jude wasn't sure she liked the sound of that. "Take care of, like what? Where?" she asked with a frown.

He picked up a pebble and threw it into the trees. Finn, hoping it was evidence of a squirrel, dashed in the direction of the sound. "You really want to know?" he responded.

"I don't think so." But she was too curious. "Just tell me where."

"Not sure, yet. Probably Louisiana." He gave her a sly grin, adding, "You may want to watch *yourself*, Miss Undercover. As far as the feds are concerned, you and The Kinship are only a notch or two below me on the terrorist watch list. What's *your* next move?"

Jude said, "I have to get to the bottom of what Wildlife Services is up to. They're decimating wildlife in horrible ways and they're totally unaccountable. Yesterday I learned that every trapper for Wildlife Services has to keep a field diary to record what animals they've caught and how often they're checking their traps. Cashman told me that they're instructed from the top to omit the non-target animals they catch, which, by the way, far outnumber the intended target animals. Negative publicity and all. But Craig Eberhardt didn't pay attention to that. Apparently, he recorded everything."

"What are you getting at?"

"It would be interesting to see what's in that diary. Maybe it would even point to someone who wanted him silenced."

"If that's so, it'll be long gone by now."

"Maybe not. Cash told me that Eberhardt got in trouble with his superiors because of the diary, so I don't think he'd just leave it lying around."

"Well, some notebook is not going to take down the big targets you have in mind."

"Livin' on dreams," she offered with a hopeful smile. "Sometimes if you grab hold of the end of the string and keep tugging, the whole thing unravels."

"Sure," said Colin dubiously. "Let me ask you something. Does Gordon know you're here? With me?"

Jude averted her gaze by way of an answer and to her surprise, Colin began to sing softly, "*She stumbles back into the shadows, where their darkest secrets dwell. And into my waiting arms, and the love we knew so well.*"

She vaguely recognized the song – one they'd listened to years before. She couldn't remember the rest of the verse, but knew she didn't want to hear it. "I have to get back," she said. "Dunne is going to wonder if I've skipped out on him without paying."

"So that's it, then?" When she didn't answer, Colin yielded to the reality that neither one of them could stay where they were for long. He took a deep breath and said. "Alright. I'll let Oliver know. But he won't be here for an hour or so. Put on some more socks and let's take Finn for a walk."

They stepped single file along a faintly-marked deer path, Finn galloping ahead. With a crust of snow covering rocks and exposed roots, Jude had to watch where she put her feet rather than enjoying the scenery. But it kept her so present that each of her senses was finely tuned. She felt the breeze cool her where it met the tiny beads of sweat moistening her forehead. Each sound from a snapping twig rang clear, the crunch of their footsteps set a natural rhythm, and the dappled light shimmered in unexpected pockets of the woods. *This moment right here*, she thought, *with Colin and Finn, this moment might be as close to domestic bliss as I ever get.*

Colin stopped to adjust his backpack into a more comfortable position. She'd teased him about what could possibly be inside to make it so heavy, wondering why he brought it in the first place. He'd tossed off something about old Boy Scout habits and being prepared for anything in the Idaho woods.

"How're you doing?" he asked.

"Good."

He stepped toward her and gave her a long hug. His hair and denim jacket smelled of smoke and pine. "Want to turn back?" he asked.

It was hard to miss the deeper meaning behind his question, and she answered truthfully. "Not just yet. A little further."

So they trekked on. At one point, Jude spotted a glistening sheen of water through the trees. "What's that?" she asked.

"It's called Freedom Lake," replied Colin. "When we were little, my dad would take us swimming and boating there. And when I got older, I'd come up by myself and sit and think. Once I saw a bear about thirty feet from me and nearly broke my neck trying to get away. I'd bet that old bear was just laughing at me."

Suddenly an unearthly scream pierced the air. It froze Jude mid-step, chilling her to the bone. The fur on the back of Finn's neck rose straight up as if electrified. The sound was the scream of a woman in agony and it came again, starting like the caw of a crow then rising to a high-pitched, throaty shriek that echoed for what seemed to be miles.

"Stay here," said Colin in a low voice. He started running in the direction of the sound.

Jude hesitated only a second. If someone was being attacked, she couldn't just stand by. Colin would need help. She started after him and a few seconds later saw him about twenty yards off the path. When she got close he put out his hands.

"It's a fox," he said. "The female makes that cry, it's called the vixen's scream."

"Are you certain?" breathed Jude, her eyes wide.

His mouth taut with anger, he stepped aside to reveal the fox, teeth bared, frantically trying to shake herself loose from a leg hold trap. The chain to which it was attached clanked and shook, but was firmly embedded in the frozen ground with a metal spike.

Jude stumbled backwards and did something rare for her – she panicked. Images of her own participation in the death of the coyote clouded good sense, and unable to help herself, she let out a small cry. Finn began barking and the fox redoubled her efforts to flee, spattering blood from the gouges in her foot.

Colin took charge. He threw his backpack to the ground and told Jude, "Get him away from here, then come back and help me."

Jude stood rooted until he grasped her shoulders. "Go!" he commanded. "He's scaring her and making it worse."

Shaking off her stupor, Jude unclipped a leash from around her waist and snapped it on to Finn's collar. She led him away from the fox and tied him to the trunk of a young tree. She returned to Colin's side.

He was stripping a tree limb with a hunting knife. His backpack was open next to him, and Jude could see wire cutters and a small crowbar inside. Deftly, he cut off the smaller branches and twigs until he had a six-foot stick with a wide, two-pronged end. He tested its strength on the ground and found it acceptable. Meanwhile, the fox had crouched low, watching him, eyes glaring.

"Okay, here's what we're going to do," he said quietly, removing his jacket. "I'm going to put this over her head. And then I'm going to hold her down while you get the trap open."

"Me?" whispered Jude.

"Yes. She's terrified, and she'll try to fight us. I have to keep her still to have any chance."

"I ... I don't know how to open the trap."

"I'll talk you through it," said Colin.

As they slowly approached, Jude finally got a good look at the fox. She was a stunningly beautiful creature with auburn fur nearly the shade of Jude's hair. Her lower legs were painted black and she had a streak of the same ebony down her bushy tail. Her amber eyes shone feral and aware, and she was ready to battle for her life. As Colin neared, she pulled back, poised to attack. Then she let loose the same eerily human screech.

"We have to work fast," said Colin. "If there are trappers around, they'll be on their way."

With his jacket in one hand and the stick in the other, he inched toward her. "Easy now, easy now. We're going to try and get you out of here, beauty." Speaking to the fox in low, calm tones, he stole closer. When he was within a few feet, he tossed his jacket forward, covering her face. She shook it off and barked a short warning cry. Colin tried again. And again, the fox escaped from under his jacket.

The third time, Colin rushed forward as the jacket landed, and he thrust the wide prongs of the stick on either side of the vixen's neck, pinning her to the ground. She struggled, but he held her firm. "Help me get the trap exposed," he quickly instructed Jude. "And watch her teeth."

Cloaked in darkness, the fox was more subdued, but it still took both of them to push her onto her side. At only thirty-five pounds, she was incredibly strong.

"Okay, do you see the two levers on either side of the jaws?" asked Colin. "Press down on them hard, and for God's sake don't get your fingers in the middle."

Jude knelt and leaned on the three-inch levers. They didn't budge. She tried again, pushing as hard as she could and nothing happened. "They're not ... moving," she panted.

"Use your feet," said Colin, his breath coming heavy with the effort of holding the vixen down.

Jude stood and maneuvered the toes of her boots on each of the levers. They were slick with snow and blood, and she'd no sooner get firm footing on one, when the other would slip off.

"Get it done," said Colin, leaving no room for mere effort.

Taking a deep breath and balancing herself, Jude got an inch more boot on each lever and willed her body weight to press down.

The jaws snapped open, and just like that, the fox had her foot out. Colin held on.

"Good girl," he said. Jude wasn't sure which one of them he meant. "Now go stand over there. I'm going to let her up and we don't quite know what's she's going to do."

When Jude was a safe distance, Colin stepped back, pulling away the stick and whipping off his jacket in one motion. The fox seemed stunned. She drew her injured foot into her body and sat on her haunches, unmoving. Colin took a careful step back. "It's all right," he said softly. "You're okay, now. Go find your mate. Go on, have a life now, my beauty."

The vixen lifted her nose into the air and as if she'd understood every word he said, began to limp away. As Colin and Jude stood transfixed, she stopped and looked back at them over her shoulder. Jude could have sworn that she dipped her head in gratitude before she disappeared, blending into the colors and silence of the wintry landscape.

Jude waited with Finn while Colin "finished up." For him it meant destroying the leg hold trap once and for all, then sweeping away their boot tracks with a pine branch. He backed up to the spot where they had left the path and covered their place of entry with a few more pieces of downed wood. They walked farther along the trail for a while, then zig-zagged back to the McIntyre cabin.

While they waited on the porch for Oliver, Jude finally asked, "Do you think she'll live?"

"I think so. She seemed to be walking okay."

Jude clasped Colin's hand. "Thank you. That was incredible, to be able to release her. I can't help but feel like God … fate, whatever, put her in my life today to give me another chance, after the coyote and all."

Colin nodded. "It's tangible, you know? We can't save them all, but we can save one. Today, we saved one."

"What now?"

"Where there's one trap, there'll be others. Oliver and I will go back tonight and look."

"I mean long term. What about us?"

The crunch of tires on gravel told them that her leave-taking was imminent. Colin tightened his grip on her hand. "It's up to you."

"Don't put this all on me," she cried. "It's not that simple."

"Sure it is. We'll save animals and figure it out as we go. Come with me."

Jude didn't respond. Oliver had driven up to the cabin and he had bad news.

Chapter 20

Two FBI agents had come into the bookstore as Oliver was opening up. They duly noted his criminal record and proceeded to question him about when he'd moved to Stanton, where he was living, and how long he'd been working at the store. And they wanted to know about Colin McIntyre.

"I told them I'd met you once in Seattle about four years ago, but that was it."

"Did they hang around?" asked Colin.

"Only long enough to threaten me with a grand jury subpoena if I didn't tell them what they wanted to hear."

Colin appeared lost in thought for a moment, then said, "Okay, take Jude back to Stanton, and then lie low for a while. I'm switching phones, but don't contact me until you've done the same. And get word to Laurel."

In the gloomy confinement of the Taurus on the ride back, Oliver made it clear with his body language that he blamed Jude for bringing law enforcement down on their heads. She refused to be pulled into a fight and withdrew, only to have the lyrics to the song Colin sang come back to her with miserable clarity. Written by a poetic rocker they used to listen to, it was a haunting acoustic track that seemed to play on an endless loop in her mind.

She stumbles back into the shadows where our darkest secrets dwell
Into my waiting arms, and the love we knew so well
They will come after, they always do, keepin' us on the run
You and me together, girl, we'll finish what we've begun

The refrain was still echoing when she and Finn returned to the guesthouse and made a beeline for their room. Safe behind the closed door, Jude finally checked her messages and found two from CJ, the last one worried that neither he nor Gordon had heard from her. But she couldn't convince her fingers to hit the call button. Instead, she kicked off her boots and collapsed on the bed. Rolling onto her side, Jude clutched a pillow to her chest in an attempt to ride out the turbulence inside.

Everything she'd worked for felt tenuous – her reputation as an investigator, her connection to Gordon and the others at The Kinship, even her sense of mission. She had built something solid and valuable for herself in D.C. She'd even gotten used to living alone. Now she could feel it slipping away. Last night, she'd had a taste of skin touching skin, the luxury of feeling him next to her through the night, and the ease in knowing each other so well. There was a piece of her that wanted to hang onto that so bad it stabbed at her belly like a cramp. Not the least of it was the cold, cast iron truth that despite her efforts, she would never see in her lifetime an end to the ingrained systems of animal cruelty. Colin offered an answer to that. Jude could still feel her fingers numb with cold, pressing down on the trap's levers, the sheen of sweat underneath her shirt from the exertion. And the release! Watching the fox escape was exhilarating. It lifted her, and Jude still felt as though she was breathing air more pure than she ever had.

But how could staying together possibly work? An impermanent life, moving all the time, distrusting anyone new and probably some old friends as well. And what would they accomplish? Defeat a few traps, save some animals who might die of their injuries anyway? Free some mink who had no experience of surviving in the wild? And the certain betrayal of Gordon – all for the tangible assurance of knowing that specific animals had been liberated.

Jude lay paralyzed, her thoughts changing, shifting, churning up silt and clouding her vision. All she wanted to do was to curl up under the quilt and sleep. She felt a light touch on her wrist. Then Finn pushed his big head to within inches of her face. She hadn't even thought about him. What would happen to Finn? If she went with Colin, could they even take him? Oliver was right, he would attract attention when they would need to stay invisible.

"Oh, my Finn-dog," she whispered, reaching out to stroke his head. "What am I supposed to do?"

He gave a little huff through his nose and solemnly rested his chin on the covers. The gesture was so innocent and trusting, it reawoke in her the immediacy of all the animals that were suffering and needed help – by whatever means. Jude pushed herself into a sitting position and swung her legs over the bed.

"You're right," she said. "There is only one way. Get out there and do *something*. Just keep working."

Finn wagged his tail in response.

* * *

This time when she passed through Fielding's Outfitters, Jude didn't stop to watch the sales clerk demonstrate the action of the Bridger Wolf Trap. She knew exactly what it could do. As she slipped into the rear hallway, the door of Sal Mayhill's office opened and a burly man sporting a handlebar mustache came out. With his hand on the door, he turned back and said, "Look at the bright side, Sal. When it all goes through us, it'll cut down on your paperwork." As he brushed past Jude, she recognized him instantly from his photo on the government website. It was Bud Grimes, regional director of Wildlife Services.

Through the open door, Jude saw Sal slam shut a file cabinet drawer with a loud clang, her face flushed with anger.

"Sorry, is this a bad time?" asked Jude.

"I'm a little busy," replied Sal abruptly.

"No problem, I can come back."

Sal waved for Jude to enter. "No, it's okay. Come on in." She moved over to the squeaky swivel chair behind her desk and peered over the tops of her reading glasses. The color in her cheeks was starting to fade. "Miz Harris, right? You find your tour guide operator?"

"Not yet," said Jude. "I'm quite taken with Stanton, though. I think it will be a terrific destination spot for us."

"Sure. How can I help you today?" She motioned to a seat across from her desk, but her mind was still on the encounter with Grimes.

Jude tugged off her gloves and sat. "I'm putting together a report about Stanton for my boss at EO Travel. And in addition to recommending activities, restaurants and hotels, I have to discuss potential issues that might pose a danger to our clients who would certainly be unfamiliar with the area. For liability purposes, you know."

Sal gave her a quizzical look.

"Well, I heard about an injury," proffered Jude cautiously, "a severe injury to a boy in Stanton from a cyanide trap."

Sal took off her reading glasses and folded them into the breast pocket of her uniform. Jude noticed how tired she looked, almost beaten down, and she wondered if it was trouble at home. There were dark circles under her eyes, and from what Jude had witnessed, Bud Grimes had just added to her burdens. Whatever it was, she had the look of someone who was resigned to simply putting one foot in front of the other because all other options were closed.

"It's true," Sal responded. "But he's going to be fine. Mind my asking where you heard that?"

"I read about them, these M-44's," said Jude, evading the question, "and they can be quite deadly, even to people. How widespread is their use?"

"I wouldn't worry. These devices are illegal, except for Wildlife Services. And if they feel it necessary to use them, they post notices."

Jude cleared her throat. "My understanding is that in the case of this child, there were no notices."

"Where'd you hear that?" repeated Mayhill. She absently picked up a pencil and began to tap it against her palm, playing out her discomfort with the subject.

"If I must say, it was from the mother of the boy herself."

"Kylie Harrington?"

"Yes, that was her name. She was kind enough to give me directions the other day. And we got to talking, and she told me what happened. The whole incident must still be weighing on her, you know?"

"I imagine."

"So you can understand my concern that our guests might step on one of these and get sprayed by cyanide, which I have to say is not a remote possibility should this ... Wildlife Services become somewhat lax about posting warning signs."

"They're supposed to, but sometimes the wind blows them down, or people take them down." Tap, tap, tap.

Jude didn't have to be a mind reader to see that Sal was no fan of Wildlife Services, and she took the opportunity to dig further. "But that's not what happened for Kylie's son and her dog," she said. "This was on her own property, and she told me she never saw any signs."

"What's your stake in this?" Sal asked sharply.

"Well, first and foremost, the use of these devices would make EO Travel hesitate to bring hikers and tourist trade to the area. But I was also moved by Kylie's situation, especially since she was apparently stonewalled when she tried to get some answers from Wildlife Services. They must have known who set that trap. They must be required to keep records of that sort of thing. I mean, there has to be some accountability, and if something like that happened to one of our clients, well..." Jude let the thought drift, and then said, "Between you and me, I think what happened to Kylie Harrington's boy and her dog is pretty horrible."

Sal sucked in a deep breath as if trying to bottle up what she really wanted to say. Finally, she released it with an audible sound, adding, "Yes, it was pretty horrible."

Jude plowed ahead. "I probably shouldn't say this, but for all we know it was Craig Eberhardt who set the M-44 that killed Kylie's dog and poisoned her son."

Sal's tapping abruptly ceased. "You're skating on thin ice there, Miz Harris," she warned. "Nobody knows who placed that trap."

Looking down demurely, Jude murmured, "Maybe someone does."

"Yeah, like who?"

"Well, I learned that Craig Eberhardt not only kept a field diary, but was meticulous about writing everything down. And I mean *everything*."

"Where'd you learn that?" Sal's eyes flashed. It was clear to Jude that she was conflicted. She was reticent to discuss Wildlife Services or Craig Eberhardt, but her interest had been piqued.

"If I tell you, will you please keep it to yourself, because it was said to me in confidence. It was another Wildlife Services guy, Orin Cashman. We were on a date, of sorts."

"Does he know where it is?"

"No, but somebody should, right?"

"The police looked," Sal blurted out. "They figured it might tell them what he was doing just before he was killed. But as far as I know they never found it."

"That's kind of unusual considering it was a work journal kept in the regular course of his job."

Sal lowered her voice conspiratorially though no one was within hearing distance. "Unless the killer took it or maybe destroyed it because something in the journal might reveal his identity."

"Oh, my! Is that what the police think?"

"I really couldn't say." She hesitated. "I do hear, though, that they're working with the FBI on the murder, and there are signs that point to animal activists."

Jude raised her eyebrows. "Animal activists? Gee, Stanton's got a lot more going on than I thought."

* * *

Sal's theory seemed plausible, even more so knowing how extensively Eberhardt had recorded his non-target kills. Had the diary itself gotten him murdered? Jude now knew that it wasn't in an evidence bag somewhere. That was something. She had just stepped out of Fielding's into the damp, gray afternoon, when CJ called, sounding quite pleased with himself.

Skipping the preliminaries, he jumped right in. "So I'm doing some research for Gordon on the AETA hearing next week, and I found something you might be interested in."

"I'm listening," said Jude.

"The guy who's pushing the amendment is Scott Olander, and as a high ranking conservative, he's got his fingers in a lot of pies. One of them is the Department of Agriculture's Subcommittee on Livestock and Rural Development, where he's the chair. Late last year when a whole lot of bad publicity on Wildlife Services came out, one of the House members proposed a bill that would have made the agency more accountable."

"Was that when they 'lost' twelve million dollars?"

"Yup. The bill demanded more oversight regarding the agency's expenditures."

"Yeah, and..." said Jude with a frown.

"It never came up for a vote. Olander buried it. And as the committee chair, he's got the power to stall the bill indefinitely."

"Why do you think?"

"How about Scott Olander and Lindsay Dahl are good buddies. They go way back to when they were both on the board of Marshfield Industries, your favorite pork producer. Small world, hunh?"

"Are you kidding me? Lindsay Dahl is the head guy at APHIS," Jude noted incredulously.

"Which oversees Wildlife Services. And if I'm right, it gets even uglier," CJ said. "You wanted to know if John Tripp was at the ALEC conference in Houston? The answer is yes. And so was Scott Olander. In fact, Olander is an advisor to the ALEC agricultural committee along with Tripp."

Jude took all this in before replying angrily, "It's all the same story, isn't it CJ? The Tysons and Cargills and Marshfields make the laws in this country. And even as they scream about regulations, they have a chokehold on the federal agencies. Profit is their god, and if farm animals are tortured in factory farms and our country's wildlife is wiped off the face of the earth so everyone can buy cheap meat, so be it. And now Olander is trying to put more teeth into the anti-terrorism statute to make sure that those of us who want to help the animals are silenced and thrown in jail."

"Welcome to twenty-first century capitalism."

Jude thought for a moment. "Remind me when the hearing is," she said.

"Next Friday."

That gave her less than a week to dig up more dirt on Wildlife Services and hopefully find the diary. Olander was going to further criminalize the fight for animal protection? Block any oversight of Wildlife Services? Not if she had anything to do with it.

Chapter 21

Ben heard tapping against the rear slider to the deck and looked up. Colin was standing with his shoulders hunched against the cold, his face in the shadow of his hooded jacket as dark as the lowering clouds behind him. Ben got up from his chair and walked a bit shakily to the door to unlock it.

"Hey, Dad," said Colin, letting in a gust of damp air.

"What's the matter with the front door?" his father asked. His gruff tone belied the flash of happiness he felt at seeing his son.

"There's a government car parked at the bottom of the driveway."

Ben grunted and cast his eyes uneasily in that direction. "I guess they didn't believe me. You, uh ... you want some coffee?" At his son's hesitation he added, "We'll hear them if they drive up to the house. And you can go out the way you came."

"Okay."

"I've only got instant, that alright?"

"Sure."

As Ben shambled into the kitchen, Colin noticed how loosely

the clothing hung on his withering frame. Yet he had taken the time to dress as if he had plans. His shirt was laundered and his trousers neatly pressed. Even if all he could do was sit and think and wait for the medication to work, he had his pride. No slippers for Ben; he'd put on shoes, shaved, and carefully combed his thinning hair.

"How are you feeling?"

"Oh, fine as can be expected, I suppose." He put a kettle on the range and took out two mugs, spooning a teaspoon of granules into each. "David and his wife are expecting again," he said, blocking further discussion about his health.

"No kidding. Rachel must be nearly three now, right?" asked Colin, referring to his niece.

"Cute as a bug. Smart, too."

"I'm going to try and get out there to see them. Soon."

They waited for the water to boil, the air still thick with bottled up feelings. Finally, Colin blurted out, "I'm sorry, Dad."

"Oh, them?" Ben waved disdainfully in the direction of the presumed FBI agents. "They'll go away eventually."

"Not that. I mean, yeah, I'm sorry the cops are bugging you. But I wanted to say..." Colin took a deep breath, "I'm sorry for what I've put you through. You and Mom. You know, I tried to get a furlough to make it home for the funeral, but I was in a max security unit and they wouldn't go for it." After a pause, he continued, "And it's not just that. I wasn't the easiest kid to live with, which you know. I ... I was just born in the wrong place, I guess. Idaho? Hunting capital of the world? If only we'd lived in Cape Cod or something."

Ben sniffed. "You probably would've bitched about the fish."

"Probably. I know it's hard for you to understand, but I see animals differently than you do, than most people do. I believe they live *with* us on the planet, not *for* us. And the way you would never want to see a dog suffer, like Far Away or Hoop or Oona, I can't accept us thoughtlessly hurting other animals who feel pain and fear as much as a dog. I just can't stand by when they're suffering." Colin saw his father's hands begin to shake. "I didn't come here to upset you, though, Dad. I came because I wanted to clear the air, you know? I wanted to say I'm sorry."

Slowly Ben poured hot water into their cups and stirred up the dark brown liquid. "Sugar?" he asked.

Colin shook his head, partly in dismay. They'd been down this road before.

"Sit down," said Ben gently. They brought their coffee into the living area and Ben took a seat in his favorite chair. "You may have a couple of things to apologize for, son. But you don't have to apologize for being who you are. I won't apologize for who I am either. People don't always see eye-to-eye, not even in families – maybe *especially* not in families. But it doesn't mean they don't feel for each other." He cleared his throat. "You know, you came along right after we'd moved here. I was nearly forty and wanted to fit in as much as anyone. It meant adopting a new culture ... huntin' deer, carrying a rifle ... being a *man* in the American west. I honestly saw your alliance with animals as being against *me* somehow. When you got older, I thought your activities were just an expression of hostility. The protests against the war and the global warming stuff all seemed so ... un-American, it angered me."

"My activism about animals wasn't aimed at *you*, Dad. And not against this country, per se. It's aimed at a culture and an economic system that profits from abusing animals."

"I know ... I know that now. And I'm beginning to think that maybe you and your animal comrades love what this country stands for more than the rest of us because you want to hold America to a higher standard. We have First Amendment rights here, but when they prosecuted you as a terrorist, they had to change the meaning of that word. If you committed a crime, prosecute you for that crime. But terrorism? No, that's totally different. And then to put you away in a maximum security prison, I couldn't see it as anything other than the government trying to shut you up and send a message to your buddies that they better not mess with big business. That's not the America I know."

"Jeez, why didn't you tell me, Dad? If I'd known how you felt..."

"I was angry. Angry at the prosecution, angry about what was happening to your mom, and I got some kind of strength from it, I suppose. You might have a bit of that in you, too." When Colin started to protest, his father continued, "But I shouldn't be trying to draw parallels between us, I've got too much to reconcile about myself. It's just ... looking back I think that if I'd let go of some of my anger, I might not have wasted all those years."

"Wasted?"

Ben stared out the window for a moment before answering. "I spent a lot of time trying to turn us both into people we weren't. Now, it's time to do what we've got to do on our own terms. You know what I'm saying?"

Colin didn't quite, but said, "It's not too late, Dad."

Smoothing a non-existent wrinkle in his trousers, Ben replied, "I'm afraid it is. You've got to move on, Colin. Those fellas at the bottom of the driveway would love nothing better than to pin a murder on you, if only to justify branding you a terrorist."

"I appreciate the thought, Dad. But they're going to catch up with me sooner or later. I've got something I have to do in a couple of weeks, but then I'm coming back. When all is said and done, they can't connect me to Eberhardt. And I know a good lawyer. I'll give her a call. Whatever this cancer is, we're going to see it through together."

* * *

Jude sat at a table with a stack of newspapers in front of her. The hushed atmosphere of the library was broken only by the intermittent buzzing of a malfunctioning fluorescent light in the corner of the reading room. She had six days until the hearing to dig up something concrete about Wildlife Services. As her inside source, Cash was still her strongest lead, and she'd called him to accept his invitation to Tripp's Christmas party. She'd see him tonight. In the meantime, she wanted to find out everything she could about Craig Eberhardt. An internet search hadn't given her much, so she turned to the local Stanton paper, hoping that accounts of the murder might open a door.

The police were quick to link the fact that Eberhardt's leg had been forced into a trap to the recent rash of dismantled traps in the area. "We've had numerous reports from local residents of missing or broken traps," said Sergeant Wheeler of the Stanton PD. "We have reason to believe it's the work of violent animal activists who will apparently break the law to advance their agenda. And I can promise that if they are responsible for the murder of Craig Eberhardt, they will be brought to justice."

In the next day's paper, Jude read a reporter's interview of people who knew Eberhardt. "I saw him at Fielding's that day," said one. "We were looking at coil spring traps what with wolf season underway." The article went on to discuss Eberhardt's work with Wildlife Services and his extensive trapping expertise. He was not scheduled to work the day he was killed. He told someone that he was going hunting – a pastime he enjoyed on his day off.

Jude leaned back and digested that last piece of information. Eberhardt's day off. She surmised that if he wasn't working, he wouldn't be carrying his field diary. And if he didn't have it on his person, his killer couldn't have taken it from him ... all of which negated Sal's theory that the killer fled with the diary because it contained clues to his or her identity. But that the cops hadn't found it in his car or at home had to mean that Eberhardt stashed the diary in a place no one would look. Jude let the thought linger for a moment then went back to the article. A minute later, she was sorry that she had.

Two officers responded to the call and Mr. Ferrow led them to the body of Craig Eberhardt, which was partially covered by the three-inch snowfall of the previous night. The victim had been shot and his leg apparently placed into a large steel-jawed trap. A full investigation is underway. Residents of the Lake Freedom area are being asked to cooperate with the police.

Jude caught her breath and hastily flipped through the rest of the paper where news of the killing continued. *The body of Craig Eberhardt, found less than a mile from Lake Freedom...* That's where Colin's cabin was.

Chapter 22

The Tripp Ranch was lit up like a gilded castle. Candles ensconced in glass were reflected in the gleaming honey oak floors; the decorations on the twelve-foot Christmas tree in the foyer twinkled with white light and gold ornaments. The atmosphere exuded warmth and wealth.

Jude handed her parka to a woman in a housekeeping uniform who gave her a numbered receipt and disappeared into a walk-in closet. Grateful that she'd packed a "just in case" black dress, Jude turned to join the other dinner guests. She'd put her hair up and added a touch of mascara and blush, about the only makeup she ever used, and wore a pair of silver earrings she'd bought at a craft shop in Stanton. She was hoping she would fit in tonight, and from a few of the smiles she received, apparently she did.

She strolled into the study where the cathedral ceiling magnified the voices and the clinking of ice. Couples mingled, the men wearing sport coats and wide-brimmed Stetsons, the women wearing satin and rhinestones, their perfume mixing with the wood smoke from the fire. A server with a tray of canapés approached. Jude smiled and shook her head, not even bothering to look at what the tray held. It was bound to be something she wouldn't eat. She made an effort to look relaxed, but since learning that Eberhardt's body had been found at Lake Freedom, her mind had been a jumble of thoughts, none of them happy.

Lake Freedom. Too coincidental. Had Oliver killed him? If so, Colin had to know. What a lame story about a piece of wood hitting him in the face. Then again, it could have been Laurel. Hadn't thought of her, but why not? She's small but surprisingly strong. Nearly tore my arm off behind the bookstore. Remember how angry she was at Wildlife Services for killing wolf pups? The possibilities fermented inside Jude all afternoon.

"Why, there's my gal," whooped Cash, coming up behind her. As if they were lovers reunited, he took her in his arms and planted a kiss on her lips. "Don't you look pretty, real pretty."

Jude drew back, replying, "Thank you, mister." She had to be nice to him this evening.

"Get you a drink?" he asked

"They have a good beer?"

"It's all the same to me," said Cash, holding up a half-finished Budweiser.

"Let's go take a look."

He led her across the foyer into the bar and dining area where the mammoth elk head stared accusingly down at the festivity.

"Do you have any microbrews?" asked Jude of the bartender.

"Sure do, ma'am." He pointed to a few bottles behind the bar, then added, "Also got a local brew in a keg called Old Gray Wolf. It's heavy-bodied and on the malty side, but it's not bitter like stout. Most women don't care for it, but you look like an adventurous sort, and this one's real good on a cold winter night."

"Sold!"

He drew a glass of the rich beer and handed it to Jude. She drank and nodded her approval.

"You a beer conna-sir?" asked Cash with a smirk.

"I like to try new things," said Jude.

He handed his empty bottle of Bud to the bartender who didn't have to be told to flick off the cap on a new one.

They wandered through an archway into the adjoining room where a four-piece country band was playing in the corner and couples were happily doing the two-step on an open parquet floor. Servers from the kitchen came and went through a set of swinging doors at the back of the room. Jude saw Abby from the Tripp Creek Café; she dangled an empty tray from her hand and was wistfully tapping her foot to the music. When she spotted Jude and Cash, she gave them a guilty little wave and ducked into the kitchen. For the next half hour, Jude played her role as dutifully as she could, keeping up small talk with Cash and feigning enjoyment as his dance partner. She was surprised at his skill, but not at how he took every opportunity to put his hands on her. Each time she had to remind herself that she'd maneuvered herself into this position and it came with a cost. She just had to keep the price as low as possible.

Meanwhile she kept her eyes open. John Tripp was playing the host; accompanied by Bud Grimes, they worked the room, shaking hands with fellow ranch owners. Cash wanted to show her off to a few of his colleagues and brought Jude into the study to meet two other Wildlife Services agents. While they chatted, Jude sized up both of them and finally targeted one. His name was Hank and he was already slightly drunk. She just had to wait for the right moment.

That moment came when the second agent excused himself and headed to the dance floor. Cash tried to pull her that way as well, but she begged off, saying that she needed to take a break. "Don't suppose you'd get me another beer?" she asked sweetly.

As soon as he left, Jude turned her attention to Hank. "You work with Cash?" she asked.

"Not exactly, I'm further north."

"And you came all the way here for the Christmas party?" Jude gave him a warm smile and his already ruddy complexion went even redder.

He began twisting one end of his thick, droopy mustache, awkward in this social situation. "It's somethin' to do," he shrugged.

Glancing across the foyer, she saw that Cash had stopped to talk with someone. "You guys don't have an easy job, that's for sure," she said.

"How do you mean?"

"I heard about your co-worker Craig Eberhardt. Did you know him?"

"Sure did."

"I'm so sorry. He was a friend?"

"You could say. We went way back."

"What was he like?"

"Bit of a loner, I guess."

"No wife or girlfriend?"

"He was married once, but it didn't work out. Can't say as I blame her. Craig was more married to his job. I think she got tired of spending anniversaries in a tree stand huntin' deer." He grinned, showing a glimpse of a chipped front tooth.

Cash was now waiting at the bar. "Did they ever catch the guy who killed him?" asked Jude innocently.

"Nope. But they will." He lifted his glass and took a swallow of straight bourbon. "Animal activists, crazy effin' people," he said, grimacing at the liquor's burn.

"Why are you so sure it was activists?"

"Because they hate us, that's why."

"Maybe there's another explanation. Cash told me that your friend had gotten into some kind of trouble at work over his ... what did he call it? A field diary? Maybe it had something to do with that."

"What does his field book have to do with the price of eggs?" asked Hank dismissively.

"I overheard someone say that the police went looking for it thinking his last entries might bear some clue about whoever wanted him dead."

Hank snorted. "It's a log for work, it ain't a personal diary."

Jude cast another look in Cash's direction. He was just getting to the front of the line. She still had a little more time. "Exactly. Which makes it that much more suspicious that the cops couldn't locate it anywhere."

"Yeah, I guess so," he conceded.

"So, if you were Eberhardt, where would you keep this book if you didn't want anyone to find it?"

"You're a regular Nancy Drew, ain't you?" Hank noted with amusement.

"And I love a good mystery," came a deep voice directly behind Jude. She whipped around to see John Tripp towering above her. She'd been so focused on Cash, she hadn't been aware of the rancher's approach. "Miss Harris, so glad you could make it this evening," he said jovially. "How's it going, Hank?" He reached out to shake the agent's hand.

"Not bad, Mr. Tripp," said Hank. "Thanks for inviting me."

"Any time. Now I see you here having a scintillating conversation with a pretty girl and I have to come over and see if I can't barge in," said Tripp, resting his hand lightly on the small of her back. "So what is all the mystery?"

Jude opened her mouth to say something, anything to keep Hank from responding. But he had already blurted it out, "We were talking about Eberhardt."

"Oh, terrible, terrible thing," said Tripp.

"Cops can't find his field book," said Hank. "And we were trying to figure out where he might have put it 'cause it might tell 'em who the murderer was. At least, that's Judy's theory."

"Is it, now?" asked Tripp. "Tell me more." He continued smiling, but his gaze had hardened.

Jude sensed a sudden tension in his body that flowed like a current through his hand still resting on her back. "Just rumors around Stanton," she said breezily, hoping he couldn't see her pounding heart through the neckline of her dress.

"Well, you shouldn't listen to rumors. They can get people into all sorts of trouble, don't you think?"

"We were just chatting," said Jude. "Didn't mean anything by it."

To her relief, Cash appeared with a beer in each hand.

"Well, enjoy yourselves now," said Tripp. "Nice to see you, Hank. And you, Miss Harris."

He sounded cordial enough, but Jude's danger sensors were firing, and when the rancher tapped Cash on the shoulder and asked to "have a word" with him, she could feel her fragile cover story fall away like flimsy clothing, leaving her naked. From the corner of her eye, she saw a grim Tripp steer Cash into the next room. She made her excuses to Hank and made a beeline for the ladies room. Once there, she locked the door and leaned on the sink, her knees feeling weak. *Damn. You were too busy keeping an eye on Cash to watch your own back. And just when you might have learned something from Hank. What the hell was Tripp so freaked out about? His comment about 'rumors getting you into trouble' – that was a warning. Was it about Eberhardt himself? Or the field diary? You'll never find out now. Maybe they don't know who you are, but they know who you're not. Cut your losses and get out while you can.*

Someone knocked on the bathroom door. "Just a second," called Jude. She flushed the toilet, straightened her hair in the mirror, and headed back to retrieve her coat. She hadn't gone far when she spied Cash in the foyer, peering one way then the other, no doubt looking for her. Quickly, she retraced her steps. The hallway hooked around into the dining area, where the band was in full swing. Tripp stood with Bud Grimes by a set of French doors. He said something to Grimes, then slipped through one of the doors to a stone patio. Grimes waited a moment, then followed.

Jude didn't hesitate. She dashed into the busy kitchen where cooks and wait staff were preparing desserts. The head chef was shouting instructions, trays and pots clanked, and the sweet smell of baked goods hung in the air. Jude spotted Abby, arranging cookies on a platter, and sidled up to her.

"Hi, you want one of these?" chirped Abby.

"Actually, I'm feeling a bit lightheaded. I could use some air," said Jude apologetically.

"I hear ya," said Abby.

"Can I get out this way?"

"Sure, through the pantry. There's a service entrance at the end."

Abby pointed her in the right direction and Jude hurried off.

The cold hit her instantly. She found herself downhill of the patio, which was rimmed with Christmas lights, and picked her way across the dirt and gravel until she spotted the outline of two figures by the railing. Tiptoeing closer, she squeezed between a few shrubs. The muted music and laughter coming from inside covered her footsteps and the rasp of the leafless branches scraping at her legs. She crouched by the patio wall, directly below the two men.

"What is Cashman doing with her?" Grimes was asking.

"What do you think?" responded Tripp dismissively.

"Did he say anything to her about the diary?"

"He says he didn't, but he'd tell her anything to get laid."

"Who the hell is she, anyway?"

"I don't know. She was out here a few days ago asking questions about wolves and god knows what else ... asking about you," said Tripp.

"Me?"

"Wildlife Services."

"She a reporter?"

"All I know is she's trouble," replied Tripp with exasperation, "and she suspects that Craig's diary got him killed."

"Shit."

"Where is it, Bud?" asked Tripp.

"I don't know," Grimes exploded. "Chief Ramey would have told me if his boys found it."

"Oh, you think so? They open up that notebook and read about the cash payments I made to Eberhardt and your other agents. They read about the plane rentals, the trash animals, endangered species, and how Shoot 'n Shovel comes right from the top." Jude could almost hear him poking Grimes in the chest with each accusation. "And you think they're going to call you and say, 'We found what you're looking for and we'll FedEx it to you.' I don't think so. I think they say to themselves, 'Good golly, look at all this taxpayer money going to private ranchers, and to our own state senator, no less.' I think they say to themselves, 'Maybe this Eberhardt guy was into blackmail. Or maybe he was going to defect and cozy up to animal rights people the way Walt Kincaid did.' No, if Ramey finds that diary, he's gonna come around sticking his nose into our business."

"But what about the trap?" Grimes argued. "With Eberhardt's

leg in there ... it points directly to those animal rights fanatics. Maybe this gal is one of them. But she's not going to find the diary, John. If the cops didn't find it, she won't."

There was a long silence and Jude became aware that she was shaking in the cold; she forced her jaw to stay open so her teeth wouldn't make a racket when they chattered.

"I'd better get back," Tripp finally said, his voice now detached as if his mind was elsewhere. "Don't do anything. Don't talk to anybody. I'll have Cash deal with this."

Jude waited until she heard the patio doors close and hurried back into the house. Keeping her head down, she took her place behind a couple retrieving their coats. Occasionally, she snuck a glance over her shoulder as she anxiously waited her turn. *Come on. Come on.*

"Coat tag?" asked the attendant.

"Uh ... yes, somewhere." Jude's frozen fingers fumbled in her purse, her fear of being seen growing with every second. "Here, here it is."

The wait for her coat felt interminable. *Let. Me. Get out of here.* She didn't know what Tripp meant when he said he'd have Cash deal with her, but she sure didn't want to find out. They were into something really dirty and didn't want it exposed. Had Eberhardt gotten greedy, looking to make some extra money by threatening to reveal Wildlife Services' corrupt war on wildlife? Had they killed him to shut him up? If so, they wouldn't think twice about silencing an animal rights activist who knew too much.

The attendant returned with her coat. Jude almost made it to the front door when she felt herself being roughly turned around.

"Hey, Cowgirl. I was looking for you." His face, lit from behind, looked gray and hard.

"Oh, Cash. I looked for you, too. But I couldn't find you, and then I … I'm not feeling all that well, so I'm going to head out."

"Nah, that's not right," he said, grasping her hands. "The evening's just getting started."

"Thanks, but I have to get an early start tomorrow."

"You're leaving Stanton?"

"'Fraid so."

"But we hardly got to know each other. Whoa, your hands are freezing and your lips are blue. Where the hell you been?"

Jude pulled her hands away. "Like I said, I think I'm coming down with something."

"I'll drive you to the Aspen."

"No thanks, I'll be fine."

"Oh, no." He took her by the shoulders and leaned in, the beer on his breath heavy and sweet. "I think you owe me. You know, after showing you all around and inviting you here…"

She wrenched herself out of his grasp. "No, Cash. Please."

He reached for her again, but a burly man in an overcoat stepped in between them. "Cash, m'boy," he said quietly, but firmly. "The lady wants to go home."

"But she don't feel good, so I'm gonna take her," growled Cash.

"You're not driving anywhere, son," said the man. "Go get yerself some coffee."

Jude didn't know who the man was, but could have hugged him when Cash backed off. "He's not a bad sort," said her rescuer after Cash walked stiffly away. "But young men these days aren't taught how to be gentlemen."

"Well, clearly you were," said Jude. "Thanks."

She hurried down the front steps and found her car. Cash did not reappear, but he knew where she was staying. Jude sped back to the Aspen, glancing behind her frequently – something that now had become as routine as breathing.

Chapter 23

The guesthouse was dark; even the holiday lights around the front window had been unplugged for the night. Jude used her key to get in and took off her shoes so as not to make any noise on the stairs. She had just started up when she heard an excited scrabbling against the hardwood floor behind her.

"Jesus, Finn! You scared the crap out of me," exclaimed Jude in a reedy whisper. "What are you doing down here?"

He wagged his tail furiously in response. A light went on in the dining room and Foster Dunne appeared. "Good evening," he said. "Would you like some tea?"

Oh, God, thought Jude. *Here we go again.* She thought if she had to play act for one more second she would explode. "No," she replied, adding even more tersely, "Did you let Finn out of my room again?"

"I did."

"Do you always go into your guests' rooms when they're not here?"

"Not as a general rule," he answered evenly. "But I felt bad for him being cooped up all evening. Are you alright? You look quite pale."

"Yes, I'm fine. Good night."

"Good night, then. I'll tell you about your visitors in the morning."

Jude stopped in her tracks. "Visitors?"

"Two agents from the Federal Bureau of Investigation came looking for you earlier."

Her breathing on hold, she repeated, "Looking for me?"

"Well, they wanted to know about your travel company."

"Come to think of it," said Jude. "A cup of tea sounds like just the thing."

She trailed Dunne to the kitchen where a kettle was starting to whistle. While he got out cups and teabags in his slow, mechanical way, he told her that the agents had asked what documentation, if any, she had provided when she checked in. The screws were tightening even further. Holding on to the last vestiges of her story, however, Jude feigned puzzlement.

"That's odd," she said. "What could they want with EO Travel? Oh, well, I'll call my boss in the morning. I'm curious ... what did you tell them?"

"Nothing, really." Dunne sat down and blew on his tea. "I showed them the business card you gave me."

"I guess they have to look at everything if they're investigating a murder," she threw out. "Did you know Craig Eberhardt?"

"I knew who he was." Seemingly disinclined to pursue the subject, Dunne sipped his tea. A lone howl sounded in the hills behind the guesthouse and Finn's ears perked forward.

"What is that? A wolf?" asked Jude.

"Or coyote."

They waited in silence for an answering yip or howl, but it never came. Finally, Dunne said, "The sound always makes me think of the Baskervilles. Do you know the story?"

Jude was happy enough to get off the subject of the FBI and responded, "*The Hound of the Baskervilles*? I read it when I was a kid, but I've sort of forgotten. Isn't that the one where Sherlock Holmes investigates a family curse?"

"The ancient curse of the Baskervilles." Dunne's voice took on a dream-like quality. "The lord of the manor Hugo Baskerville was so madly desirous of a neighboring farmer's daughter that he kidnapped her and imprisoned her in his bedroom. She escaped in the middle of the night and he became enraged at the thought of losing her. He mounted his steed, let loose his hunting dogs, and went after her on the desolate moor. Later, they were both found dead. The girl had perished of fright, but Baskerville had a more grisly end. A supernatural beast, a huge black hound, had torn his throat out."

There's definitely something wrong with this guy, Jude thought.

"Arthur Conan Doyle had it right," Dunne concluded.

"Had what right?" Jude asked hesitantly.

"The link between hunting and predatory sexuality." Dunne smiled. "I cover this in my psychology class on gender and domination."

Jude was wary, but intrigued. She couldn't help but think of Cash and nodded for Dunne to go on.

"Hunting in modern times, and I include trapping as well, is experienced as an erotic activity in our patriarchal society. You often hear hunters speak of their appreciation or love of the animals they capture. They are adamant about 'thanking the animal' for her sacrifice; they speak of the grace and beauty of their prey; they'll stroke the dead body and take photographs of themselves touching their victims. The sport is one of dominance and possession. And of course taking possession entails killing the animal, eating its flesh and often mounting the head on the wall."

"It sounds so ... deviant put that way," said Jude.

"I suppose it is, but certainly something that has attained a cultural acceptance."

"Around here, there's so much antagonism towards wolves and coyotes," she noted. "Clearly hunters and trappers don't see them as beautiful or seductive."

"That's true, and it brings up the interesting correlation to rape. There's a common perception by the rapist that the victim provoked the act – in the way she dressed or enticed him. Similarly, you see hunters cling to the notion that they have been the victims of animal invasion and are completely justified in striking back. Everyone around here knows that disease and weather are responsible for many more livestock deaths than wolves, but the predators are given demon status, which for many heightens the thrill in killing them."

Jude was decidedly uncomfortable with this midnight discussion of rape and sacrifice, especially with someone as unpredictable as Dunne. She wondered if she ought to be afraid and glanced at Finn to make sure he was close. Yet what Dunne was saying matched up with Lisbet's theory that imbuing wolves with mythical powers made killing them that much more exciting. Jude wondered if he could shed any light on the riddle of Craig Eberhardt and asked, "What would you say about a person ... a hunter or trapper ... who felt compelled to record all the animals he killed in a journal?"

"It wouldn't surprise me at all. Criminal profilers have long since made the connection between the hunting mentality and serial killers. In fact, when it comes to violent crimes against people, law enforcement lexicon classifies those who seek out nearby victims as *hunters*, those who travel to locate their prey as *poachers*, and people who have a position or occupation that brings potential victims to them as *trappers.* Moreover, we know that many serial killers, particularly in sexual crimes, crave a trophy from their victims – a ring, a lock of hair, sometimes a body part. The trophy helps them re-live the thrill of the killing itself. Similarly, the head of an elk or a lion, a deer's antlers, these are all souvenirs that allow hunters to re-experience the flush of the kill. So to answer your question, this person you describe is akin to a serial killer. He is proud of his kills and probably wants to list them, count them, and read about them over and over again. I would venture to say that he is taking physical trophies from the animals as well."

"And where might someone like that keep his trophies?" asked Jude.

"Depends on the trophy, I suppose. Culturally, we think that the head of an animal mounted on a wall is perfectly fine décor. But perhaps this person is hunting or trapping animals that he oughtn't. Can't very well put those heads over the mantel, now can he? So he might find someplace safe to do that. A place where he feels in his element."

Jude let that sink in for a moment, and it took her somewhere so dark, she wasn't sure how to get back. Animal heads mounted on walls. All because humans felt superior. And what about the humans who felt superior to other races, other religions ... might it be culturally acceptable to mount their heads in prominent places?

"Are you alright, my dear?" asked Dunne.

Jude nodded, fatigue leeching into her very bones. "I really must get upstairs," she said. "Thanks for the tea and the conversation." She had to push herself up from her chair. "Finn and I will be leaving in the morning, I'm sorry to say."

"Too bad. I've enjoyed this fella's company," he replied, scratching Finn behind the ears.

"Well, good night." Then, glancing back over her shoulder, Jude asked casually, "Do you need to ... lock up or anything?"

He smiled. "Not to worry. You're safe here."

Before she got through the doorway, Dunne stopped her. "Miz Harris, I hope you find what you're looking for." His look was so penetrating that she thought, *He knows. He knows you were asking about Eberhardt. And he knows who you are. I don't know how, but he knows and he's trying to help.*

Jude shook off the feeling. She was just tired, that's all. She gave him a genuine smile and said, "Thank you, Professor. I hope so, too."

* * *

Jude swung her backpack over her shoulder and grabbed the handles of her duffel. She'd donned an extra layer of fleece in an effort to get the zipper closed on the overstuffed bag. The air was heavy with impending snow, due to start late in the afternoon, though she hoped to have crossed the Colorado border by then. With her free hand she gathered up the bag with Finn's food and water bowl and they made their way downstairs for a last breakfast.

An unexpected visitor sat at the long table in the dining room. Sal Mayhill. She wore a worried expression as she talked with her brother. Jude only caught a bit of what she was saying, but *FBI* and *arrest* were the words that stuck out. Sal changed course as soon as she caught sight of Jude.

"Oh, Judy. Hi there. Ah, this must be the famous Finn," she said. "He's made quite an impression on my brother."

"There's coffee on the hutch," said Dunne. "And Mary made oatmeal 'cause she knew you liked it so much."

"Tell her thank you," said Jude, helping herself from the sideboard. "Please don't let me interrupt."

"I should be off," said Sal, pushing her chair back.

"So they're going to make an arrest?" Dunne asked her.

"That's the plan."

"What arrest?" asked Jude.

When Sal hesitated, her brother said, "Tell Judy what's going on, so she doesn't worry about them looking for her."

"The FBI is all over Stanton this morning," said Sal. "They're ready to make an arrest on Craig Eberhardt's murder."

Jude was stunned. "They are?"

"Yes. They got a DNA match from the trap on Eberhardt's leg. It belongs to some member of a radical animal activist group. They have reason to believe he's in the area and they're mounting a manhunt."

"I know the boy," said Dunne, shaking his head. "I'm sad for Ben, the boy's father," he explained to Jude. "He lives in Saint Claire, and we both have known him for many years."

They exchanged a few more words about the McIntyre family before Sal left. Foster Dunne glanced occasionally at Jude's white face and if he guessed anything, he didn't say. It was all Jude could do to go through the motions of paying her bill and checking out, all the while feeling that the ground beneath her had opened up and she was being sucked into the darkest depths of the earth.

Chapter 24

A black Ford Explorer with tinted windows idled in front of the Eat, Sleep, Read bookstore. An identical vehicle was parked about fifteen yards away, giving the occupants an unobstructed view into the alleyway behind the store. If the FBI was trying to be unobtrusive, they were failing miserably. For them, DNA was incontrovertible evidence, yet Jude refused to let go of her belief that it was a terrible mistake or there was some other rational explanation. *If Colin was guilty, why would he even think about staying in Stanton with his father? If he was guilty, I would've been able to see it in his face. Wouldn't I?*

She'd been up half the night battling with herself over saying goodbye to Colin, and the morning light hadn't done much to ease her conflict. Once before she had left him without a proper explanation and she didn't think she could do that to either of them again. The decision was made when she heard about his imminent arrest. Someone had to warn him.

Jude drove slowly past the bookstore, piecing together the

scene. Laurel and/or Oliver were inside and the agents were waiting to see if either panicked and led them to Colin. Alternatively, Colin was already in custody and the agents were sitting on the location ready to pick up his friends should he decide to talk. In either event, they were wasting their time. She continued up the street toward Fielding's Outfitters, where she saw two more government vehicles and a half a dozen men and women in navy flak jackets printed with large FBI yellow letters on the back. A few wore bulletproof vests. Jude had to shake her head. *We're animal activists, folks, not heavily armed white supremacists.* Two of the agents were apparently impressed with a resident's pickup truck and the canid carcass that had been tossed into the back. *Terrorism is in the eye of the beholder*, thought Jude, ticking off another in the escalating count of dead wolves. She made an angry u-turn and drove back into town.

Abby was working at the Tripp Street Café.

"Hey, how's it going?" asked Jude with forced cheer.

"Not so good," responded the waitress. "I partook ... is that a word? Partook? Partaked? Alls I know is I drank too much last night. But that band was good! Did you enjoy yourself?"

"Sure did. Say, Abby, do you have a phone book I could look at? A white pages?"

"Over by the take-out counter. Cash ever find you last night, honey? After you came into the kitchen, he poked his head in looking for you. I sent him out through the pantry, told him you were feeling poorly."

Jude fought the urge to check behind her. "Mmn, yeah," she mumbled. "I'll take a black coffee to go and have a look at that phone book."

She hurriedly flipped through the pages under M and found a McBurnham, McIntosh, and McMillan. But no McIntyre. Her heart sank. Then her eye caught the heading; she was looking in Stanton. Ben lived in Saint Claire.

Yes. There it was. Ben & Joan McIntyre, 54 Tolan Way. If Colin wasn't home with his father, he was still at the cabin. Ben could tell her where it was.

She turned onto Tolan Way and drove nearly a mile and a half along the sparsely populated road until she found the mailbox for number 54. Taking a deep breath, Jude turned into the rough, pebbly driveway to the house.

She cracked a window in the Subaru for Finn and rapped on the front door. After a moment she heard shuffling footsteps. A thin, drawn man with his hair freshly combed opened the door part way. She saw a much older version of Colin in the shape of his jaw and the tiny frown lines at the center of his brow.

"Mr. McIntyre? My name's Jude. I'm a friend of Colin's. Is he here?"

He scrutinized her face before replying, "No, he isn't. What do you want?" He made no move to allow her access.

"I don't know if Colin has ever mentioned me," said Jude. "We were ... very close in college. We've been friends for a long time."

"So?" he asked distrustfully.

"I think he may still be at the cabin. I have to find him."

"I have no idea where he is."

"It's important, Mr. McIntyre."

Ben growled, "Look, I told you people I haven't seen him and I don't know where he is."

Oh God. He thought she was a cop or with the FBI trying to scam him. "I'm not what you think. I really am a friend."

Glaring at her, Ben asked, "Is Colin alright?"

"I think so, but..."

"But what?"

"Mr. McIntyre, there are quite a few federal agents gathering in Stanton. They're going to arrest him. They have DNA evidence that links him to the murder of the Wildlife Services agent."

"That's a lie," snapped Ben.

"I don't think so. I'm told they found his DNA on the trap."

For a moment Ben looked utterly confused. His already pale face went a shade grayer as he sagged against the door frame.

"Are you okay?" Jude asked, alarmed.

"It's not possible," he cried. "You have it all wrong."

"Mr. McIntyre, please–"

"Go away. Get out of here!" he barked and shut the door in her face.

Jude lifted her hand to rap on the door again and heard a low moan on the other side of the door. He must have been deeply distraught, unable to accept the fact that his son might be a killer. And he thought she was a cop – he would never tell her where the cabin was. A stomach-churning sense of failure washed over her and she kicked herself for handling the situation so badly. Now she had to go back to Stanton and find a way to get to Oliver or Laurel. As she headed slowly back across the front yard, her foot kicked something and it rolled away, bumping down a gentle slope. Layers of snow fell away revealing a flash of yellow. She saw what it was now – a tennis ball. From the yip inside the car, so did Finn. His favorite game was chasing tennis balls, the older and smellier the better. There were a few more yellow orbs dotting the yard, some half-covered by snow.

This must be where Ben threw tennis balls for his dog Oona. Jude could picture her, tail flying, ears flapping, chasing them down and dropping them at Ben's feet, looking up at him with shining eyes and a wagging tail. *Do it again, do it again!* And he would. Oona ... who went everywhere with Ben, according to

Laurel. In the back of her mind, Jude heard again Colin's lament that his father kept no photos of his children, "but he keeps the dog collars." Except Oona's. Why? Ben had buried her when she got hit by a car. Isn't that what he told Colin? If so, why didn't he keep her collar with the others? The questions circled and then were drawn as if by a powerful magnet to one thought – one re-calculation. Ben's cry *You have it all wrong. It's not possible!* Dear God, he meant it. Not theoretically, but factually. Colin a murderer? It was *not possible.*

Jude did an abrupt about-face. She pounded on the door, calling, "Mr. McIntyre, open the door." Nothing. She knew he could hear her. "I am not who you think I am. My name is Jude Brannock and I'm an animal rights investigator. I was with Colin at the cabin at Lake Freedom yesterday. He told me that he'd seen you and that you were talking about your dogs ... Hoop and Far Away, right?"

"Get out of here!" Ben bellowed from beyond the door.

Jude wasn't going anywhere. "You're right, they have it all wrong. I know what happened. Oona got caught in Eberhardt's trap, didn't she?"

She could almost hear him holding his breath. "Go away," he tried again, though his voice had weakened.

Please, Ben," implored Jude, willing him to open the door, "if you want to help Colin, you've got to talk to me."

There was movement inside, and a moment later Ben unlatched the door. His eyes burned, dark and glazed, as if with fever. He turned and stumbled to a nearby armchair where he collapsed. Jude went over to where he sat with his head in his hands.

"Can I get you something?" she asked.

He shook his head.

"Let me help you," Jude pleaded. "Let me call somebody."

"No," he said sharply. "Don't you dare."

"Okay." She knelt by his side and asked gently, "What happened to Oona? She wasn't hit by a car and you didn't bury her. If you had, you would've kept her collar along with the others. Colin told me about finding them all, but not Oona's. Because Eberhardt took it, didn't he? She got caught in one of his traps and he took her collar as a trophy."

Ben did not protest, he just continued to stare at the floor. His passivity angered Jude and she snapped, "You're going to let Colin take the rap for his murder? Is that what you're going to do?"

"No!" exclaimed Ben, coming to life.

"Tell me what happened," she demanded.

Finally, he lifted his head and shed his burden. "She liked to wander. Ever since she was a puppy, she'd go walkabout, every year farther and farther. But Oona always came home. She was my shadow, my friend, and after my wife died and I found out about my cancer ... she was all I had. One day she didn't come home. I went out looking for her that night, the whole next day. I called and called. I knew something was wrong.

"I thought she might have gone up by the cabin. It's far, but she loved it there with the lake and all. I drove up and started walking around. I don't know how she knew I was there, but she began to howl. I found her in a leg hold trap, a big one." Ben shut his eyes against the memory. "She was almost gone. Her teeth were broken, her mouth a bloody mess. Her leg was all torn up. She'd lost so much blood. I don't know how long she'd been there. Dear Jesus, my girl was hurtin' so bad, but when she saw me, she tried to wag her tail. She trusted that I would save her. But I couldn't open the trap. I'd been walking all day and my strength was gone. I didn't have tools with me. Even a year ago, I could've opened it somehow. But not with this damned cancer." He clenched his fists, ready to fight with his disease.

"Go on," Jude prompted.

"I had tools at the cabin, but how could I leave her? She wouldn't understand. And I knew she didn't have long. So I lay down and held her. She passed not long after." Rubbing a hand across his face, Ben continued, "I was going to bury her down by the pond here – close to my other dogs. So I went back to the cabin for tools and some kind of litter to carry her to the car. Maybe the hardest thing I've ever done, walking away and leaving her there ... and when I got back, she was gone. And the sonofabitch had reset the trap." Ben's voice cracked with fury.

"How did you know it was Eberhardt's?" asked Jude.

"It had a government stamp on it. And he was the only one working the woods around the lake."

"What did you do?"

"I waited to see if he'd come forward like a man and tell me what he'd done. The tag on her collar had my address and phone number. And we'd met, he knew who I was. But he never did."

Jude nodded encouragement.

"I went looking for him in town. When I found him, he said, 'How's it going, buddy?' like nothing ever happened. If I'd had a gun then, I woulda shot him right there, right through the smirk on his face. I said, 'You killed my dog.' He tells me I'm crazy, then says even if it was his trap, dogs get caught in traps all the time, he has *immunity* with the government. He pushes right by me and says he's got more important things to do than talk about an old dog stupid enough to walk into a trap. I heard him tell someone he was going deer hunting. So I went back to get my rifle. I used to hunt up by Freedom Lake and I'd seen where his tree stand was ... a big one you could practically sleep in that he'd slapped together between a couple of trees. Anyway, I found him alright and threatened to go to the authorities, get him fired. 'No one's gonna believe an old man like you,' he says. 'And if even they do, I got the U.S. government behind me.' All the while I see him fingerin' his trigger like maybe he's nervous or something. Suddenly, he raises his gun ... and I shot him."

"So it was self defense," Jude suggested hopefully.

"Don't know exactly. I can't rightly remember what was in my mind just then."

"But he wasn't dead."

"He went down, alright, but I only got him in the shoulder. Maybe I could have let it go at that, but he ... he wouldn't shut up. He was saying stuff, was going to get me put in jail, all over an ugly bitch of a dog. Sayin' awful things about *her*, like how she pee'd all over herself in the trap, whining and crying like a baby. And I blew. I just lost it. I found a leg hold trap in his ATV. And while he's still cursing and screaming at me, I set it and jammed his foot in there. He howled just like an animal when those jaws bit into his leg."

A silence descended in the wake of the violent images. Finally, Ben said, "I meant to go back. I was going to leave him 'til the next morning – way less time than my pup'd suffered in his trap. But I got real sick that night and the next day. I didn't even know where I was. And by the time the fever let up, it was too late. I dragged myself back to the lake, but when I got close I saw the police cars. I knew he didn't make it."

Jude let her head drop. "You're going to have to turn yourself in, you know."

"I know, and I plan to. But not until Colin gets clear of Stanton. They're going to ask me a lot of questions ... about what I've done and all what I know about him. I'm going to tell them the truth. Don't know how his DNA got on that trap, I swear to God. But he's probably been screwing with those things for weeks. Eberhardt's trap must have been one of them." Ben looked directly at

Jude. "There's a good chance, too, they're not going to believe me. You should know as well as I do that the FBI wants *him.* I could confess six ways to Sunday and they'd only think I'm covering up for my boy."

"But the truth will come out eventually," protested Jude.

"Eventually is too long. The last time, my wife and I didn't even know where he was for months. They treated him like a goddamn terrorist. He could disappear again. You've got to help him get away from here."

Jude was stunned with the illegality of what he was asking. A career-ending move if ever there was one. "I can't ... do that," she sputtered.

Ben grasped her hand. "Please, I'm begging you. Colin is innocent. He's at the cabin, closing it up. He told me he's going to stay with me. But I don't want him to." His eyes searched hers for some semblance of pity. "I'm dying, Jude. It scares the bejeezus out of me, but I can handle that. I can bear anything if I know my son is not going back to jail."

His cold, vein-topped hand gripped hers with as much strength as he could muster, and it wasn't a lot. *Oh, shit.* She squeezed back. "Okay," she said. "Okay. Tell me how to get to the cabin. In return, there's something I need to know about Craig Eberhardt."

Chapter 25

From the looks of it, no one had been there for months. Sheets of plywood were nailed over the cabin windows, the door padlocked, and the dirt driveway raked of all footprints. Colin had been thorough. For a worrisome minute, Jude thought she had missed him and that he was en route to his father's. But Finn sniffed him out and the two of them emerged from the trees behind the cabin.

"Fancy meeting you here," he said, relief brightening his face. There was something else, too, that seemed to smooth the crease in his brow. Jude thought it was happiness, and she had to look away, knowing she would be the one to extinguish it. Colin wrapped her in a bear hug, asking, "Did Oliver tell you where I was? He's actually a closet romantic, if you can believe that."

Jude drew back and dealt him the first blow. "Colin, it's bad. They have a DNA match to you on the Eberhardt trap."

"Me? No way."

"The FBI says they do."

"That's bullshit. It's a setup."

"Maybe not. How many traps have you sprung? You always use gloves?" Jude asked.

His eyes flickered anxiously as he ran through the possibilities. "Yeah, I do, but I've torn holes in them plenty of times. I could have gotten blood or some skin on any one of them. Probably one of them was Eberhardt's. *Jesus!*" He took Jude by the shoulders. "You have to believe me. It wasn't me. I swear to God."

"I know that." Jude shook her head sadly. "Colin, I know ... who killed him. I just saw Ben. He told me the whole story. Eberhardt killed his dog Oona."

Colin's face darkened with anger. "What the fuck are you saying?"

"Your father shot Eberhardt and put him in the trap."

"My dad? I don't believe you."

"I'm telling you the truth."

He wheeled away. "Why are you doing this to me?"

Jude trailed after him. "He found Oona in one of Eberhardt's traps up here by the lake. She was still alive, but she died before he could get her out. He went to get something to open the trap, but when he got back, Eberhardt had taken her body ... probably to get rid of the evidence. That's why Oona's collar wasn't with the others."

Colin had his hands on the porch railing, his back curled as if he might throw up. Jude continued, "Your father knew whose trap it was and confronted him. Eberhardt raised his gun first, so there may be a case for self defense. But Ben shot him."

"And then put him in a trap? I can't ... I can't believe that. He's saying these things to protect me." With his head bent, Colin's rejection was muffled, unsure.

"No, I saw his face when he told me what happened. Your father loved that dog and seeing her die that way. I think he just went mad for a moment."

"I've got to go to him," said Colin, straightening slowly as if it hurt him to stand.

"No. You cannot show up there now."

"He needs me."

"Colin, he doesn't *want* you to stay. He sent me to convince you to leave. Look, I'd be the first one to tell you that it's the right thing to stay with him now. But he doesn't want you to risk it. He begged me. He knows as well as anyone that even if he confesses, they're going to arrest you. Christ, they have your DNA on the trap! They're going to think exactly what you want to believe ... that your father's trying to take the rap for you. But by the time it gets sorted out ... *if* it gets sorted out, you'll be long gone into maximum security again, and your father may be dead."

Jude had to say what she knew in her heart was true. "Ben loves you. He says he's going to give himself up, but not until you're far away from here. Look, he knows they're going to question him hard about you. Don't make him have to lie or be complicit in your arrest. He wants to make up for the past, Colin. Give him his chance. He needs that more than he needs your company now."

Colin threw his head back and drew a deep lungful of air into his chest. "Okay," he said on the exhale. Then he looked at Jude. "I left my wheels down the road. We'll meet up in Saint Claire."

She had been dreading this moment. It seemed so unfair to throw this final punch, but Jude couldn't pretend she didn't know what he meant. "Colin, I'm not coming with you."

With this one he was left breathless. She reached out and touched his arm. "I can't. And right now there's something I have to do. I don't have time to explain everything right now, the light is fading by the minute."

He withdrew from her touch and folded his arms, taking a

stand. "I don't know what the fuck you're talking about, but if you're running off again, at least I deserve an explanation."

Jude listened intently for the sound of tires on gravel. She was sure that no one had followed her, but she was still worried. If the FBI suspected that Ben did in fact know where Colin was, they could have checked his property records and learned that he owned land at Lake Freedom. They might be on their way even now. "I hope you left the cycle where no one could see it," she conceded, motioning to the Subaru. "Come on, get in. I'll give you a lift."

He led her to a neighbor's cabin, closed up now that deer and elk season was over. On the way, Jude did her best to tell him what she surmised about Eberhardt.

"Remember I told you about his field diary and how he recorded every animal he trapped and killed? I think he stashed it at his tree stand."

"A tree stand? They're nothing more than little platforms with a seat."

"Not Eberhardt's apparently. Your father's seen it and says it's something much larger, built between two trees. At Fielding's the other day, I saw one the size of a tree house. It was advertised as 'Your Home Away from Home.' I think that if Eberhardt was keeping obsessive records of the animals he killed, including non-target animals, he fits the profile of a serial killer – someone who might also be keeping physical trophies. Just maybe he took trophies from the *non-target* animals as well, and those he would have to hide somewhere."

"And you think they're in his tree stand."

"It would make sense. The cops have looked everywhere for the field diary and they've never found it. Last night I was talking with Foster Dunne about where a hypothetical serial killer would keep trophies that he doesn't want anyone to find, and Dunne said he'd keep them somewhere he felt completely safe and 'in his element.' After what your father told me about the tree stand, it just clicked. What could be more remote and more in his element than Eberhardt's 'Home Away from Home?'"

After a moment, Colin asked, "You think he kept a trophy from Oona? Like her collar?"

"Could be. He removed her body before your father could get back to open the trap."

Jude pulled in to a narrow driveway that dipped down a hill until it arrived at a small house with boarded-up windows. No one could see them from the road and Jude decided to leave the car there.

"So I have to find that field diary," she announced. "Before someone else makes the connection."

Shaking his head in disbelief, Colin said, "You can't be serious. You're going to try and find Eberhardt's tree stand now?"

"Your father made a kind of map for me."

Colin barked out a harsh laugh. "You're out of your mind. You think you're Daniel Boone? You'll never find it on your own. There's a hundred square miles of *nothing* around Lake Freedom." He unbuckled his seatbelt. "I'm coming with you."

"No, you can't risk it," Jude exclaimed. "They're all over Stanton looking for you."

Colin began marching resolutely up the driveway.

"What are you doing?" called Jude angrily.

"I'm going to get Oona's collar. It's the least I can do for my dad."

Jude let Finn out, and he raced after Colin. There wasn't anything else to do but zip up her coat, shoulder her backpack, and trot after the two of them. When she caught up, she asked Colin, "Don't you want to see the map?"

He kept walking. “I don’t have to,” he said. “I’ve been working this area for almost a month. I know exactly where it is.”

A few snowflakes had begun to drift out of the leaden sky. The storm was moving in.

Chapter 26

About thirty minutes later, they found it – a platform of rough-hewn planks hammered into the trunks of two close-growing Douglas firs. Eberhardt had cobbled together waist-high walls made of split logs on three sides. Thick, overlapping branches formed a natural roof and helped to camouflage the structure which had weathered over time and turned the same color as the bark.

Colin found a ladder nearby and shook off the snow. It was coming down harder now, gathering on their hoods and shoulders.

"Let me see how secure it is," he said. He set the ladder up against the tree and started up, testing it one foot at a time. At the top, he stepped onto the platform and disappeared into the gloom for a moment before motioning for Jude to follow.

The space was cramped and dark. Colin fished out a flashlight from his backpack and aimed it at a large beer cooler tucked into the corner. Covered with a mildewed cushion, it likely served as seating when Eberhardt waited for an unsuspecting buck. Colin threw off the cushion and lifted the top of the chest. They both gagged at the smell coming from inside. The Wildlife Services agent had taken pains to dry out his trophies and seal them in plastic zip-lock bags, but they were still decaying animal parts. Jude reached in and brought out a bag of feathers. Unusually large, they had the white and black shafts of eagle feathers. She pulled out another plastic bag filled with bits of fur and more; Jude made out a pointed ear of some mammal. One particularly large bag contained paws – paws from coyotes, wolves, maybe dogs ... others from smaller mammals like martens or beavers. Jude could feel the stiff, matted fur and nails through the plastic and dropped the bag in revulsion. It was like something from a horror film.

Colin sat on his haunches opening a canvas sack. He withdrew a handful of dog collars. Most had ID tags still attached. He held up a jeweled pink collar that might fit a dog of twenty pounds and read the tag aloud. "Lola – The Remsens, Saint Claire, Idaho." He lifted a frayed leather collar, shiny and dark with wear. "Earl – Bobby Hill, 320 Route 9D, Stanton, Idaho. Then another, and another. He read each tag as if memorializing fallen soldiers. Finally, he found the one he was looking for – a blue nylon collar, grimy with age. Colin's voice cracked with emotion as he read, "Oona, Ben McIntyre, 54 Tolan Way ... " He shoved the collar deep into his pocket and said, "Let's go."

"No, not yet. I haven't found the diary," said Jude. She picked up the flashlight and began to shine it around the floor and walls of the tree stand, but there wasn't anything more to see except a pile of dirty rags and some leaves that had blown in. She was rattled. It *had* to be here. Unwilling to admit defeat, she trained the light above their heads and spotted an oval hole in one of the tree trunks. A home for a squirrel perhaps. She rose up on tiptoe and thrust her hand in, feeling around. Her fingers finally touched something smooth, with defined edges. She pulled out Eberhardt's diary wrapped in black plastic cut from a garbage bag. Clever.

"Is that what you're looking for?" asked Colin.

"Yes, I think so." With growing excitement, she stripped off her gloves and began thumbing through the pages. In small, neat handwriting, Eberhardt had noted the dates and times he checked his traps, and when and where he killed an animal, adding comments about species, size, and gender. "Oh, look," she said victoriously. "Here he puts that he caught a golden eagle and writes, 'Called Boise for instructions. Per BG, bury and do not record.' I'll bet BG is Bud Grimes, the regional director of Wildlife Services. And here," she had turned to one of the last entries. "'White, female Labrador, 65 pounds, trap #0172, Lake Freedom, sect. 86.' That's got to be Oona. That's going to prove that Eberhardt was killing domestic pets and covering it up. This is really important. They want to debate the AETA? These politicians want to strengthen the laws prosecuting animal activists? When I bring this evidence that the *government* itself is so corrupt, so depraved ... wow, the press is going to have a field day."

Colin eyed her sadly. "You wish."

"It's not just one employee," insisted Jude. "This implicates the regional director of the entire program. You don't see how big this is?"

"Yeah, big for about five minutes," replied Colin bitterly. "And then it's gone, replaced with important news like what some asshole celebrity is wearing to the Academy Awards."

"It's going to have an impact," Jude insisted.

He winced as if the idea hurt him. "It all comes back to the same story. You and Gordon think you're going to save all the animals. You go hunting for evidence, get your undercover videos, draft the petitions, hand out your leaflets, and post it all on your ridiculous Facebook wall, as if the bureaucracy will suddenly acknowledge their own corruption, the public will wake up and take notice, and then all the animals will live happily ever after."

"God, you're cynical. How dare you belittle our efforts. We've had successes, you know."

"Successes? You're more naïve than I thought. Listen, I don't have a thousand fucking Twitter followers, but today I can save an animal from being tortured to death. You can't say that."

"How does your way change anything in the long run?" Jude flashed back. "Talk about being naïve ... you can't make people see the value of animals by breaking the law. You don't change a cultural mindset by freeing one fox."

"It sure makes a difference for that fox. But that's only part of it. You have to make people sit up and notice, and sometimes you have to get up in their faces. And that's exactly what we did in Colorado and what we're going to do in Louisiana."

"So you can be a radical hero? An outlaw?"

"I break the laws because what they're doing to animals is diabolically *wrong*," responded Colin bitterly. "And I cannot let them get away with it."

"But it's not the real world!" cried Jude.

"Okay. Let's talk about the real world. You know what's going to happen in the *real world*, don't you?" He snatched the book from her hand and flipped to the last page. "This right here about Oona? It's going to set off alarm bells for the cops and lead them right to my father." He jabbed an irate finger at the diary. "This maniac killed hundreds, probably thousands of innocent animals for the thrill of it. And you're going to put my *father* in jail?"

Jude was silent. He was right. Ben had assured her he would turn himself in, but was *she* going to be the one to bring the cops down on him before he was ready?

Just then, Finn began to bark. Jude peered over the wall and saw him holding his tail high and stiff – a warning she knew well.

"Someone's out there," she rasped. "You'd better go. Now."

Colin pushed her toward the ladder ahead of him, but she drew back. "Just you," she said. "Look, I don't know who it is, but if the FBI found out about the cabin, they could have tracked us from there. For me, all they can do is make life difficult and get Gordon pissed off at me. You're a different story."

Through the trees, they could see a flickering light, and Finn's bark became more insistent.

"Go, go," hissed Jude, fear taking hold. "They've got guns, Colin."

He waved a truce flag by holding out the diary to her. But she pressed it back into his hands. "Take this. I'm not going to say anything about your father. But if you're caught, you might need it."

He leaned in and put his forehead against hers. "It isn't over for us," he said.

"No," breathed Jude.

Colin wrested himself away and clambered down the ladder. Night was falling as fast as the snow and Jude never even saw which direction he ran. She thought that if she could stall the FBI for a few minutes, the snow might fill in his footprints so there would be no sign of him at all.

She gathered up the sack with the remaining dog collars and put it in her backpack. Then she descended the tree stand and grabbed hold of Finn's collar as she waited for the bobbing light to get closer. The last thing she needed was Finn to attack someone – possibly a federal officer.

Holding her ground and putting her hand up to shade her eyes against the bright beam, she called out, "You can see it's just me and my dog. I'm not armed. I'm holding on to him out of caution, but he's not a problem."

There was no response, just the continued approaching light now pointed at her face. Finn had stopped barking, but a menacing growl rumbled deep in his throat. She yanked on his collar to shush him.

It was weird. They should have identified themselves by this time; that's what cops did, wasn't it? Shout out instructions to put your hands up, don't move, right? But no one said a word. For a moment she welcomed what seemed to be indecision – it would give Colin more time. She tried to extend it by identifying herself. "My name is Jude Brannock. I'm an investigator. I have a driver's license in my backpack if you want me to get it out."

The light switched off. Still blinded, Jude squinted, trying to see how many men were there. But only one figure took shape, and it said, "Tie up your dog."

Icy adrenaline shot through her as she recognized the voice. "Listen, Cash, it's not what you think," she said.

"I'm not paid to think anything, Cowgirl. Now tie up your friggin' dog before I shoot him. And I will."

"He's not going to–"

"Do it now or he gets a bullet."

Jude heard the click of the hammer on his pistol. "Okay, okay." She retrieved a long leash from her backpack, then clipped it to Finn's collar and walked him to a nearby tree. She talked to her nervous dog all the while, reassuring him that everything would be all right. But she didn't believe it. *How had he followed her? What did he want? How dangerous was he right now?* Then she tried to form a plan. Talk, keep talking until you know what he wants, and just in case, tie a loose knot in the leash.

As if he heard what she was thinking, Cash said, "Don't mess around. Tie it good. If he comes at me, I will kill him."

Jude hesitated, but ultimately yanked the knot tight. Finn

would normally do what she said, but the second he perceived she was in imminent danger, he'd go after Cash. She turned back, keeping her voice calm to keep Finn from lunging.

"I guess you know by now I'm not a travel agent," she said. "I'm really sorry I told you that I was, but I had a job to do in Stanton that had nothing to do with you, and I had to maintain this–"

"Shut up," he cut her off.

"This has nothing to do with you."

"You played me, you bitch," he snarled. "Nobody does that to me. Nobody, you hear?"

Jude was scared. They were in the middle of nowhere and her worst fears about working undercover had come true. Not only did her mark know he'd been deceived, he felt humiliated, and he had no reserve when it came to killing animals. "You know, when I first saw the light, I thought it was the FBI. They put a tail on my car today," she lied, "so they probably followed me here, too."

"Nice try, Judy or whatever your name is. There ain't nobody within ten miles of us. So you're some kind of animal rights person? We thought you were."

"Look, I understand you're angry. You have every right to be. All I can do is apologize, but I promise you, it's not personal. This was never about you."

"You used me." There was a steel edge to his voice that raised the hairs on Jude's neck.

"I'm sorry, Cash."

He seemed to let that settle before saying, "John Tripp wants a word with you. He also wants Eberhardt's diary."

"I don't have it."

"Bullshit."

"I'm serious. It's not here."

"This is the only place it could be. You must be pretty smart to figure that out. I figured it out," he boasted. "Just didn't know where his tree stand was."

"I'm telling you the truth. It's not here."

He motioned with his hand to give up her backpack. She did as she was told and set it on the ground. Still pointing his gun at her chest, he crouched and rifled its contents. Jude thought her best course of action was to keep him talking. There wasn't much chance that anyone was coming to her rescue. He might give her an opening to say or do the right thing to get out of this jam.

She asked him, "Is the diary for Tripp or for your boss Bud Grimes?" When he didn't answer, she continued, "They have a lot to lose in this, but you don't. Not unless something happens to me. You've just been doing what Grimes tells you to do. No one is going to hold you responsible for that."

"You got no business meddling where you don't belong."

"And the U.S. government has no business lying to the American public," burst out Jude. "And you have no business killing thousands of innocent animals and covering it up."

He retorted, "To the contrary, doll. That *is* my business. You don't know shit about livin' out here."

"I know enough to cost Bud Grimes his job. But you don't have to lose yours, Cash. If you help me, I could put in a good word for you."

"Oh yeah, I'm going to help out some animal rights freak," he jeered.

Frustrated at not finding the diary, he upended the backpack and dumped all its contents in the snow. "What is this?" he demanded, emptying the sack of dog collars.

"They're from all the dogs Eberhardt trapped and buried."

Cash tossed them aside in disgust. He turned his attention to the tree stand. "He kept it up there, didn't he? Come on, let's go look."

Jude protested, but he spun her around and pushed her up the ladder in front of him. In the tight confines of the platform, she pointed out the blue cooler and said, "He kept pieces of his trash animals in there."

Even Cash recoiled at the stench. "What the fuck for?"

Now was not the time to explain about Eberhardt as a serial killer, so she simply said, "Look for yourself. It's not here."

After he rummaged through the cooler, failing to find it, he shoved the revolver into his belt and started to roughly pat her down.

"Get your hands off me!" cried Jude.

But Cash continued his probe, feeling for the diary under her thick coat, feeling for other things as well. "We never did finish what we started," he growled into her ear.

"Don't do this, Cash," warned Jude. "You don't want to spend the rest of your life in jail. Cooped up in a cage. No more wild. No fresh air. Just metal bars."

She'd hit a nerve, and he backed away. He swept the rest of the platform with his foot to make sure the diary wasn't hidden in a corner, then went down the ladder and waited for her.

Once on the ground, Jude scavenged the snow for some of the things he'd strewn about – an extra pair of socks, her phone, and when Cash's attention was diverted by the agitated Finn, the satchel of dog collars.

"Get up," instructed Cash. "You're coming with me."

"Where?"

"I told you, Tripp wants to see you."

"What about Finn?" A germ of panic had sprouted and was growing quickly. "We can't leave him here."

"He stays."

Jude straightened and took a bold step toward Cash. "I'm not leaving without my dog," she stated.

"Fine," he said, swiveling and aiming his pistol directly at Finn.

"No!" screamed Jude. "I'll go. Don't hurt him."

Cash eyed her coldly and motioned her ahead. She started on the path with Cash at her back and Finn's protesting barks burning a hole in her chest.

She rationalized that if Cash had meant to kill her he would have done it already. But with each step, the alleged meeting with Tripp seemed less likely. If Cash hadn't committed a crime before, he certainly was now, and he had to know she'd go to the police – if she got free. The idea that she was to become the next victim of Shoot, Shovel and Shut-up seemed the more plausible scenario. Jude began to look for a chance to escape.

He'd left his ATV far enough away that neither Jude nor Colin had heard it approach. Cash instructed her to get on. He started it up and drove on his own tracks back through the woods. It crossed Jude's mind to try overpowering him from behind, but she let that idea go quickly – he was much stronger and he had a weapon. She was afraid to vault off while the vehicle was moving, imagining a broken leg that would make escape impossible. They turned onto a wider trail, which offered a vague hope that they would eventually end up on a road where she had a chance of finding help. But Jude decided to take any opening that presented itself.

It came when Cash veered a couple of feet off the trail. The ATV's tires could navigate the four inches of snow on the trail, but when he tried to avoid a tree limb, one of the front wheels dipped into an unseen hole, nearly toppling them. The abrupt stop jolted them both forward, slamming Jude into Cash's back. The engine stalled. He sat still for a moment and cursed.

As soon as he dismounted and knelt down to inspect the undercarriage, Jude bolted.

"Hey!" he yelled. "Get back here."

Encumbered by her backpack, Jude lurched in the direction they had come, trying to keep her feet on the fresh tire tracks where the snow was packed. Cash came after her. The beam of his flashlight danced wildly from the path ahead of him to the bulls eye on her back. But she dared not go into the woods on either side. At least here she could run.

"Don't be an idiot," he shouted. "You won't make it out of here by yourself."

She kept running, her breath coming in gasps. She could hear and feel him gaining on her. It was only a matter of a few seconds before he brought her down. No more time. Jude veered from the open trail and plunged into the cover of the woods. Holding her hands in front of her, she staggered through brush and saplings that whipped her upper body and face. Her shoulder slammed into a tree trunk that seemed to spring out of nowhere, spinning her around and nearly knocking her down. Thirty yards behind her, Cash's light winked through the tree branches.

He called out another warning, "You'll freeze to death, Cowgirl."

Jude looked around, aware of how easy it would be for him to track her in the snow. A series of black shapes rose out of the white powder. Rocks. She wouldn't leave footprints on rocks. On all fours, she scrambled over the boulders and then up an embankment. When she looked back, she saw Cash's light flicker below. For a moment it looked as though he might climb up after her, but he retreated. Fearing that he was going back to get a rifle or a stronger light, she started running again. But seconds later, over her own hard breathing, she heard the ATV rumble away.

In the ensuing, surprising silence, Jude dug out her cell phone. It had some battery life left, but there was no service. She slowed to a walk, trying to stay parallel to the ATV trail – until she found Finn. Her boots made whooshing noises each time she took a step, and to her own ears it sounded loud. Every so often she stopped and pushed back her hood to listen for footsteps behind her, while the powdery snow accumulated on her hair and eyelashes.

Soon her path was cut by a small stream. The sight of it caught her off guard because they hadn't crossed a stream that she recalled. She decided that she must be going in the wrong direction and changed course. She began to sweat under her parka. Her ankle twisted on one awkward step, and she forced herself to slow down to avoid the roots, rocks, and broken branches buried under the snow cover. She couldn't afford a more serious injury. The only good news was that the snow had let up, though huge clumps dropped from the upper branches. A front was coming through, driving the fast-moving storm away, and moonlight peeked through the racing clouds. It felt like she was heading toward Finn, but she had yet to come across the ATV tracks, or any other tracks for that matter.

The even ground gave way to an incline that kept stretching upwards, testing Jude's knees and pounding heart. But she climbed, hoping to see a road or a house from the summit. Finally, she reached the top, only to see more forest below ... miles and miles of forest. Snow had gotten into her boots and her hands were ice cold in her wet gloves. The wind was sharp. She was glad for the extra layer of fleece under her jacket, but now, aware that she was shivering, it didn't seem nearly enough.

She hadn't allowed herself the luxury of reflection. But it came now. *I'm in trouble. I'm in big trouble.* Panic threatened to take hold.

Then in the moonlight she spotted a patch of black in the distant landscape. It had to be a body of water. Probably Lake Freedom. *I have to get to Finn.* She fumbled with the zipper on her parka, trying to close it further, but it was up as far as it could go. Her shoulders ached from the weight of her backpack. Jude headed downhill, the lake her target.

She walked for another twenty minutes before she fell. The ground simply dropped away and she slid down an embankment, landing in a heap. The full body slam hurt like hell, and rising through the pain was an intense fury. Lying on her back, looking up into the starlit black sky, it erupted. "Why?" she screamed. "Why do you have to make it so hard?" Silence was her answer. "Yeah, I'm talking to you, God, or whoever you are. Don't you care? I thought you made it *all*, the land, the water, the animals. Are you going to let them all die? Don't you fucking care?"

That's when she heard the wolves. The same careening howls that a week ago had sounded so eerie and beautiful now sent waves of fear coursing through her. One second they sounded far away, the next very close as the echo of the howling pack cut through the night. Jude knew full well that there had only been two fatal wolf attacks on humans in the last hundred years, but she had nothing to fight back with if they decided she was prey. There was only one thing to do – keep walking. Jude sat up and opened her backpack. She fished out the extra pair of socks, her phone, and the dog collars and stuffed them deep into her pockets. Everything else was meaningless. She got to her feet and ditched the backpack.

She never got to the lake. Over the next hour, the vast landscape of Idaho swallowed her, sapping her energy, her body heat, and her courage. Every once in a while she heard a wolf or a coyote. But mostly, all she heard were trees groaning like old hinges and her own faltering footsteps. After awhile, even her senses shut down. She couldn't feel her fingers and toes, her body was exhausted. All she wanted to do was lie down, just for a minute, just a minute, that's all. But somewhere inside she knew that if she did, she would never get up. Survival meant one more step.

She entered a pine forest where the trees towered above her head. The moon was bright and filtered through the branches, casting shadows everywhere. One more step. To her right, a large shadow moved at the edge of the trees with the stealth of a panther. Her breath quickened. It was a wolf or some large animal. The shadow slunk along the ground tracking her. Jude tried to speed up, but her legs wouldn't go any faster. Then suddenly, it bounded out from behind a fallen tree and leapt at her.

Jude dropped to her knees, ready to be taken, grateful that she could rest now. A large, dark animal whined and pushed her over. A raspy tongue licked her cheek. It was not the sight of him or the sound, but his smell that Jude, in her disoriented state, finally recognized.

"Finn?" she whispered. *Was she only hoping it was Finn?*

But there was his scent, warm on her face, dog-like, familiar. She wrapped her arms around his neck. And it felt like ... home. His strong, noble face swam into view.

"Oh, Finn. Good boy, good boy." Her face was so cold, her lips so dry, she could barely form the words.

If it was an illusion, she clung to it. Using Finn's bulk, Jude pushed herself to her feet. He danced at her side, a three-foot piece of leash hanging from his collar dragged on the ground. She grabbed hold of the end, but it slipped through her useless fingers. She reached for it again and wrapped it around her hand, letting Finn take control.

One step at a time. With Finn. One step at a time.

She didn't know how far they'd gone, but he finally stopped. He was crouching and pawing at the ground in front of a huge tree that had toppled by its roots. The root ball rose from the earth like a wall, creating a protected hole, and branches from another tree taken down in a previous storm formed a kind of canopy. Finn was now on a mission, exploring the space underneath, seeking out any other animal that might be living there. Finding none, he wriggled on his belly into the tree cave and whined at Jude to do the same. She collapsed next to him and inch by inch worked her way into the protected darkness where there was room for the two of them. The ground was damp, but soft with layers of leaves and pine needles. And they were out of the wind.

Jude folded her frozen body around her dog. With trembling fingers, she removed her wet gloves and buried her hands in the ruff of Finn's neck. Slowly, slowly, they began to regain sensation. His body heat was perhaps enough for the two of them. When she thought she could manage it, she eased off her boots and wet socks, replacing them with the pair in her pocket. Then she dug her toes under Finn's haunches and drifted into a cold, light sleep.

At one point she was aware of Finn moving. She woke long enough to find that he had placed himself at the entrance to their little cave, lying with his head down, but his eyes and ears alert. She pressed herself against her protector and allowed herself to be pulled back into unconsciousness.

CHAPTER 27

Her fingers throbbed. Unclenching them slowly, Jude smoothed down her skirt, the bandages scraping lightly on the fabric. She was three rows back from the witness table where Gordon was undergoing questioning. Next to him sat Elizabeth Crowley, The Kinship's attorney and Gordon's lover. Jude always felt slightly dog-eared next to Elizabeth (no one called her Liz) who everyone considered breathtakingly lovely and wickedly smart. She'd been nicknamed the Vegan Goddess by a few of the investigators, and although she waved them off, Jude thought she privately liked it. Facing them on the dais was the congressional panel. Something had gone awry with the sound system and while they fixed it, the members talked among themselves.

One of the congressmen kept glancing in Jude's direction, and she couldn't miss the malevolence in each sideswipe of his eyes. Scott Olander was prepared to take Jude apart when she testified. He'd been filled in by John Tripp; he knew who Jude was and what she was likely to say. Despite the time she spent with Elizabeth going over her testimony, Jude felt her confidence draining by the minute. She was scared of being attacked by a congressman, scared of messing up. Ever since the night in the woods, she was having trouble concentrating, as if the deep freeze had numbed her ability to think. She'd find herself explaining something to Gordon as her thoughts drifted to Colin or re-lived the terror of being lost, only to realize that her boss was waiting for her to continue. And there was still the ongoing ache in her feet and hands, though it was nothing compared to the agony of what they'd called "re-warming" in the emergency room. Many of the people at the subcommittee hearing had removed their suit jackets, but Jude kept hers on, wondering if she would ever feel truly warm again.

She and Finn had crawled out of their makeshift shelter at first light. Mercifully, there was no wind, but she knew they had to keep moving. She told him to "go find home" and prayed he would lead her to civilization. He did. It wasn't long before she heard the rumble of a snowplow, and she slid most of the way down an incline to where a road was being cleared. The plow operator called an ambulance while she and Finn began to thaw in the cab of the plow.

The next twenty-four hours dissolved in a haze of pain medication. Jude suffered superficial frostbite that left blisters on her feet and hands. The tips of nearly all her fingers turned a mottled blue and the sensation that returned to her extremities came back as burning and throbbing, making her wish for the numbness again. But the doctors said that in time she would be fine; she was fortunate that she'd worn layers underneath her parka, and even more fortunate that she had Finn. All the nurses came around and wanted to meet the dog that saved her life.

As word spread, Foster Dunne came to the hospital and offered to take Finn back to the Aspen to care for him. Gordon flew out as soon as he'd heard, bringing Lucas with him. The brightest moment of her hospital stay was when Lucas arrived, bearing an armload of warm vegan burritos. A fellow investigator and her closest friend at The Kinship, he was to drive Finn back cross country in Jude's car, while she flew back to Washington with Gordon.

Not all her visitors were friendly faces. Two FBI agents arrived to interview her. They'd asked in a variety of ways if she knew Colin, if she knew where he was, if she knew his friends... She mostly told the truth. She knew him from college days, she'd seen him in Stanton, but didn't know where he was. Beyond that, she'd followed Elizabeth's advice to say as little as possible. They promised another visit and, as they had done with Oliver, threatened a grand jury investigation, but so far they'd taken no action.

When she returned home, the first night in her apartment nearly crushed her. The loneliness was worse than the frostbite. Lucas and Finn were still a day away and no matter how she tried to distract herself, she couldn't stop thinking about Colin. Elizabeth told her in no uncertain terms not to contact him – even if she knew how. Jude's thoughts, too, drifted to Ben. She believed he would turn himself in and hoped that at trial – if his body held out that long – the jury would feel compassion for him. Perhaps some jurors might think about how they loved their own dogs, sometimes as much as they loved another human. Love was love, wasn't it? Yes, but the law was the law. Ben had killed a man and would go to prison. Until she knew that he had shown up at the police station, however, being the keeper of his confession was a torment. Jude hadn't said anything about him, not even to Gordon.

Finally, there was the lingering fear. Was Cash or someone else on Tripp's payroll going to come after her again? Before she'd left the hospital, the Stanton police had picked him up, but the D.A. was reluctant to prosecute. Cash claimed he'd followed Jude to apologize for being drunk the night before and was going to give her a ride home. She jumped off his ATV – what could he do? He tried, but couldn't find her. Her word against his. And in light of her being an animal activist posing as a travel agent, her credibility was already in question. The cops had retrieved Eberhardt's cooler, but they seemed to shrug it off. So he kept pieces of animals he trapped – no harm there. Gordon thought that Jude's best protection was to tell her story to *The Washington Post*. A reporter interviewed her, but later got blanket denials from John Tripp and Wildlife Services. With just Jude's statement and a handful of dog collars that Eberhardt could have found somewhere, he felt he didn't have enough to run a story about Wildlife Services.

Jude was left with the chance to appear before the subcommittee. In his efforts to bolster the provisions of the anti-terrorism statute, Scott Olander planned to bring in an FBI agent to testify that it was the agency's belief that Eberhardt's murder was the work of animal activists. Once they did that, Gordon was able to pressure the committee chair to let Jude speak.

"You're up," Elizabeth was gently shaking her shoulder.

Jude wanted to climb under her seat. "I don't think I can," she said to Elizabeth.

"Of course you can," replied the attorney, unmoved by her anxiety. "Here, maybe this will help. It was just delivered by messenger." She handed Jude a padded envelope that for security reasons the guard had insisted on opening at the door. Jude reached in and pulled out an old blue dog collar and a notebook wrapped in black plastic. Elizabeth glowed with a jubilant grin; she knew what it was.

Jude turned the package over in her hands, her heart beating so fast she could scarcely breathe. It was addressed to her at The Kinship, and the return address drew a big smile. It was from "John Tripp" in Stanton ... Colin's sense of humor. All at once, she didn't feel cold anymore and the pain in her fingers didn't matter. She clutched the package to her chest and limped up to the table to take a seat.

* * *

Sal climbed out of her rubber boots for the third time that morning. Two hunters, one trapper, five coyotes, and another wolf. The end of the hunting season for wolves was months away and her district's quota was nearly met. But she knew it didn't mean the killing would stop. She gazed out the window to see if it had started snowing. All the weather reports said this storm was going to leave at least a foot. She had four-wheel drive, but didn't want to set out for home too late. The phone rang.

"Sal Mayhill here," she said, sliding behind her desk.

"Sal, it's Ben McIntyre."

"How are you, Ben?" she asked, surprised to hear from him. She knew he was ill and wondered how he was dealing with the fact that his son was still a wanted man.

"Well as can be expected," he said. "Listen, I ... I called because I've got something to say. We've known each other a long time and I would like you to handle this. You can contact anyone you need, but I just ... want to tell you first."

He sounded so somber that Sal pulled her eyes away from the computer screen and sat up in her chair. "How can I help you, Ben?" she asked.

"Sal, I killed Craig Eberhardt. He trapped my dog Oona and I shot him."

His blunt statement came as a shock and she couldn't speak for a moment. Finally she found her voice and asked in disbelief, "What are you saying?"

"I'm telling you that I shot Eberhardt. With my Winchester. It's right here and the ballistics will match up, I'm sure. Then I set a trap 'round his leg and let it fly. Same kind of trap that got Oona, so it seemed fitting, I suppose. I want you to know that I was going to go back and release him, but I got real sick and then it was too late."

Sal felt her scalp tighten like a vise.

"You still there?" asked Ben.

"I'm here ... I just don't know what to say." She wasn't entirely sure she believed him. "Is this about Colin? Because of the DNA on the trap?"

"It wasn't him. I'm telling you the truth. The kid was sabotaging traps. He probably left traces on some of them, which could explain the DNA. But what you'll find at my place is solid proof. I'm no forensic expert, but I still have the boots I was wearing and there's some of Eberhardt's blood on 'em. Cops are welcome to the clothes, my rifle, and anything else they can find. I've written up a full confession. It was me, Sal. Nobody else. I didn't plan it. I only wanted him to admit what he'd done. He was a vicious man when it came to animals. One thing led to another, and the bottom line is I shot him and left him to die."

She could hear the truth in his voice and sighed from a place deep in her chest. "Have you called the police?"

"Nope. I'm calling you."

"I'm going to have to get them in on this, you know."

"I understand. You do what you need to do."

"Oh, Jesus. I wish this wasn't happening," said Sal.

"You've got to do me a favor, Sal. Make sure they call off the hunt for my son."

"Is he with you?"

"No, I don't know where he is. I hope he's long gone."

"Where are you, Ben?" she asked.

"I'm home."

"Okay. I have to tell you to stay put. I'm coming out with the police."

"You do that." There was a long pause, and Ben added, "Thank you, Sal."

He hung up.

* * *

The subcommittee chairman was a Democrat named Jensen from Maryland. He put on his reading glasses before shuffling his notes, then took them off again to address the next witness. "The chair recognizes Jude Brannock, an investigator with Mr. Silverman's organization The Kinship. As you've been told, Miss Brannock, this committee was not intending to add a discussion of Wildlife Services to the agenda, but since my Republican colleague here has interjected the issue of escalating violence by animal activists in Idaho, we agreed that a witness who has some knowledge of such activities should have an opportunity to respond. I would ask you to keep it brief, however."

She brought the microphone closer and began to read from her prepared statement, "Chairman Jensen and distinguished members of the committee, I want to thank you for the opportunity to testify here today. I was sent to Stanton, Idaho, on December 12th by The Kinship to look into a rumor that animal activists were responsible for the death of Wildlife Services agent Craig Eberhardt. I went in my capacity as an undercover investigator because we thought that my association with an animal advocacy group would be a barrier to my investigation..." She proceeded to testify that while in Stanton she learned several things about

Eberhardt specifically and Wildlife Services in general that were deeply distressing to many residents in the town. "These activities could logically provide a motive for the killing," she continued. "For instance–"

Olander leaned in to his microphone and cut her off. "You don't have to tell this committee about what Wildlife Services does."

She looked up from her notes and met the warning in his gaze. "I have no doubt that you are aware of what Wildlife Services does, sir. Like how they conduct aerial gunning of wolves and coyotes. But did you know that this killing takes place not only on public lands, but also in areas where there are no sheep and cattle grazing? Of course you know that amongst many poisons, the agency uses M-44 cyanide ejectors to kill coyotes. But did you know that those same devices have killed family pets and injured people, including children? And that Wildlife Services refuses to take any responsibility for this?"

Olander started to interrupt, but Jude raised her voice and boldly carried on. "I'm certain you must know that from time to time, animals who are not targeted for death by Wildlife Services get caught in their traps. But did you know that these non-target animals outnumber the targeted animals by two-to-one, or three-to-one, as one Wildlife Services agent informed me? And did you know that Bud Grimes, the regional director of Wildlife Services in Idaho, instructs his agents to hide evidence of these non-target animals, a policy otherwise known as Shoot, Shovel, and Shut-up – even when the non-target animals are endangered species? And quite naturally, sir, you are aware of the fact that millions of taxpayer dollars have gone missing or are unaccounted for in the Wildlife Services budget. You know this because the bill that seeks accountability is before the committee of which you are the chair–"

Olander banged his fist against the table. “Enough!” he roared. “You’re here to answer questions, not ask them.”

He went on a blazing offensive, probing her relationship with Cash and making it appear as though she might be a spurned lover, then trying to paint her as an ALF sympathizer with her own illegal agenda. Finally, he sought to link her to Colin and pin her with obstruction of justice, asking, “What precisely is your relationship with Colin McIntyre?”

“We were friends. I hadn’t seen him in many years,”

“Were you aware that Mr. McIntyre was wanted by the FBI for the murder of Craig Eberhardt?”

She’d discussed this with Elizabeth and answered circumspectly, “When I came to Stanton, I heard that there were FBI agents looking for a particular individual, but I did not know who that individual was.”

Olander sensed something slippery about her answer, but couldn’t immediately pin it down and felt he had to keep at her. He shuffled his notecards and asked, “Were you aware that McIntyre was committing a crime by interfering with traps? Government traps in particular?”

“I did not have any direct personal knowledge that he was destroying traps, nor did he admit to me that he had.”

The congressman kept at her. “Miss Brannock, you’ve made a serious allegation that a regional director of Wildlife Services was instructing his employees to hide evidence of non-target animals.”

“That’s correct.”

“What is the basis for this allegation?”

“For one, I overheard a discussion between Idaho Senator John Tripp and Mr. Grimes himself concerning a field diary kept by Craig Eberhardt. They were worried that the diary would be found by the police or the FBI because not only would it implicate Mr.

Grimes in his instruction to cover up the non-target animals, but it would also document suspicious payments from ranchers to the agency and vice versa."

"That's preposterous hearsay, young lady. Do you have any reliable evidence outside of this alleged field diary that no one has seen?"

"Well, I learned about it first from Orin Cashman, who works for Wildlife Services" said Jude. From the corner of her eye, she saw Elizabeth hide a smile and remembered what the lawyer always said about examining a witness: never ask a question you don't already know the answer to – you might get an unwelcome surprise. "Cash ... I mean, Mr. Cashman was the one who revealed the existence of this diary," she continued. "He said that Eberhardt had angered a lot of people because he was writing down all of his non-target takes, even after he was told not to record them."

Olander knew that no one had found the diary. They all surmised that it was still missing. "And just where is this alleged diary?" he challenged with a smirk.

"It's right here," said Jude, pulling it out of the package and placing it in front of her. The look on Olander's face was one she would always remember.

* * *

By the time Sal rounded up the police and they got to Tolan Way, it was snowing heavily and visibility was poor. No lights showed in the house. Sal led the way and knocked firmly on the front door. "Ben?" she called. "It's Sal Mayhill. Can you open the door?" The snowfall muted the sounds of their boots, their breathing, and the squeaking of leather gun belts as they waited for a response, but it was eerily quiet.

Chief Bill Ramey pushed past Sal and tried the door. It opened easily. He dropped back and withdrew his service revolver.

"He's not going to do anything, Bill," rebuked Sal.

But he motioned her and the other officers to the side. "Ben?" he called out. "Come on out, Ben. It's time."

The returning silence told them that only bad news waited on the other side of the door. Ramey nodded to his officers and they stormed into the house.

It was cold and still. The fire in the wood burning stove was long since extinguished. Two officers checked the bedrooms, while the sergeant went outside to search the garage. Ben was gone.

But he had left something for them. On the kitchen counter lay his Winchester rifle and a stuffed plastic garbage bag. Ramey snapped on a pair of latex gloves and slid out the contents of the bag – a pair of jeans, a down vest, and a worn pair of boots, smeared with a rust-colored substance. There was also a pair of gloves which appeared to be spattered with blood. Next to his wallet, Ben had left an envelope with Chief Ramey's name printed on the outside. He opened it and scanned the contents.

"Mind if I look?" asked Sal.

Ramey set the letter on the counter.

To Whom it may concern:

My name is Ben McIntyre and I shot Craig Eberhardt with my Winchester, then put his leg in a spring coil trap, the same one as killed my dog. He set the trap and then took her body so that I couldn't bury her.

My son Colin is innocent of this crime. He may be guilty of others, but not this. I love my son and have come to admire him. In his own way he is trying to ease the suffering in this world. If he tries to do that on his own terms, he might pay the consequences and I accept that. But he had nothing to do with Eberhardt.

You may think me a bad man for what I have done, and maybe I am. But I do not want to die in jail. I believe in God and have gone where I hope to find his forgiveness. – Benjamin James McIntyre

The sergeant burst in through the front door. "Chief, come take a look at this," he said.

He led them outside around the back of the garage. "There's footprints going that way," he said, pointing to dull indentations in the snow that were already filling in.

"What's up there?" asked Ramey.

"Nothin' but wild," replied the sergeant. "If you keep on over Mount Owyhee you might hit Saint Claire, but that's a good four, five miles and not an easy hike."

Ramey crouched down to examine the prints. "He must have left right after he called you, Sal. Sonofagun."

"Where the hell is he gonna go in this?" asked one of the cops, holding out his gloved hands and letting the snowflakes collect.

"I don't know," responded the sergeant. "There's a pair of snowshoes in the garage and unless he's got a second set, he won't get very far. You want me to go back and get a search team?"

The Chief looked up in the direction of the peak and nodded uncertainly. "Yeah, sure. And get cars on Tolan Way at both ends."

The sergeant hurried off, barking out instructions to the other officers. They left Sal and Chief Ramey standing in the falling snow.

"What do you think, Sal?" he finally asked.

"He left his wallet," she noted.

Ramey nodded. "He'll be tough to find," said Ramey. "Another twenty minutes and we won't see any tracks. And if we don't find him soon..."

They both left the sentence unfinished. There was no need. Both of them knew there would be no arrest, no trial, no jail. Ben was gone – on his own terms.

Chapter 28

"Merry Christmas," said Lucas, raising his glass.

Jude clinked her glass against his and took another sip of wine. Lucas had stayed behind to help clean up after their holiday dinner, which had become a tradition at The Kinship that Jude was happy to host. Everyone brought a vegan dish and they exchanged little gifts, often silly things like the costume that now adorned Lucas's companion animal Habib.

"You know, I don't approve of dressing up animals," said Jude solemnly, as she watched Habib's little whiskers poke out of the front of Lucas's shirt. "I think it demeans them. But that is so cute, I can't stand it." She bit her lower lip to keep from laughing out loud as Habib the rat scurried up Lucas's arm with his red cape flying.

Finn watched disdainfully from his bed near the Christmas tree. He adored Lucas and had come to tolerate the rodent – but that's as far as he would go.

"Too bad Gordon couldn't come for dinner," said Lucas.

"They had to make an appearance at some other gathering, but he said they'd stop by later."

"Boss-man ought to be here celebrating. No more AETA amendment."

"Well, technically, they're just tabling the amendment, but apparently when the press got hold of the field diary, they decided to drop the attack on activists for a while."

"Beautiful, man. I love it. And that was a kickin' headline *Who's the Real Terrorist?*"

"Yeah, Congressman Jensen says he's going to form his own committee to take on Wildlife Services."

Lucas picked up Habib to give him a kiss on the nose, adding, "One step at a friggin' time, right?"

Jude folded her legs underneath her on the sofa. The good food and wine, the friendships, and the festive lights on the Christmas tree threw a dreamy spell over the apartment.

"So, Miss B, how you doin' ... really?" asked Lucas.

Jude held up her hands. "Not bad, see? Almost healed."

"Dude, I mean here," he said, pointing to his heart.

"Almost healed," she said with a tentative smile.

"And what's up with your boyfriend?"

"He's not my boyfriend, Lucas," Jude chastised. "I don't know what he's up to."

"Does he know about his father?"

"I'm sure he does. It did make the news."

"How's he taking it?"

"I don't know ... I haven't spoken to him."

The doorbell rang and Finn leapt to his feet, barking a deep warning. He'd been more protective than usual since the night in the woods. But his bark quickly turned into a giddy whine when Jude opened the door to Gordon and Elizabeth.

"You made it," said Jude happily.

"Merry Christmas," said Gordon, giving her a hug.

Elizabeth gave Jude a peck on the cheek and took off her coat. She looked positively glamorous.

"I brought someone else," said Gordon, his eyes shining. He stepped aside to let in Lisbet Hammond.

"Oh my goodness," exclaimed Jude, embracing the wolf biologist. "Come on in. What are you doing in Washington? How are you?"

A flurry of introductions filled the small apartment as the new group settled in and Jude retrieved drinks and some dessert for her guests. Elizabeth was none too pleased, however, to see Habib.

"Don't worry, Goddess, he's chill, he ain't gonna hurt you," drawled Lucas, defending his buddy as usual.

"I know," she responded uncomfortably. "I would just prefer he not ... crawl on me."

"Habib don't crawl, Goddess, he *strides*. He's super dude now. Marches to the beat of his own drum."

"Fine. Just don't let him stride or march on me," she demurred.

"Love the cape," said Gordon. "Lisbet, tell Jude why you're in Washington."

All eyes turned eagerly in her direction. "Well, as you all probably know, since the federal delisting, wolf populations out west are declining. They're at the mercy of the state wildlife agencies and the animal agriculture and hunting industries that fund them. But, we have an idea. It's in the early stages and will take some time, but we're mounting an effort to help wolves recover their original range in the northeast," she announced excitedly.

"There are no wolves there now?" asked Lucas.

"No. Occasionally one or two make their way down from Algonquin Park in Canada, but they're either shot or they hybridize with the eastern coyote and aren't able to re-colonize as a distinct population. But we think we have a good chance to convince the states, namely New York, Vermont, Maine and New Hampshire, to set their own standards for protecting wolves even if the federal government won't. With protections in place, we might be able to reintroduce wolves someday, the way we did in Yellowstone."

"What makes you think that the hunting industry in those states won't do the same thing it's doing in Idaho and Montana?" asked Jude.

"They'll probably try, but we've got a couple of things going for us. First, people in the northeast are a little more environmentally sympathetic, and they aren't as fixated on the wolf as the boogeyman. Secondly, wildlife watching is a big money-maker in the northeast, and it could be even bigger if wolves are part of the equation. That's certainly true at Yellowstone. They draw huge numbers of people just for the chance of catching a glimpse of them, and that brings revenue to the whole community. But unlike Yellowstone, a wolf habitat in the northeast would be much more accessible to a large number of people – just a day's drive from New York or Boston."

Jude had a visceral memory of that early morning on the Lamar Valley ridge and the thrill of seeing the Stone Mountain Pack emerge from the pine trees. She saw once more the alpha male with his thick silver and black coat, his keen almond-shaped eyes, and the sprinkle of frost on his muzzle. Feeling the hunger and excitement of possibilities for these amazing creatures, she asked excitedly, "When, Lisbet?"

"Well, it's a heavy lift and a long process, but–"

"There's hope," finished Jude.

Gordon's cell phone chirped. He looked at the screen and frowned. "CJ says to turn on CNN right now."

Jude jumped up and turned on the TV, flipping channels until she found the story. A young female reporter was on location, standing by the side of the road in front of a white van ringed with yellow police tape and lit by the news station's arc lights. Police cars were visible on either side of the van. Jude turned up the sound.

... The transport truck was on its way from the University of Wisconsin earlier today en route to the Tulane National Primate Research Center in Louisiana. It is believed that the assailants knew the transport's route and schedule. The driver and a technician left Wisconsin with the young primates to deliver them to the Center's biomedical testing labs. The driver told police that they had just turned onto this road when a car and a large minivan pulled in front of them. Four individuals wearing black hoods and believed to be members of a group calling itself Animal Liberation Front ordered the driver and technician out of their truck. They were then tied up and left in the back. The assailants took the eleven baby macaque monkeys out of their cages and loaded them in a getaway van.

The driver told police that the ringleader of the group was male. But he was masked and not otherwise identifiable. He did, however, leave a message.

The camera panned around to the side of the white van, where the words "Animal Liberation Now" had been spray painted in large letters.

This is the first known hijacking of a transport vehicle carrying animals used for testing. I contacted an administrator at Tulane to ask him what tests were going to be performed on these baby monkeys, but he did not wish to comment. Tulane does do research into Ebola, SARS and West Nile viruses using nonhuman primates. So perhaps for a few monkeys ... this is a Merry Christmas. Back to you, Bob.

The news anchor went on to the next story, leaving Jude and

company speechless. Lucas broke the silence with an "Awriiight" and thrust his fist in the air in a gesture of solidarity. Jude looked over to Gordon and thought she could see him already calculating what impact the event would have on their own work. But the story had left him misty-eyed, of that she was sure.

After everyone left, Jude cleared the last of the dishes. The silverware clinked in the empty apartment and from somewhere outside came the sound of late, tipsy carolers. She opened her laptop to search for more news about the ALF operation, but quickly closed it down again, deciding instead to give herself a gift. Tonight she would bask in the warmth of good friends, the possibility of wolves roaming a wilderness without traps and poison, and the promise of a life for eleven baby macaques finally free of suffering at the hands of white-coated men in sterile labs. She padded over to where Finn was snoring on his dog bed and lay down next to him. Above her, the Christmas tree lights twinkled. On the top was perched Oona's collar. Its weight bent the frail tip of the evergreen, but it seemed the right place for it – the one reserved for angel ornaments. Finn opened one eye, then closed it again.

"You see, Finn? There's hope," she said softly.